FOREVER
BY
AVA FARREL

For Collette

Who stopped me from giving up

All characters in this book are entirely fictional. Any resemblance to persons alive or dead is purely coincidental.

Copyright © Ava Farrel, 2020

ISBN 9798640745320 All rights reserved. No part of this publication may be reproduced without the permission of the copyright owner.

Prologue – Me

I am a seventeen-year-old girl from the north of England. My life at home is a lonely, unhappy existence; my parents just don't understand my generation. They brought my sister and myself into the world quite late in their life, due to this my mother expects us to behave as she had done during her teenage years, staying at home in the evening, either sewing or reading. But, being the two girls that we are this is never going to happen. The reality is that we like to go out and party.

Being four years apart in age doesn't stop us being close. We socialise together and generally have a good time.

My sister has somehow managed to become a single mother to two small girls, having a place of her own; where I spend every weekend, helping her with the children and of course just getting away from my parents. She is my sister, my best friend and my complete lifeline.

I work hard during the week at my job as a weaver in a cotton mill, for which I am paid a handsome amount of money. However, I need to stay at home during the working week, since my home is much closer to my place of work. My time at home on weekday evenings is spent alone in my bedroom, rather than sitting downstairs with my parents; not wanting to listen to them criticising my lifestyle.

My main obsession in life is a singer who is currently one of the biggest stars on the planet. I am completely besotted with him and spend far too much time alone in my bedroom, staring at posters of him on my wall, and listening to his records playing on my ancient record player. I have never laid eyes on anyone who is so gorgeous, with the sexiest voice I have ever heard. I am totally in love with him, and my ultimate fantasy is to meet him and somehow get him into bed.

Although I am only 17 years of age, I have been sexually active for the last two years. Therefore, although he is almost six years older than me, I feel confident and mature enough to seduce him; that is if I ever manage to get close enough to him.

The only problem is that he is American and at the moment there seems to be no sign of him visiting the UK to perform, and so, every Friday when I am handed my pay packet, my first point of call is to the bank where I deposit a large chunk of my hard-earned cash.

If he isn't coming to me, I will just have to save enough money to go to one of his concerts in America.

One way or another, I will try everything within my power to meet him. This is my dream, and somehow, I will achieve it.

Prologue – My Idol

I am an American guy in my early twenties. All I have ever wanted to do with my life is to sing, write music, and play my guitar.

However, something seems to have gone wrong with my career. Instead of being a respected musician, I seem to have become a heartthrob to the teenage fraternity, which isn't the image I want to portray.

Don't get me wrong; being what I've become has some significant advantages. Girls are falling at my feet, and my sex life has never been more active. The choice of a different girl as often as I want, always up for a session between the sheets.

But - this is now starting to bore me. Sure, I can pick the one I fancy the most, yet knowing I'm getting what I want, I also know that sleeping with me is nothing more than a fantasy achieved on their part. And although I seem to have as many girls as I want, I have no desire to form a relationship with any of them. Get them in bed, thirty minutes of sex and I can't wait to see the back of them.

I am well aware of the reputation this is giving me but, guess what – I don't care. This lifestyle seems to have been thrown upon me, and so I am taking full advantage of it; whatever my reputation becomes.

My stardom seems to have taken over my life. I don't feel like a real person anymore; just someone to ogle over and meet in person, if they're lucky enough.

I'm not a young kid anymore; I am now in my twenties and want to meet a girl who loves me for who I am, not what I have become. I want a girl I can care for, rather than throwing her out as soon as my sexual frustrations have been satisfied, needing her by my side to love; someone who will love me in return.

How my life is at present, I don't seem to have time to go out and look for the girl of my dreams, but I live in the hope that maybe - one day.

Chapter 1

As I stared at the newspaper, excitement bubbled inside me. He was doing concerts in the UK, at long last. Having waited two years for this moment, I knew I would be there watching him; nothing on this earth would stop me.

A TV music show I had watched a few nights earlier had announced that the dates and locations for his concerts would be in the Sunday papers. So, I had happily climbed out of bed at six o clock and walked down to my local newsagents to buy a copy. Hardly having slept the night before, I couldn't wait to find out where he would be performing and how I could get a ticket.

He was to perform in the north of England and London, and so, taking the newspaper into the garden, I studied the venues and dates. The northern site wasn't that far from where I lived and was relatively easy to get to, being only a thirty-minute train journey. It would be easy to travel there to buy a ticket when they went on sale and then a few weeks later for the actual concert, without any problems.

But, studying the northern ones, my eyes started to wander down the page to the London concerts, listed below. I had no idea why I was even looking! London was at the other end of the country, and to get there would be much more difficult. Almost impossible to travel to and much more expensive; but as I looked at the dates for London, I knew in my heart this was where I wanted to watch him. The northern concerts made much more sense, but this wasn't where I wanted to be.

I wanted to go to London.

The problem was, getting hold of a ticket. It was impractical to go all the way to London on the day they went on sale, and this would also mean taking time off from my job—then travelling there again a few weeks later for the actual concert. Putting the paper down, I went inside and lay on my bed, dreaming about the forthcoming shows and staring at his poster on my wall. Yet, I couldn't shake away thoughts of travelling to London to watch him perform.

Although my biggest fantasy was to meet him in person and get him into bed, the tight security surrounding him made this almost impossible. Making it nothing more than a fantasy, it didn't stop me dreaming. Somehow, I knew, something was telling me to go to London.

I was aware that I was utterly obsessed with him. Half of my bedroom walls had his face plastered on them. I also spent more time than was healthy sitting alone, listening to his records, while crying and longing to meet him.

After spending hours daydreaming about watching him sing and flash his gorgeous smile, trying to think of a way to get hold of a ticket for one of his London concerts, I was still no nearer to an answer. I was so in love with him, and this was the most important decision I would ever make and somehow, I didn't care how, I had to get that ticket, I had to go to London.

Needing to talk to someone about it, as always when I had a problem, I went to see my sister.

Being close to her, I spent much of my time at her house. She was a one-parent family, with two small girls who were a big part of my life.

When I got to her place, I didn't mention the concert straight away. However, as I had virtually ignored her as she had been telling me about my nieces' school play, she knew there was something on my mind and finally got it out of me.

When I told her which of the concerts I intended to go to, she looked at me as though I was stupid. Her first question was, okay, "If you could get a ticket, I would like to know how you're thinking of getting to London and back on the day of the concert, it's miles away and will cost you a fortune on the train".

"I'll hitch-hike," I simply said, like it was but a few miles away; not having given a thought to transport. Getting hold of a ticket to his London concert meant I would be able to watch him there, which I had now decided was all I cared about, walking there if I had to. I had hitch-hiked many times before, but never as far as London.

Trying to persuade me to get a ticket for one of the concerts in the north; and after throwing arguments of north versus London at me, she gave up.

She sat there thinking for a few moments and then suddenly jumped up, "Watch the kids for a minute, I'm just nipping next door" she ordered me and disappeared out of the door.

My sister's next-door neighbours Andy and Cath were a couple in their fifties who had no children of their own. They often looked after the girls for my sister and helped her out in many other ways.

Knowing how much I adored him and understanding my lonely home life, she knew the reasons why I wanted this so much. I knew she would do anything to help me achieve my dream.

After a few minutes, she was back with a big smile on her face. "What are you grinning at?" I said, smiling too and somehow knowing I was going to like what she was going to say.

"Andy is working in London on the day the tickets go on sale, he's going to go to the concert venue to get one for you," she said, with the same silly grin on her face.

Looking at her, I screamed.

"And don't be doing that at his concert like all his silly little fans, you're older than most of them. How do you think you're going to get him into bed behaving like that?" my sister replied, laughing.

"Oh yes," I said, laughing, "Like that's going to happen! Even though it's what I want more than anything, this won't be like the type of concert you go to, where the band join you at the bar for a chat afterwards. He's the biggest star on the planet with the tightest security ever, I've got no chance."

Standing next to the kitchen worktop watching the kettle boil, I started to think about what my sister had said. Now that she had planted the seed in my mind, it had made me wonder if I could manage it. Getting so close to him was beyond my wildest dreams, and even though I dreamed of it every day, I still didn't think it was possible. Could I pull it off, get to meet him and get him into bed? The thought of his hands touching my body and his lips on mine made me go weak at the knees and brought a massive smile to my face.

I knew it would be no more than quick sex and then goodbye, but hell! Getting him into bed was still beyond anything I had ever thought possible. Having lived out my fantasy, I would have a great memory to bring home with me.

My sister looked at me as I walked back into the lounge, smiled and said, "I know how much you want to meet him, so go all out and try to get in there but remember, you have to be prepared for it to fail. As cruel as this may sound, even if you do manage to get to meet him, he may not fancy you. Just because you're in love with him doesn't mean he will feel the same way". And laughing, she added, "Andy will also run you to the motorway on the day of the concert. So, believe me, when you leave here, you'll look a million dollars, which will at the very least give you half a chance."

After I made the tea, we sat and talked about what I would wear and how I could hatch a plan to meet him.

Not being able to buy black denim in the UK in the 1970s, my sister had managed to get hold of some black industrial dye, and so we had decided to dye two pair of light blue jeans in her washing machine.

Being pleased with how they had turned out and how they looked when I had tried them on, I had put them away in my wardrobe for when I went somewhere special. Well, this was just the occasion to wear the jeans. Being skin-tight down to my knees, they then came out in a flare and really flattered my figure.

Not having the longest of eyelashes and wanting to look as glamourous as possible, I suggested to my sister that I would buy false ones to wear on the day.

Looking aghast, she laughed and related a tale to me when one of hers had fallen off while she had been in bed with someone. Saying that she hadn't realised it had become detached until she had seen it stuck to the cheek of the man who was lying beside her.

The thought of this happening if I did manage to meet him made me go cold.

"Don't worry," she said, laughing at my reaction. "We'll get up extra early, and I'll put your mascara on so all you'll need to do is top it up during the day."

Somehow, after the concert, I would need to get away from all his other fans. Needing to be stood-alone somewhere, where his car would pass me and hopefully stop. To do this, I would need to be in London a few hours before the concert started. I would have to explore the area around the concert venue and find somewhere to wait and also be able to get to this point without any of his other fans seeing me. I couldn't run the risk of being followed by any of them.

After we had got the girls to bed and bought a few beers from the local shop, we talked well into the night. It was late when I eventually got home and into bed, but found I couldn't sleep for excitement.

I had to meet him, and he had to like me; just one chance to get this close to him would be enough. It was all that mattered. I had no love in my life, apart from my sister and nieces. Having parents who were entirely out of touch with reality, the only time we spoke was to argue. I was a disappointment to them because I worked in a cotton mill. I was a tart because I went out every night and, in their opinion, dressed like one. The money I provided each week from my wages was all that interested them!

Finally falling to sleep, my dreams were full of his face close to mine, lying by his side in bed.

The concert was still six weeks off. How on earth was I going to wait so long?

Spending the next week worrying about Andy getting a ticket for me, when the day came for the tickets to go on sale, I was a bag of nerves.

My job as a weaver in a cotton mill was complicated and needed total concentration. However, being so worried about my ticket, I spent most of the following week in a dream world making several mistakes, prompting a dressing down from my supervisor.

What if Andy forgot when he was in London, or there were no tickets left; hundreds of reasons why I couldn't get a ticket went through my mind.

Andy, however, was true to his word. The minute I had finished work, on the day the tickets had been on sale, I went straight to my sister's house. Sitting on the bus that took me to the area where she lived, I was a bag of nerves, and as I got off at the bus stop around the corner from her house, I ran the rest of the way.

Walking in through the front door, I looked down onto the coffee table. There was my ticket. Walking across the room, I slowly picked it up and held it in my hand as tears rolled down my cheeks. Finally, I was going to see him in the flesh, and hopefully, if I could put my plan into place, I would be seeing a lot more flesh than anyone else! I was now more determined than ever to accomplish my dream.

Chapter 2

I can't tell you how excited I was to be flying to the UK for my first overseas tour. Sure, playing all over the USA was fun and I'd also had more than my fair share of girls along the way. However, not one of them interested me any more than the excitement of a quick sex session, but, the thought of seeing another country had me tingling with excitement. And then there were those British girls of course, with their cute little accents.

I made sure my manager booked me into the best hotels in each of the cities I was playing. Not that it mattered to me, but if I did meet one of those British cuties then I wasn't going to take them back to some dive in a rough part of town.

The schedule was packed; six concerts in two cites, all in just over a week, before flying back home, but I had a driver to get me between gigs. It's just a shame he had to be such a prick, trying to ruin my time here with his lousy stuck up attitude. Who the hell did that guy think he was?

As I arrived at the venue for my first performance, thoughts of private hotel performances disappeared in an instant! None of these girls looked over fourteen years of age. Where the hell were all the cute girls who would want to get to know me a little better? And just why were they all screaming and crying? I was here; just give me a wave and blow some kisses, show me you love me; even though not one of you are old enough to give me any real love.

Stunned, I entered the building to prepare for my performance; still shocked at what appeared to be my fans; both their age and the way they had behaved.

The intro to my first song began, and I walked on stage, smiling and waving. As my performance progressed, I had no idea if I was singing in time to the band, my voice and the music being drowned out by the horrific noise from over a thousand girls. By now they seemed to have upped their crying to actual wailing!

And what was this ripping at their hair all about. How these fans were behaving wasn't music appreciation as far as I was concerned. If you liked what was being performed, you listened to it!

My ears were ringing from the sheer amount of screaming along with the fact that I knew I would end up with a banging headache later. My record sales here had been immense; did this mean they acted like wailing banshees every time they listened to one of my records? Shaking my head, my only thought being, just get me out of here.

The following two concerts had been every bit as bad as the first one! When I waved, they screamed; while I was singing, they screamed, and if I should dare blow a kiss, well, they went crazy. I'd had enough!

I was off down to London next. A new city, a new driver and maybe older, more sophisticated girls. Although I wasn't counting on this, expecting the same lonely experience I had found in the north. No female company, a driver who thought he was superior to me, and the inside of a hotel room, alone.

On my internal flight from the north, I had a look at the arrangements I had scribbled down, where I was to meet my new driver. Probably another obnoxious prat, the same as the northern guy, I thought to myself. Well sod him; I would get through this tour without his or anyone's help, I didn't need these stuffy Englishmen trying to tell me what to do.

Get these next concerts over with and fly back home. How excited I had been at the prospect of visiting the UK. Now I couldn't wait to see the back of it.

Chapter 3

Finally, the day of the concert arrived. Having stayed with my sister the night before, we had both been up by five; giving me plenty of time to get ready.

My clothes had been ironed and were hanging on the wardrobe door upstairs, and my bag was ready with all the essentials I would need.

The black jeans I had planned on wearing would be complemented by a sexy Basque top for the concert later that day. But I didn't think it was a good idea to wear such a revealing top while I was hitch-hiking, and so I was wearing a plain black vest top under my new jacket. I would also be wearing sparkly, heeled shoes later that day which I couldn't possibly travel in; never having been very good on heels. I was determined to wear them, however, as they gave me height and looked glamourous. And so, they were also stowed away in my bag, while I travelled in a pair of pumps.

Arrangements had been made with Andy. He would be driving me to the start of the motorway in his work van.

Andy was expecting me to be ready for seven. So, the next two hours passed as my sister applied layer after layer of mascara along with the rest of my makeup. My blonde hair, which was past my waist, was wavy, which I hated. However, after my sister had spent over an hour blow drying it while using a brush to straighten it; finally, it was how I wanted it. Straight and even longer. When at last, my makeup and hair was how I wanted it, I went upstairs to dress.

Although I was only wearing jeans and a vest top, as I looked through the long mirror in the bedroom, I grinned. The reflection that stared back at me didn't look like me; I was genuinely amazed. I looked so sexy and beautiful.

Thinking I was alone in the room, I looked through the mirror and spoke. *"You don't know it yet, but you're going to have the most amazing night of your life tonight?"* I whispered. Just thinking of this made my head spin.

"Just believe it, you can do it and make it come true," my sister whispered from behind me and gave me a big hug. "Good luck."

Andy drove me to the motorway, although I was so nervous, I thought I was going to be sick! Usually being a chatty type of person, I was so quiet Andy gave me a worried look, asking me if I was okay.

My sister had made me eat toast before I left. "I know you won't stop to eat before you get to London," she had scolded. Being thankful for this, I knew she was right; I just wanted to get there as fast as possible. Once I was in London, I could worry about food.

We arrived at the motorway junction, and Andy pulled up at the top of the slip road; I felt like crying with relief.

Courtesy of Andy; I had a ticket, had given myself enough time to make plans for later that evening to get away from his other fans, spent a fortune on clothes. Now I was on my way to London.

"You sure you're okay," Andy asked, looking concerned. Nodding I climbed out of the van, thanking him for the lift. "Knock him dead," Andy said, smiling, "You look amazing, believe in yourself."

Moving lower down on the slip road, I stuck my thumb out. Yes! I was going to London to see my idol.

What the coming day had in store for me I had no idea, but I couldn't wait to find out!

Chapter 4

Touching down at the airport from my internal flight, I was met by some airport guy who ushered me into a poky little room to meet my new driver. Some other stuck up idiot who thought he was better than me I presumed. Well stuff him I thought, as I sat down and picked up a magazine from the seat next to me, I didn't even care that he wasn't already there to meet me. I was in a foul mood.

Roughly fifteen minutes later, the door opened, and a man who looked to be in his mid-thirties walked in. As he smiled at me, I stood up, crossed the room, shook his hand and introduced myself. Although he was probably every bit as unbearable as the one up north, I always tried to be polite and do the right thing.

In a worried sounding voice, he told me his name and explained how he had become caught up in traffic crossing London, and from the expression on his face, I had a feeling he thought I was about to shout at him for being late. So, he had kept me waiting, but I didn't care; he was at least smiling now and seemed cheerful, which gave me hope that he would be more tolerable than the prick up north.

Walking out to the waiting car, I decided to find out just how approachable this new driver was and so I asked him, "Gerry, what's the hotel like?" Expecting a one-word answer like the idiot up north, I was shocked when he laughed, telling me he had got lost twice in the hotel corridors, on one occasion ending up in an upstairs kitchen area.

Before I knew it, we were in the car and driving out of the airport, still talking and laughing.

Feeling much better, I had a feeling I was going to enjoy London. I don't know why but having Gerry as my driver was undoubtedly going to make life more enjoyable.

Chapter 5

Climbing down from the driver's cab, I was careful not to catch my jacket; having bought it especially for this occasion. It had cost me nearly a full week's wages, but what the hell, I wanted to look as sexy and glamorous as possible, and so it had been well worth the extravagance.

Slamming the door shut, I blew a kiss to the driver. It had been a good lift, all the way from the Coventry area and the driver had been friendly, but not too familiar, chatting about this and that. It helped that I had a good knowledge of football, a subject most men liked to talk about, and had found in the past that I could hold a good conversation on the topic. It turns out that he was a West Brom fan and as I was a Wolves fan, we had a bit of friendly banter, which had been a good laugh.

As the lorry pulled away, I took in the surrounding area, excitement coursing through me. In the distance I could see the famous white towers of Wembley stadium, where I had been to in the past, to watch football. So, I knew that I was quite near the arena I was heading to, Wembley Empire Pool, where the concert was that evening.

Now suddenly, I felt overwhelmed, and at that moment I wanted to do nothing more than make my way to the arena, sit on the doorstep and wait until eight o clock when the concert started. However, I had plans to make, important plans!

Deciding to find somewhere to eat, I started to walk down the road. Once I had eaten, I would then check out the area around the concert venue, finding out the route that his car would take after leaving the arena. I still had no idea how I was going to manage what I planned, but I was so determined to meet him, my idol; but alone, not in the company of hundreds of screaming girls, getting into his car and hopefully into his bed!

After walking in the direction of the arena for about fifteen minutes, I came to a small café. It looked quite seedy from outside with steamed up windows and net curtains which could have done with a good wash. However, I was hungry and not planning on eating the curtains anyway.

Once inside, I was pleasantly surprised at how clean and neat it was with checked tablecloths and small vases of flowers on each table. After ordering a bacon and egg sandwich, a cake and a cup of tea, I found a table in the corner, sat down and looked out through the steamy window.

As I sat daydreaming of the day ahead, my food arrived, which I devoured like I had not been fed for a month. Feeling better after eating I drank my tea and sat wondering for what must have been the hundredth time that morning, just how on earth I was going to achieve what I wanted

Hitch-hiking to London to see his concert and try to get to meet him. God, I must be mad. I could have gone to the northern show without all this trouble but knew, somehow, I was in the right place. The thing was, I wanted him that bad all logic went out of the window; I would have travelled anywhere for the chance of getting near him.

My appetite satisfied, I left the café and walked down the road in the direction of the white towers. As I crossed the road at the next junction, I walked past the football stadium and made my way to what I could now see as the arena.

When the actual building came into view, I stopped dead and stared; the reality that I had travelled to London hit me like a ton of bricks. The venue was much bigger than I had expected it to be, which meant, of course, even more, screaming girls than I had anticipated.

What if one or more of his other fans had the same idea as me. If I did find somewhere to wait after the concert, what if there were other fans in the same spot as me. He wasn't going to stop if there was a few of us, was he? I would just have to cross my fingers and hope this didn't happen!

As I stared at the front entrance of the arena for a few minutes, I became quite emotional, thinking of him performing on stage later that evening. Tonight, would be the first time I had seen him in the flesh, making me tingle inside as I visualised his face and his gorgeous smile.

Standing there on my own, I suddenly shouted out loud, "I'm having you tonight, darling, I don't know how but whatever it takes, I'm gonna do it." Looking around sheepishly, in case anyone had heard me, I heaved a sigh of relief. Luckily there had been no one about to hear me.

Now it was time to have a walk around the building, get an idea where the back of the arena led to and where the rest of his fans might assemble, once the concert was over.

To the right of the main doors, I found a path leading around to the back of the arena. Following it, I found myself behind a secure parking area, big enough to hold several vehicles, with a road that led away for a few hundred yards and then veered to the left and went out of sight. This was where the fans would make their way to after the concert, to get a glimpse of him in the car as it left; and was not where I wanted to be.

Retracing my steps back to the front entrance, I walked past the main doors and round to the left of the building. From the corner, I could see an industrial area containing several buildings and some open land. This was secured by a metal gate of around six foot. As

I walked up to the gate, I could see there was a huge padlock securing it. Bollocks! Not letting this put me off I concluded that I would just have to climb over it.

The height of the gate meant that I would need to change from my heels and back into my pumps before I attempted to climb over it. No way was I scaling this massive gate in heels; I would need to change my shoes over, climb the gate and then switch back into my heels before I stood waiting for the car. That part of the plan sorted, I now needed to find out where I would be when I had climbed the gate and crossed the area that I could see in front of me.

Making my way past the main doors again, I walked up to the main road I had walked down earlier, then turning left I walked parallel with the side of the building keeping an eye out for a sight of the gate.

Once I had made my way back onto the main road, I walked past a row of shops, situated at the corner of the next junction. Looking down the road to my left, I could see a set of traffic lights in the distance. Walking down the road until I came to the lights, I looked to the left again and down the road that led away from the traffic lights. Anticipation rippled through me; this was the road leading from the back of the arena, I was sure of it. Starting to run down the road, I prayed that I was right.

As I rounded a bend in the road, the back of the arena came into view. "Yes!" I screamed. Now I felt like I was getting somewhere! This was the road the car would use after leaving the arena. With him in it! All I had to do now was to find out how to get to the traffic lights after climbing over the gate.

Standing there, looking at the back area of the arena, I wondered if it would be easier, after the concert, just follow all the other fans to the back of the arena and then to carry on walking up the road to the traffic lights. It would cut out climbing over the six-foot gate and finding my way to the lights. But what if I did this and some of them started to follow me for some reason? It would then ruin everything I had planned – and so, I decided to stick to my strategy. I would find out where the area on this side of the gate led to.

As I sauntered back up to the lights, totally out of breath from running, I turned left onto the road I had walked up a few minutes earlier, continuing to look across for a sight of the gate. After going past some industrial units, it eventually came into view.

Pleased with myself, I stood and took in what was between me and this side of the gate. It was quite some distance away from where I was; meaning I would have to move as quickly as possible.

I could quite easily see across the area between where I was standing now and where the gate was. Observing that a few feet away from the gate there was a small wall, which I assumed I could easily climb over, this then led onto what looked like a field of rubble and bricks, with a broken wire mesh fence at this side of the field. A path then led up the side of a small warehouse building.

That was what was between me and the gate. So, I would have to do an obstacle course. Big deal! If I got what I wanted, it was a small price to pay!

Sitting down on the warehouse step, I was exhausted but unbelievably happy; it had been much easier to put my plans into operation than I had thought it would be.

That done I decided to go and find a pub, I felt I deserved to treat myself to a drink, I also needed to calm myself down, my heart was beating so fast I thought it was going to burst through my chest.

Having five hours to kill before the concert started, I needed to find something to occupy my mind.

I walked away, singing one of his songs with a massive smile on my face.

Chapter 6

Being in London with Gerry as my driver was a whole lot better than being with the prat of a driver I had been assigned for my concerts in the north. He was a great bloke and finding that we shared the same odd sense of humour, meant that we found it was easy to talk to each other and have a good laugh together. The only time I had seen the driver up north was on the drive to and from the concert venue. Gerry, however, had joined me in my room for most of our meals and a few beers, watching some TV, or just talking and laughing.

He had even drove me around the London area in the car; me sitting beside him rather than in the back and wearing a hooded top and sunglasses so I wouldn't be recognised. He knew how lonely I was and tried his best to be a friend and help me, rather than just treating me as a job he didn't want to do.

Although having Gerry around to talk to and keep me company was great, I was still feeling mighty lonely. I needed female company, badly. When I did concerts at home, I would somehow manage to get a girl into my hotel or at least into my dressing room. My fans at home were older and of course almost always up for sex. But here, well! I had no chance; nothing but underage girls who screamed and cried all the time.

I now had two concerts left, and although I was feeling needy and frustrated, I resigned myself to having to wait until I got back home. Perhaps I could call one of the girls I knew on my first night home, get them to come round to keep me company for a few hours. By this time, I would be desperate, but even so, a few hours would be long enough to put me right, as truth be told the girls I knew were fine for a quick sex session and a bit of fun, but none of them interested me any further than this.

I wanted a girl to love but didn't hold out much hope of finding the right one any time soon.

Gerry I

My name is Gerry Holden.

Recently I started to work for a security company in the Midlands. As a company, we undertake a variety of security jobs and being one of the new boys I got allocated the jobs no one else wanted. So, when a job came through babysitting a young pop star for five days in London, guess who drew the short straw. Taking it in good humour, I laughed along with my colleagues about pop star tantrums and demands; I wouldn't always be new, and in time I would be able to take my pick of the jobs available.

Catching the train to London on the day he was due to arrive on his internal flight from the north of England, I picked up the hire car I was to drive him around in, then checked into the hotel for both of us. There would only be the two of us in this hotel; as a kind of decoy, his fans were the type to storm hotels, screaming everywhere and making a real nuisance of themselves.

Going up to my room, I threw my bags inside and went to check out his 'suite', as I had been instructed.

Opening the door, which led into a long hallway, I could see several doors leading off it. Opening the first one, I found I was in a massive lounge with doors that opened onto a balcony, on which there was a table and four chairs. After having a look around and checking the balcony door were secure, I walked to the other side of the hallway, where the next door I opened led me into a huge bedroom with a bed bigger than any I had ever seen in my life. The last door was a bathroom that was big enough to throw a party.

How the other half lived, I thought.

Everything seemed to be in order and so walking back down the hallway, I locked the door and went back to my room to relax, until it was time to leave.

The arrangement was for me to pick him up from an airport an hour's drive from London, where he would be arriving on his internal flight from the north.

However, not being used to the sheer volume of traffic in central London, this took me longer than I had anticipated. As I drove through the city, I knew that I had no chance of arriving at the airport by the allotted time, and knew he would already have landed, waiting to be collected.

As I entered the private room where he was waiting, I found him sat reading a magazine. When he saw me, he jumped up and came towards me. Expecting him to have a rant about me being late, I was shocked when instead he shook my hand, introduced himself and asked about my journey from London. I was speechless for a moment; not expecting him to be so personable and polite.

As I found my voice, I told him my name and explained that I had got caught in traffic on the way to the airport. He didn't seem to mind at all that I had kept him waiting. Walking out to the car, he asked about the hotel, and before I knew it, we were laughing and joking like two old friends.

Over the next few days, we fell into a comfortable working relationship.

He was a nice person, no tantrums, no demands, in fact, the only time he rang my room was to tell me his balcony door wouldn't close and would I go over to his room to take a look at it, before he reported it to the hotel.

I had thought he would want his privacy when we were in the hotel, but it seemed he was quite happy for me to spend time with him, sharing a meal or watching TV in his suite. We had the same type of humour and found it easy to laugh together.

He was doing three concerts in London, so obviously he sat in the back of the car when we travelled to and from the concert venue, although on a few other occasions when we went out, he was quite happy to sit in the front with me.

He was chatty and had a great sense of humour, nothing like the picture that had been painted of him when I had talked to my colleagues. He related stories of the driver he had been given while in the north, making me laugh with some of the names he called him. I had to laugh; this was such an easy, enjoyable job.

One thing I did learn, though, was that he was lonely.

The papers painted pictures of him being with a different girl every night, when he was on tour. Here in London, this was as far from the truth as it could be, as most of his UK fans were too young to accompany him to his hotel room.

Knowing if he needed help finding a girl here in London, I would be only too willing to help him.

Chapter 7

After treating myself to a pint of cider in a nearby pub, I made my way to the underground station at Wembley, deciding to catch a train into central London. Studying the list of stations on the board outside the station, I decided on Kings Cross. It was the only destination that I had heard of on the same tube line as Wembley!

Alighting from the train at Kings Cross station, I made my way up to the road via the escalator. Standing on the pavement outside the tube station, I stopped and stared in amazement; I was astounded at the sheer volume of people. I knew London was busy, but the vast crowds still surprised me.

Walking away, down the bustling road my mind returned to the plan I had made for later that day, and although I had been happy when I had put it in operation, I was now finding fault with some of it; one big problem was who would be travelling in the car with him. I needed him to be alone in the car, apart from the driver, and the thought had crossed my mind that any number of people could be travelling to the arena with him; his manager maybe or any one of the minders that always seemed to be around him. Even a girl.

There had been some footage on television from a concert he had done in his own country, and it seemed that there always seemed to be lots of people around him, everywhere he went.

Crossing the main road, I was so deep in thought as I glanced to my right, I suddenly saw a bus heading straight for me. Diving back onto the pavement, bumping into several other people who were also waiting to cross the road, I thought to myself, whoa, if you're not more careful, you won't be going to any concert tonight!

Waiting for the traffic to pass and being more alert on my second attempt, I crossed the road and walked along the pavement on the opposite side. Looking down each side street, I noticed the entrance to a small market on one of them, and so I turned and headed towards it.

As I walked onto the market, I began to feel much better, thinking to myself, this is much safer! No main roads or traffic, and wandering in and out of the stalls, looking at the brightly coloured goods on display, my mind went back to my plans. Needing to watch the back of the arena when he arrived to see if he was alone in the car seemed my best option. The problem was, If I sat at the back of the arena, waiting for him to arrive, I wouldn't be near the front of the queue, so obviously wouldn't be near the front of the stage. No way did I want to be near the back, or even halfway. I wanted to be at the front. As close to him as possible!

Deep in thought, I suddenly felt something moving, right in front of me. No! I had walked straight into a display stand, knocking it to the ground, scattering hats and scarves everywhere.

Alarmed, I started to pick up the scattered goods, as the elderly stallholder appeared, "Don't worry, dear," she said, smiling "No harm done." When I had helped her to pick everything up from the ground and return the display to its former glory, I apologised to the lady.

As I turned to go, she touched my arm to stop me, holding out a beautiful scarf in black and gold. "It matches your outfit," she said and then wrapped it around my neck, saying, "Take it."

Feeling guilty for knocking over her display, I smiled back at her and took my purse from my bag." Pushing my hand away, she smiled back at me. Then completely astonished me by what she said next.

"Wear it tonight and whatever you're dreaming of will be yours……but not forever." Wanting to laugh at her words but of course, not wanting to offend her, I thanked her and kissed her weathered cheek.

As I walked past her stall, I noticed some pretty, dangly earrings, that would also match what I was wearing. Wanting to buy something from this lovely lady, who had been so gracious about what I had done to her display, I once again took my purse out to pay for the earrings. Taking them from me to put them into a small paper bag, she looked down at them, then back up at my face, saying quietly, "Don't wear these tonight dear, he won't like them."

Now she was freaking me out, and so as politely as possible I thanked her once more and said goodbye, before walking away.

Leaving the market, I realised I was trembling. Although I didn't believe in what I considered as mumbo jumbo, the stallholder's words had unnerved me; it was as if the lady knew what was going to happen.

It was almost five o clock as I headed back to the tube station. I needed to be back at the arena early, whatever I decided to do, either get in the queue or wait at the back of the building; I would make my decision during my tube journey back to Wembley.

Before going down to the tube station, I found a public toilet across the road from the station. I needed to change from the black vest top which I had worn to travel down to London and replace it with a deep yellow Basque top with black ruffles across the top edge. Being wired underneath my bust meant I didn't need to wear a bra and made it quite revealing.

Putting it on, I pulled it down as far as I could, making sure it showed plenty of cleavage. With a bit of luck, I might be able to flash it to him when he was on stage later!

A liberal squirt of perfume and I was almost ready. Taking the earrings that I had bought at the market out of my bag, to add to my outfit, I stopped and stared down at them. As I held them in my hand, what the stallholder had said to me went through my mind. Somehow, the lady on the market had known something, and although I still didn't believe it, I put them back into my bag.

But I knew for sure that I would be wearing the beautiful scarf that she had given to me. Although I didn't understand why the stallholder had said what she had, her words wouldn't leave me. As I tied it around my neck, I knew; I was leaving nothing to chance.

Chapter 8

Sitting on the balcony outside my room looking out over the rooftops of London, I wondered what it would be like to have a normal life. Be able to walk out of the front doors of this hotel, walk down the street, call into a coffee shop, and look into some of the shop windows on the road outside the hotel. Act like any other joe on the street.

But, no, I couldn't! Because my fans here were crazy young kids who wanted to rip my clothes off if they got chance, and just generally grab at any part of me.

At one of my, northern concerts I had jumped down from the stage, to shake hands with some of the girls who were at the front; give them a peck on the cheek as I did at home. Big mistake! One girl had pulled the sleeve of my suit so hard it had torn. My hair had been pulled, and somehow, I had a huge scratch across my left cheek. Luckily, security had rescued me, ensuring I was firmly back on stage. Physically shocked, I didn't understand why they behaved in this way; okay, they were young, but that was no reason to assault me.

But I was so incredibly lonely stuck in this room by myself. It had been the same every night since I had been in the UK; performing every night and the rest of the time holed up in a hotel room. Although here in London had been more enjoyable than up north, due to Gerry's company, I had still seen far too much of the inside of hotel rooms.

All this makes it sound like I love myself, but in all honesty, I don't think I'm anything special, although most of the UK female population under sixteen seemed to think I am. Girls everywhere seemed to want to gain my affection, and I was under no illusion; it was because I was famous, rather than wanting to know the real me.

One girl back at home had said I was good in bed, but as sex had lasted no longer than twenty minutes, I suspect she had told me to flatter me. It didn't work though, as all she had wanted was for me to sing to her, which I would have been happy to do until I found she only wanted me to sing my songs, which I spend enough time singing on stage.

There was no one from my tour in this hotel, apart from Gerry and me. It was a decoy, me and Gerry in here and everyone else in another hotel. That way if the fans saw my manager and the crew, going through the front doors of another hotel, they would assume I was in there too. When the hotel I was in with Gerry was on the other side of London.

Earlier that day Gerry had called my room, asking if I would be okay on my own for a few hours, so that he could go out for a while and see some of the London sights. Yes! I had told him immediately, of course. It wasn't fair for him to be cooped up in a hotel room just because I had to be. He had already spent more than enough of his free time with me, keeping me company. How I wished I could have gone with him, but as he was planning on walking and using the tube, this of course was out of the question.

Sitting in my room alone was driving me crazy.

Walking back into my room from the balcony, I flopped down onto one of the sofas and closed my eyes, dreaming of being here with a girl, any girl. But finding one that was old enough seemed to be impossible.

I must have dozed off as the next thing I knew Gerry was shaking me awake. "Time to get ready to go, mate," he said. Standing up I stretched, resigning myself to performing another concert to a bunch of girls who wanted to do nothing more than scream for the whole of the concert, then back to this same hotel room for the night – on my own, as usual.

How I wished I could pick a girl from tonight's crowd, drag her in the car and bring her back here, for some fun and of course the inevitable, as much sex as I could manage, which I knew wouldn't be much; but hey! It would be better than nothing. But as none of them were old enough, this was never going to happen. Also opening the car door when a few hundred girls surrounded it was virtually impossible.

I quickly showered, grabbed my guitar and was ready to go.

Chapter 9

Standing on the platform waiting for the tube back to Wembley, I started to fantasise about my dreams for later that evening. Could I make them become a reality? Closing my eyes, I dreamed how his lips would feel locked with mine and how wonderful it would be to lie next to him, feeling his touch on my body.

Suddenly, I felt people pushing past me. My train had arrived, but I had been so engrossed in my fantasies I hadn't even heard it pulling into the station. Bringing myself back down to earth, I moved forward with the rest of the crowd and boarded the train.

Once I was on the train, I found myself a seat in an empty carriage, needing somewhere quiet to sit and think; deciding what I was going to do when I got back to the Wembley area. Should I wait outside the back of the arena, to see if there was anyone in the back of the car with him, or should I join the queue, giving myself a better chance of being near the stage once I was inside?

The train continued its journey to Wembley, filling up more at every station, mainly with groups of teenage girls accompanied by adults; the average age I guessed seemed to be roughly thirteen or fourteen years old.

It was evident that they were all going to the same destination as me as I could see that they were all wearing t-shirts and scarves adorned with his name. No one took any notice of me; I had deliberately not worn any fan merchandise to make myself look older and more mature than his other fans.

He was nearly six years older than me and couldn't possibly be interested in any of these girls with their little hairclips and gaudy make-up.

By the time the train arrived at Wembley, it was packed. Pushing my way through the crowd of people getting off the train, I ran down the steps from the station and along the road to the arena. Luckily, I had kept my pumps on, and although I've never been much of a runner, I made it to the arena before the rest of the crowd from the train.

Travelling back to Wembley, I had decided to hang around near the back area of the arena. What was the point of making sure that I was at the front of the stage, only to find that when I was standing at the traffic lights later that evening, the car didn't stop because there were other people with him?

And, if I was at the back, I could try to push my way through to get nearer to the front.

Out of breath, I ran around the back of the arena intending to sit on the grass verge to watch the car arrive. However, as I rounded the corner of the building, I realised what a lousy idea this was, as the sound of teenage voices greeted me; chanting and screaming. Were they for real these kids, he wasn't even here, and they were going crazy? Also, I took one look at them all and suddenly felt incredibly old.

Not wanting to hang around with a bunch of kids, I wandered up the road towards the traffic lights, where I had planned to wait after the concert.

Half-way up the road, after I had rounded the bend and was now out of sight from the back of the arena, I came to a small office building with a metal fire escape on the outside. There was no one around by this time, and I was now completely out of sight of the fans who were congregating outside the back of the arena. Crossing the road, I walked up a few of the metal steps. Sitting down on one of them, I smiled and took in the magnificent view I had from here. I could see the junction clearly, and so whichever way the car approached the junction, I would notice it.

Perfect. Keeping my eyes trained on the traffic lights, as I had no idea what the car would look like, but I needed to see it before it passed where I was sitting; having the chance to see inside.

Around thirty minutes later I was still in the same position and looking across the junction I saw the car, as it waited for the traffic lights to change to green. It knew it was the right one; big and classy.

The lights changed, and it crossed the junction, driving quite slowly down the road. Drawing almost level with me, I could see inside clearly, and to my relief, I could also see that he was alone in the back seat.

Standing up, I bounced down the last few steps, to get another glimpse of him before the car was too far away, when no! The car had stopped to allow a large vehicle to pass the opposite way. Standing on the pavement, level with the back window of the car, I became rooted to the spot. His head turned, and he looked at me, and although his look was one of surprise, he smiled and waved. Realising I was behaving like an idiot, just standing there staring at him, I waved back as the car set off again.

Sinking back down on the steps, I could hear my heart beating far too fast and a strange dizzy feeling in my head. Had that just happened? Had he looked at me and waved to me; only me? This was the first time I had seen him in the flesh and how incredibly gorgeous he had looked completely took my breath away.

When my breathing had returned to normal, I ran through what had just taken place and then wondered? When I was standing at the top of this road later, would he recognise me; and would that be a good thing or a bad one? Having no idea what the answer was, I knew if I didn't get in the queue soon, I would definitely be at the back, which would never do!

While I wandered back down the road to the front of the arena, I thought again about what had just happened; trying to picture the expression on his face as he had waved to me. The whole thing had lasted no more than ten seconds, but as I closed my eyes, I could see the look on his face. Although it seemed to be one of surprise at seeing me standing there on my own, had also been one of lust. Laughing at this, I could only think that was the look I wanted. Wanting him so badly, if what I had just seen in his eyes was correct, then yes! Get to the traffic lights later, and I would give him all the lust he wanted.

Rounding the corner of the arena, I stopped dead! The queue was snaking across the front of the building and up onto the main road.

As I walked past everyone to join the end of the queue, I noticed many of them were adults. They would no doubt be leaving their offspring to attend the concert on their own and would then be waiting out here to collect them once it was over.

After walking past what seemed like hundreds of people, I joined the queue at the same time as a lady with a girl who was obviously much younger than the average fan, and was in floods of tears; the girl's mother nearly in tears herself, trying her best to console the girl.

Smiling at me the lady said, "Our bus got held up because of an accident, we should have been here over an hour ago; now we'll be near the back, so Melissa probably won't see a thing."

Looking down I could see the little girl (whose name I now knew was Melissa) was now sobbing, tears flowing down her pretty face.

This was a great opportunity, and one I wasn't about to pass up.

Crouching down so that I was level with Melissa's face, I spoke to her gently, saying, "Do you want to be at the front?"

Sniffing, she nodded, and so I continued, "I'll get you to the front, don't worry. You'll have the best view in the room." A huge smile appeared on her face as she took hold of my hand.

As I stood up, her mum looked at me, laughed and said, "And how are you going to that then?"

Taking a deep breath and speaking as quietly as I could, I explained to Melissa's mum, where I had just come from and about my plan for later. Explaining what I had in mind once we were inside the arena, as I too wanted to be at the front.

Looking at me in astonishment, she answered, "And do you think it will work?"

To this question, I laughed and answered, "Which part, getting to the front – no problem. As to the plan for later, I have no idea, but I do hope so".

Melissa's mum laughed again, and squeezing my hand, said, "Go for it girl, you deserve it. I wish had been as brave as you a few years ago. There were a few pop stars I would have loved to have got into bed." Looking at her, I wondered if she was right; was I brave – or was I just plain stupid.

It was now twenty minutes to seven, the doors were due to be opened at seven-thirty, and the concert was scheduled to start at eight. Time passed slowly, although talking to Melissa and her mum helped to pass the time.

Sitting on the ground I changed into my heels, stowing my pumps near the top of my bag for when I needed to change into them later, touched up my mascara, and thoroughly brushed my hair. Looking through my small compact mirror, I was more than happy with my reflection.

Melissa and her mum watched me, Melissa saying how pretty I looked while her mum just looked even more astounded.

Eventually, the doors were opened by two burly security men, and everyone started to pour in.

By the time we got inside the building the girls who had entered the building before us had started to scream, chant and cry to the point where I wanted to scream myself, just for them to cease their unbearable noise.

Once we were inside of the arena, I said to Melissa's mum, "Stay right behind me, I'm putting Melissa in front of me." With that I started to push girls out of the way, while at the same time shouting, "Move please, this girl is only small and suffers from claustrophobia, she needs to be at the front."

I could hear Melissa's mum laughing while holding onto the back of my jacket, which felt good as I knew that she was still behind me. Eventually, after giving a mouthful to a few of the girls who didn't want to move, we reached the barrier at the front, just to the left.

My sister, who had been to many concerts herself had advised me not to stand in the centre, as in her opinion solo singers didn't spend much time standing in the middle of the stage, but preferred to move from left to right.

The noise was deafening from what seemed like thousands of girls. I had been to quieter football games, how on earth could all these little girls manage to make so much noise?

There was still twenty minutes to go until he came on stage, and I was now a nervous wreck. The noise was driving me mad, and the prospect of my plan failing was making me feel sick. Melissa's mum could see what a state I was in and was constantly assuring me that everything would go to plan.

As she admired my scarf, which I suspect was to take my mind off the state I was in, I told her I had only got it that day.

Telling her the story of what had happened at the market, her eyes widened, as I related what the stallholder had said to me. Although I didn't believe in any of it, she went on to tell me that she did and 'Yes!' Some people could see what was going to happen.

"See!" she said, "I told you, you're in there. Just believe in yourself." Well! That was the second time that day that someone had said this to me. Okay then, I would try to believe in myself; hopefully getting what wanted.

Suddenly a voice came over the speakers, which silenced everyone for a moment. After a few security messages, finally, his name was

announced, and he walked onto the stage.
The screaming resumed.

Chapter 10

After exiting the back door of the hotel and getting into the car, which was parked in the hotel's yard, we began to move slowly through the early evening traffic, on the drive to Wembley.

Chatting to Gerry, I asked him where he had been that afternoon, on his journey around London.

Laughing, he told me he had seen Tower Bridge and Buckingham Palace and had tried some jellied eels, which he had found disgusting.

He was so enthusiastic about his afternoon which made my mood even worse; I wouldn't be able to go anywhere here in the UK, because of all these crazy fans wanting to rip away at me.

Approaching the arena, we stopped at the traffic lights across the road that led down to the arena. From here we could hear the roar of girl's voices, screaming and chanting my name.

Driving down the narrow road towards the back of the arena, we stopped to let a lorry pass on the other side.

As the car stopped, something caught my eye outside, and as I turned my head, I saw the most beautiful blonde girl standing alone just outside the car.

Wow! Where did she appear from, I thought, and before I missed my chance, I gave her a big smile and waved to her. As the car began to move again, she waved back to me. Leaning back in my seat I closed my eyes for a moment, thinking, now there's a girl who's pants I wouldn't mind ripping off.

She was still on my mind as we approached the caged area at the back of the building. Her face etched in my mind.

The outside was a mass of teenage girls and security men. Edging closer the car was surrounded by girls screaming and banging on the car windows, mixed with security, who were trying to pull them away. The car approached the gate as it was swung open by more security.

Doing my usual waving and blowing kisses which only made the girl's even worse, we managed to get into the caged area, the gates being closed behind us.

I heaved a sigh of relief. Arriving at the venues in the UK was horrendous, all those girls and I still hadn't seen one that looked over fourteen years old. Suddenly I stopped and thought! Recalling what had just happened on the road outside, I realised; the girl out there had definitely been older than the crowd outside.

"You okay mate," Gerry asked. Nodding I got out of the car. The girls behind me were still there, screaming like a bunch of banshees. Giving them a quick wave, I headed through the backdoor.

Being allowed a little time before going on stage and my usual bottle of cold beer to calm my nerves; I sat and thought about my life.

Wanting to sing and be a musician was all I had wanted since I had been a young boy but, never in a million years had I wanted this.

I wanted fans who appreciated me for my music, not girls who wanted to scream my name and rip my clothes off, if they got near enough. As I sat and drank my beer, my mind wandered to what had happened on the road outside, and the girl who I had just waved to. Her face wouldn't leave my mind, even though I had only looked at her for a few seconds.

Who was she and how could I find her, as I realised that she wouldn't be near the front of the stage, because of the time she had been on the road at the back; by this time the queue for the venue would be huge? This saddened me as I knew there was no chance of me ever seeing her again, and although I had only had a short glimpse of her, I knew I wanted to meet her.

Sighing I finished my beer trying to wipe the memory of her face from my mind.

All too soon, it was time to prepare for tonight's performance. After changing into my stage clothes, my make-up and hair done, I could hear my name being announced, and, if possible, the screaming got even louder. The intro to my opening song began, and I walked onto the stage, with a massive smile on my face.

Two hours of singing and pandering to a bunch of girls who wanted to do nothing more than scream, cry and tear at their hair.

Then back to my lonely hotel room. This was what my life had become.

Chapter 11

Wow! He was standing there right in front of me. I don't think I heard a word of that first song!

He was gorgeous on pictures in magazines, but up there in the flesh, he was amazingly beautiful in a way I can't even start to explain. Having waited for this moment for two years; looking at him singing and smiling up there in front of me made me so emotional, and even more determined to have him.

After a few minutes of being overwhelmed, I started to enjoy myself, holding Melissa's hand and swaying to the music, clapping enthusiastically at the end of each song.

At the end of one of my favourite songs, he came closer to the edge of the stage, and the front house lights came on. Starting to walk up and down the front of the stage, he said how nice it was to be in London and thanked everyone for coming.

Starting to cheer, he stopped right in front of me, stopped and looked straight at me, an astonished look on his face. I'm sure my heart stopped beating at that moment, as his eyes locked with mine for what seemed like forever, when it was probably more like five seconds.

Had he recognised me from the road at the back of the arena? No, I thought to myself; don't be so stupid, of course, he hadn't.

As he started to sing the next song, I convinced myself that I had imagined it. There were hundreds of girls in here; he could have been looking at any of them; even though Melissa's mum assured me it was.

However, a moment later, he appeared again, right in front of me, and this time there was no mistaking where his eyes were looking, they were staring directly into mine. Smiling at him, my heart was thumping inside me, and my knees felt like they were about to give way. How was this happening! Staying in the same position looking around the crowd, his gaze returned to me again and again!

It was like being locked inside a dream. Well, that was until the girl next to me, who was probably about fourteen years old started screaming on top note, "He keeps looking at me, he wants me!" She screamed it over, and over again. Stupid bitch! As if he would take a second look at her, she had mousy brown frizzy hair and big buck teeth. If I hadn't been so annoyed at her for spoiling my moment, it would have been hilarious.

She then pushed right in front of me, almost knocking Melissa over and although I was slightly taller than she was, there was no way she was ruining this for me; this was beyond my wildest dreams! With a swift kick to the side of her right ankle, she screeched and doubled over, giving me the chance to elbow her out of the way. Melissa's mum couldn't stop laughing.

The concert continued and two songs later, he was back in front of me.

Feeling as if he was singing just for me, the look in his eyes as he looked into mine were full of longing. Then suddenly he held out his hand to me! Unreal! Without thinking, I did the same, except I held out both my hands, wanting him to know how I felt, and that the reaction he was getting from me was serious.

It felt like we were the only two people in the room.

I knew I was drawing attention to myself, but I didn't care one little bit; sure now that there was something between us. If I could make it to the top of that road at the back, I was in there. Tears trickled down my cheeks, and at that moment, I felt so much love for him. I didn't care about anything else, apart from meeting him.

The concert was now over half-way through.

One of his songs was a slow ballad, where he sat on the edge of the stage and threw roses into the crowd while singing.

At the start of the song, he sat on the right side for a while, then got up and made his way to the left.

What happened next was both amazing and funny.

As he sat on the edge of the stage, he took one of the roses and placed it apart from the others. While continuing to sing, he lifted his feet on to the edge of the stage, so that his knees were near his chin and then! He opened his legs as wide as he possibly could. The crowd went wild. His suit was skin-tight and everything he "had down there" was on show! Laughing, I dropped my eyes to what I took to be on display for me and me alone, then back to his face, while unbuttoning the top two buttons of my top, revealing even more cleavage.

I couldn't help but laugh at the fact that he was advertising everything he had to a bunch of underage girls, but all the same I still looked straight into his eyes—as much longing on my face as I could possibly manage.

As the song was nearing its end, he picked up the rose he had placed apart and held it in his hand, while signalling to the security guard who was standing close by.

As he was doing this, I heard Melissa say to her mum, "Is that flower for me mum, it's the last one!"

Knowing he was going to ask the security guard to pass the rose to me, I grabbed Melissa in my arms, and as the security guard was level with me, I all but threw her at him, while looking straight into the eyes of the wonderful man on the stage.

Understanding me, he smiled and held out his arms to take Melissa from the security guard, sitting her by his side on the edge of the stage.

After ending the song, he spoke to her, (although the only people who knew what he was saying was himself, Melissa and the security guard) she positively glowed. Giving her the rose, he then kissed her cheek, and she was passed back to me.

Melissa's mum hugged me, and with tears in her eyes said, "Thank you so much, without you, we would be standing at the back, and none of this would have happened."

Smiling at me, she said, "That man up there has fallen for you, big time. The market lady knew, now go and make it happen and have a wonderful night. You deserve it, you lucky girl."

As the song ended, I blew what I hoped was a sexy kiss. Blowing one back to me, he looked down at my unbuttoned top; giving me the sexiest smile I could ever have imagined.

Was this happening; it was like it was meant to be.

Suddenly, there was something I needed to know.

Bending down so that I could speak to Melissa, I asked her what he had said to her. As she told me he had asked if I was her sister, I looked up at him and smiled. So, he had wanted to know if I was alone. The thought of this made me hope with all my heart that the reason he had asked her this was because he wanted to meet me.

Oh! How I hoped that he did.

I was in heaven, watching him sing and gazing into his eyes when he came to stand in front of me. He spent so much time in front of me, his fans on the other side of the room must have thought he had gone home.

I was in a world of my own; no one else in the room existed, just us two.

Until a voice from my side caught my attention. "Why are you blowing kisses and being so stupid, you've no chance with him, he's just being friendly?" It said.

Yes! The same annoying girl, I just had to shut her up. Turning to face her, I looked her up and down and said, in my haughtiest voice: "Is that a fact love, well did you see what he just put on show up there on the stage, well that's mine tonight, it's you who's got no chance".

She looked gobsmacked and turned away from me. I knew there were tears in her eyes, and I was a bit sorry for what I had said. However, there was no room for sentiment in tonight's plans; I had to keep focused if I was going to make what I had just said to the annoying girl come true.

Spending most of his time standing opposite me while he was singing, I was confused when he suddenly disappeared to the other side.

Looking at Melissa's mum, I saw that she was smiling at me. "What!" I asked her.

"Don't you know why he's gone to the other side?" She laughed.

Looking puzzled, I answered her, "No, why?"

Laughing, even more, she told me, "So he doesn't have to stand in front of you and look at you!"

As tears formed at the back of my eyes, she took hold of my hand and whispered to me, "You didn't see what was happening inside the bottom half of his suit. I just hope none of these kids saw it, but I did. He was becoming turned on, and I assume he has moved over to the other side of the stage until he has calmed down a little."

Was she right? Even though I had only met her a couple of hours ago, I trusted what she said, and if she was right, that meant he at least found me attractive.

When he eventually came back to stand in front of me, I tried to give him a more serious look and mouthed the word 'sorry'.

What he did next shocked me completely. Rubbing his hand over what he had displayed to me, he smiled, pointed to me and mouthed the words, "Yours tonight?"

Gasping, I could do no more than stare in astonishment, while Melissa's mum squeezed my hand and said, "Told you."

All too soon, he was announcing his last song.

Right! I needed to get out of here to have any chance of making it to the top of the road, in the short time I had. And so, while he was on one of his rare trips to the right side of the stage, I said goodbye to Melissa and her mum, thanking them for giving me the opportunity to get to the front.

Melissa's mum took my hand and said in a stern voice, "No doubts now, he wants you as much as you want him, I know it." Hugging her, I just hoped she was right.

Soon he was in front of me again and so blowing him another kiss, hugging and kissing Melissa, I turned and made my way through the crowd to the main doors.

Once outside, I found I was shaking. "Pull yourself together you silly cow; you've got this far; you can do it" I said silently to myself. Taking a deep breath, I made my way to the left side of the building.

Chapter 12

Walking onto the stage singing, with a smile plastered on my face, trying to make myself heard over the constant screams was horrific. What was wrong with these kids, if they liked my music, then listen to it, don't scream over it.

Going through the motions of singing each song on my playlist and shouting "Thank you,", at the end of each song was horrendous.

So, deciding to interact with the crowd (although I had no idea how) and needing a couple of minutes break from singing, I signalled to the stage crew to put the house lights on at the front of the arena.

Now that I could see the front of the crowd, I started to walk along the front of the stage from right to left. As I said how nice it was to be in London and thanked everyone for coming, my mind was thinking that even if any of them appealed to me, they were all much too young. But as I approached the left side of the stage, something stopped me in my tracks.

She was here! The beautiful girl I had seen on the road outside the arena. Somehow, she had managed to get to the front of the room and was standing right up against the barrier, and although she was not any taller than the girls around her, I had been right, she was most definitely older and more mature than all the others.

Also, she was standing there with her head on one side, smiling – no screaming or tearing at her hair, she looked so classy.

My heart was doing somersaults, as I locked my eyes with hers. Staring into this girls' eyes for far longer than I should have, I realised I should be getting into my next song, yet, all I wanted to do was stay exactly where I was.

As I started my next song, I couldn't shake the girl's face from my mind, finding myself wandering to the part of the stage where she was standing.

Two songs later as I wandered back to stand opposite her, I gazed into her eyes, again, and trying to give her my best sexy smile, I did something quite outrageous. Holding my hand out to her as I sang, she looked up at me, giving me what I can only describe as a shy sexy smile, and she then held out both of her arms to me. Staying like that for a few seconds – our hands held out to each other, it was then I saw she had tears in her eyes.

I really can't explain how this made me feel; but knew at that moment, I had to meet her; desperately wanting to feel her body up against mine. And, I wanted to know if her actions were because of the thrill of the concert, or did she want more.

The only issue I could see was that she was holding the hand of a girl who was younger than the other fans, probably about ten years old and maybe her younger sister. Questions went through my mind as I sung. Was the younger girl the reason she was here, and did she not want to see me perform? Why had she been standing at the side of the road alone?

One of the songs I had on my playlist was a slow ballad.

The usual performance ritual was to sit on the edge of the stage and sing, while throwing roses into the crowd, sitting on one side then moving to the other.

For the first half of the song, I sat on the right, then jumped to my feet and walked over to the left side. Sitting directly opposite her, I looked straight into her eyes.

As I continued singing, my legs dangling over the edge of the stage, I placed one of the roses apart from the others. Then I lifted my legs so that my feet were on the edge of the stage.

Looking straight into her eyes and smiling, I opened them as wide as possible; knowing how tight my suit was and that I was showing off 'everything I had' down there. Knowing this was kind of unethical in front of so many young girl's, I wanted a reaction from the only girl in the room that mattered to me. Looking into my eyes, then dropping them a little lower and back up again, she smiled such a sexy smile; my heart did summersaults.

Wanting to pass her the rose that I had placed apart from the others, I beckoned to the security guard standing to my right. As he approached, I was astounded as she lifted the little girl and threw her to him, while giving me a pleading look.

Laughing and understanding exactly what she wanted me to do, I took hold of the little girl and sat her next to me.

Finishing the song, I asked her name, which I discovered was Melissa. I then asked her if the girl who had lifted her up was her sister.

Looking up at me, she said shyly, "No, she's a lady we just met here, who got us all the way down to the front, I'm with my mum,"

Relief flooded through me; seemed she was alone, as I had initially thought.

Asking Melissa another couple of questions, I thanked her for being here, kissed her cheek and passed her back to security. As I did, I saw a lady who I now knew must be Melissa's mum, hugging the beautiful blonde girl.

Turning back to the stage, she laughed and then blew me the sexiest kiss ever.

Although I had started to sing, I wanted to cry. Even in a room packed with people, I felt that this was the start of something between us.

It had to be.

I knew I was spending too much time in front of her and that I was ignoring my fans on the other side. The thing was, as much as I kept moving to the other side of the stage, I instinctively moved back to stand in front of her!

Gazing at her, I let my mind wander, wondering what it would be like to kiss her and run my hands over her body.

Fantasising about what she would look like naked I was suddenly aware that I was becoming turned on. No! I couldn't have this happening in a room full of young girls, and although I didn't want to, I moved to the other side of the stage until my body returned to normal.

Moving back to stand in front of her once I had calmed down, I saw her mouth the word 'sorry' to me. Smiling at her, my only thought was, don't be sorry, this is only happening because I find you so damn sexy. Feeling reckless and needing her to know how I felt, I ran my hand over my lower parts, pointed to her and mouthed the words 'yours tonight'.

An amazing look appeared on her face, and at that moment all I could think was, I hope that look is because you want me as much as I want you.

When it was time for my last song, I was still straying in front of her as often as I could.

When she blew me another kiss, turned and disappeared into the crowd, I started to panic. No! I didn't want her to go, but then I realised or hoped, she would be at the back of the arena.

Swearing to myself that if she was there, then whatever it took I was getting her in the car with me. I had to, the alternative of never seeing her again was unbearable.

Ending my last song, I waved to the fans, blew little Melissa a kiss and disappeared backstage.

Chapter 13

Pulling myself together, I edged my way down the passage at the side of the building, moving slowly towards the gate I had found earlier that day. It had been light when I had checked out the area earlier; it was now pitch black with no lights anywhere in the vicinity.

When I got closer to the gate, I sat down on the ground and unbuckling my shoes, I took my pumps out of my bag and put them on, stuffing my shoes into my bag near the top, for when I needed to change back into them.

The gate looked much bigger in the darkness, but I was more than determined to climb over it, and so grabbing the metal with both hands, I said to myself, "Here goes!".

Putting one foot on the lowest part of the metal slats that ran across the frame of the gate, I heaved myself up and grabbed hold of the top one, as my other foot found a higher slat; I was now halfway up.

As I swung my leg over the top of the gate, I very nearly fell off as a voice behind me said,

"What the hell are you doing love; you're going to do yourself an injury?"

Turning my head gingerly round, I expected to see the police, but to my relief it was a guy in jeans and a leather jacket grinning up at me.

"Well give us a hand then" I replied cheekily.

"Get your other leg on this side, and I'll lift you down," he said in an amused voice.

Doing as he said, I lifted my other leg over the top of the gate, and when I had both legs on the other side, I felt two strong hands lifting me away by my waist and putting me carefully down on the ground.

Still looking amused, he asked me where I was going. There was no alternative but to tell him the truth, which he found hilarious.

Not wanting to waste any more time I thanked him, said goodbye and made my way towards the road.

Climbing over the small wall, which also seemed to be bigger in the dark, I ran across the area covered in bricks and rubble, being thankful that I hadn't changed back into my heels once I was over the gate; I would have ended up breaking my neck.

Going through the wire mesh fence, I was careful not to snag my clothes or get my hair caught, and then making my way to the warehouse I found the path which took me past the warehouse, and out onto the road.

So far so good, although by this time I was completely out of breath.

After running up the road to the traffic lights, I heaved a sigh of relief. I had made it here without any significant problems, which was a miracle! I now needed the miracle to continue.

All the time I had been heading towards my destination, I had been aware of the faint hum of girl's voices, shouting and chanting, which meant that he had still not come out of the arena.

Sitting on the ground, I once again swapped my shoes over. Brushing my hair which had become somewhat dishevelled during my assault course, I checked my appearance and was just deciding whether to touch up my make-up when the distant sound of the voices grew much louder.

"Oh my god," I thought! That must mean he had appeared from the back of the arena. Shoving my mirror back into my bag, I waited, my heart beating loudly. The voices got louder and louder, then suddenly faded away.

Standing there with my heart in my mouth, a million butterflies in my stomach, I saw the headlights of the car appear before it came around the bend. Holding my breath, I tried to look sexy while leaning on the traffic light.

If the car drove straight past me, all of this would have been for nothing. I tried not to think of this happening as it drove towards me.

As it approached where I was standing, I was aware that it was slowing down. Stopping next to me, the rear door opened, and the sexiest voice in the whole world spoke to me, "Would you like a ride somewhere?" it asked.

In a complete dream, I climbed in through the open door and sat next to him. As I looked into the eyes of the most gorgeous man in the world, I was rendered completely speechless, but inside I was thinking just one thing. "Yes, I've done it!"

This was where it all began.

Chapter 14

Heading for my dressing room, I stripped off and wrapped myself in the blanket that had been left there for me.

Lying back and closing my eyes, her face swam in front of me, making me fantasise what it would be like kissing her, touching her body and having sex with her.

I couldn't wait to cool down, get dressed and out to the car. She had to be at the back of the arena or why would she have left the concert before it ended.

How was I going to get her into the car when she would be one of several hundred screaming girl's I had no idea? I would talk to Gerry as soon as I was ready to go.

Gerry was sound. He knew how lonely I had been since I had been in the UK, and I knew if there were a way to get her into the car, he would be only too willing to help me.

Picturing her beautiful face and her sexy smile, I knew I couldn't face another lonely night alone, now that I had found a girl who I wanted to share my bed.

A voice broke through my thoughts, "Time to get dressed; you should be okay now," it said before the door closed.

Jumping up, I got dressed in record time, grabbed my guitar, and made my way out of my dressing room. Walking into the corridor that led to the back door, I waited for Gerry.

Catching up with me after a couple of minutes, he started to walk towards the back entrance. "You ready mate," he asked.

Grabbing his arm, I stopped him. "Gerry, there's this girl," I said, "Can you help me get her in the car if she's at the back, please?" The 'please' was more of a plea than merely good manners.

"Shit mate, that's a bloody tall order" he replied, looking at me like I had gone completely crazy.

"I know," I said but…. my voice trailed away; I couldn't even begin to explain what this meant to me.

Putting his hand on my shoulder, he answered, "Come on, I'll see what I can do, I promise."

We opened the door to a frenzy of screams, and once I was in sight, they grew ten times louder. For once, I took no notice, trying to scan the faces of the girls up against the fence. I couldn't see her and expecting her to be up against the fence as she had left the concert early, I started to panic. But by then, the crowd was at least ten people deep, and I could only assume she had been pushed back by the multitude of girls.

As we got in the car, me in the back and Gerry obviously in the driver's seat, we moved towards the gate where security positioned themselves, ready to open it. As it opened, the crowd surged forward, and the girl's faces surrounded the car.

Looking around, out of the front and side windows, and even behind me, there was no sign of her. "Where is she? She has to be here?" I said out loud, yet still there was no sign of her.

By now, we had edged forward, and most of the crowd were behind us. Trying to hold back the tears I stared out of the window, my emotions in tatters. I had been so sure she would be here in the crowd, now feeling that the connection we had made while I was on stage was nothing more than a bit of fun on her part and gratitude for giving Melissa the rose. Bitch! She had been stringing me along for her own amusement.

She had probably left early to meet her boyfriend. I should have realised that someone so beautiful wouldn't be unattached, she was probably having a good laugh at my expense. Putting my head in my hands, I closed my eyes, feeling like an absolute idiot. I was unable to hold back the tears any longer, wondering how I was going to get through yet another lonely night alone.

As we drove away from the arena, the loneliness inside started to engulf me, making my tears turn to sobs, when suddenly a voice broke through my thoughts. "Hey mate," Gerry shouted, "Is this the one you're looking for?"

As I lifted my head, I saw he was pointing to the top of the road, at the set of traffic lights, close to where I had seen her earlier. A massive smile broke out on my face, making all the nasty thoughts I had been having about her disappear in an instant! "Yes, it is" was all I could say in reply, as my heart started racing.

She was standing beside the traffic lights looking even more beautiful than earlier. My heart hammered in my chest, and my mouth felt like sandpaper.

Managing to wipe away my tears as Gerry pulled up beside her; I opened the door and spoke. "Would you like a ride somewhere?" I asked.

She didn't reply, just got into the car, sat close to me and looked straight into my eyes.

So, she wasn't only beautiful; she was intelligent too!

She had realised she had more chance of getting to meet me by being away from all the screaming girls. Speechless, I did no more than gaze at this beautiful girl who was now in the car with me. At last, here was a girl who was old enough to share my bed, one I fancied like mad!

I couldn't wait to be alone with her; knowing I was in for one hell of a fantastic night. But, at that moment, I had no idea how the next few hours would change my entire life!

Chapter 15

The car set off again for the drive away from the Wembley area.

At this point, neither of us had spoken; sitting there doing nothing more than gaze into each other's eyes.

Eventually, he spoke to me, asking me where I wanted to go. What was I supposed to say, "To your bed?"

Shrugging my shoulders, I tried to look cool, which just made him laugh.

"Would you like to come back to my hotel for a drink?" he said shyly.

Staring at him and thinking that this was going entirely to plan, what he said next completely blew my socks off!

"Please" he added, with a worried look in his eyes.

Reaching over, I took his hand in mine before answering him. "Yes, I'd like that," I said. We continued to gaze into each other's eyes.

He then leant back in the seat and taking my hand, pulled me towards him. As I slid across the seat, he wrapped his arm around me, pressing my head down onto his shoulder gently and began to run his fingers through my hair.

Wow, was this a dream? My whole goal had been to be here in this car with him, yet I still couldn't believe I had managed it and that he was treating me so lovingly. I was surprised at his behaviour; his reputation was that he treated girls as objects to be used for sex. But hell! I was going to enjoy this, before we got back to his hotel and it turned into 'quick sex' as I knew it would.

The car continued its drive through London, and soon we were crossing over the River Thames. At this point, neither of us had spoken, until suddenly he asked me what the name of the river was. Telling him, it was the Thames; this seemed to break the ice.

Asking my name and how old I was; I was sure I saw the relief on his face as I told him my age; realising, I was old enough for what I hoped he had in mind.

Soon after crossing over the river, we left the main road and drove down a side street, into the back entrance of what I took to be a large hotel.

As the car parked up inside the yard, his driver turned around in his seat. "Stay here, you two," he said, "I'll go and find Bill". He then got out of the car and disappeared.

"We need to go in through the kitchen area so that no one sees me" he explained. He then went on to tell me the "decoy hotel story" and that his driver, who I then found out was called Gerry had gone around the front of the hotel to find the night porter, who would let us in the back way.

Several minutes later, Gerry was back, accompanied by an older man with distinguished grey hair, wearing a smart black suit.

Before we got out of the car, he turned to me, "Are you sure you want to come up to my room?" he said gently. "I can get Gerry to drop you somewhere if you like."

Why was he saying this to me? Was he being considerate? Or did he want to get rid of me? Smiling, I answered him by saying, "If it's what you want, then yes I do?" As he took hold of my hand, giving it a squeeze, we got out of the car, following Gerry and the porter through the backdoor of the hotel.

After walking through a kitchen area, along a corridor and through another door we came to what I took to be a goods lift.

This lift took us up to the second floor, opening out onto another corridor, which took us through a large ballroom, to the hotel's main corridor.

Gerry and the porter walked in front of us until we came to another lift. As Gerry and the two of us got into the lift, the porter bid us goodnight and walked off down the corridor. This lift took us up to the seventh floor, where we got out and walked down the final corridor.

As we had travelled through the hotel, he had kept hold of my hand, even putting his arm around my waist when we were in the second lift; how loving he seemed to be acting had surprised me.

A little further along the corridor, we stopped at a door, and Gerry handed him his key, said goodnight, and walked further along to his room.

Unlocking the door, he turned to me and touched my face. "Thank you for coming back here with me," he said quietly. He then took my hand and led me through the door and down the corridor to the lounge.

The room, or should I say suite was beautiful, with big comfortable sofas and secluded lighting.

Standing there in the middle of the room, looking around at the beautiful surroundings, I suddenly felt completely out of my depth. What on earth did I do next! I had no idea what he expected me to do; his behaviour had been so loving and caring that I had become puzzled.

Did I sit down, rip my clothes off or turn and run, so I smiled at him and like an idiot, I said, "What do you want me to do?" No! What a stupid thing to come out with, I could have kicked myself and thought, this is where he throws me out for acting like an idiot.

The reality of what happened next was, however, quite the opposite. He looked at me lovingly, and walking across the room towards me, put his hands on my waist and brushed his lips against mine before saying, "Can I kiss you?"

What! He was asking permission to kiss me. What on earth was happening here? I had expected him to be ripping my clothes off by now, not acting like a scared teenager! Looking into his eyes, I smiled and replied, "Yes, if that's what you want?" And so that was what he did, gently and oh so sensually. As his lips met mine, a massive shiver ran through my body, and although I wanted to act mature, I was unsure how to respond. Did I let him kiss me how he wanted to, or did I try to respond in a way that would turn him on? Too late! I was responding to this breathtaking kiss with every inch of my body, pushing myself against him, and if he had ripped my clothes off, right there and then, I would have been powerless to stop him.

He was now as close to me as he was ever going to get, the smell of him so close to me was tantalising. I could smell the odour of his hair mixed with his body smells from him being under the stage lights, the reality of it making me feel dizzy inside.

My hands at this time were by my side until I realised that I should be doing something with them, so I wrapped them around his neck and pulled him even closer. Doing this seemed to work some kind of magic as his kiss became even more demanding.

I had kissed lots of boys in the past but "phew" this was some kiss. I wanted it to go on forever.

Suddenly there was a knock at the door. Pulling his lips away from mine, he kept his hands around my waist. "Sorry," he said, "Stay there, I'll be one minute."

As he disappeared towards the door, I stood there waiting, in a complete trance, wondering if the last two minutes had happened or whether it had been a dream. Seconds later, he returned, with an ice bucket, two glasses and two bottles of champagne on a large tray. "Champagne alright?" he said frowning, as though he should have consulted me first.

Champagne! I drank cider at home and had never even tasted champagne. As I nodded, he poured two glasses and handed one to me.

As we sat on the sofa, side by side, the conversation was, shall I say, a little strained!

Although we had shared the most fantastic kiss, it seemed that now he didn't want to be near me. He was sat next to me looking so worried I could only think he was looking for an excuse to ask me to leave.

What had I done wrong? Was I supposed to do something while he was kissing me? Had the way I had kissed him not turned him on enough? Drinking my champagne, I could have cried. I had got this far! So close! Now I had destroyed everything. Thinking I was mature enough to seduce him, I should have known better. He now saw me as another silly little girl because of how I had behaved and wanted rid of me.

If he wanted me to stay, then why wasn't he ripping my clothes off? Even though he had asked me back for 'a drink' it was obvious what he had meant, and yet he was sitting two foot away from me as though he had completely changed his mind.

Not knowing how this was going, I decided to pour myself another drink. This champagne was lovely, and if he did ask me to leave, I was at least having another glass of the stuff, before the inevitable happened, and he threw me out. As I did, he seemed to relax. Jumping up off the sofa, he pulled me into his arms and kissed me again, which astounded me. God! I was so confused, but this time I made sure I kissed him with as much passion as I could.

As this second 'amazing' kiss ended, he sat back on the sofa and patting the space next to him, asked me to sit next to him. Sitting close to him as he had asked, he wrapped his arm around my shoulders. By now, I didn't know what to think. He wasn't ripping my clothes off. He was acting considerate and caring, so trying to lighten the mood I started to ask him questions about himself, careful not to dwell on the fact that he was a big star, but questions about his home and his childhood.

He seemed to enjoy talking about his earlier life and told me about school and his first job.

He also told me that the girl's he had met while he was on tour in his own country just wanted him to sing his own songs to them while they sat there and cried.

He looked pissed off by this.

By this time, I had drunk another glass of bubbly. The drink was now taking effect on me, so glancing to where his guitar was propped up by the wall, I smiled sexily and said, "Sing whatever you want then."

He turned to look at me, and then kissed me so passionately I was the one who wanted to rip his clothes off, right there and then. Stopping suddenly, he jumped up from the sofa and went to get his guitar.

Sitting on the arm of one of the sofas he seemed to think for a moment and then started to strum his guitar, smiled and begun to sing, "Will you still love me tomorrow", which had been a big hit for Carole King.

All the time he was singing, he was looking at me. Tomorrow! More like forever! I had now perched on the opposite arm of the sofa, which was just as well, as my legs had gone so weak if I hadn't been sitting, I would have fallen over. He was sat here singing to me!

Was this happening, or was I going to wake up at any moment?

After he had sung another two songs to me, he had put down his guitar and flopping down on the sofa he had pulled me down beside him, kissing me passionately, but had not attempted to take things any further.

Somebody once told me that champagne goes straight to your head and makes you feel incredibly sexy. Well, they certainly got that right.

After three glasses, my shyness and nerves had gone, and I was talking nineteen to the dozen, laughing and being flirty with him. Although I was aware of how I was behaving, I didn't seem able to stop, which seemed to be having the desired effect.

Holding me gently in his arms, although we spent some of the time talking to each other, every time he kissed me, I had been expecting his hands to start wandering to other parts of my body; yet the furthest he had gone was to kiss my neck and run his hands across my back.

I was now laying with my head across his knees, looking up into his eyes. Moving his hand and touching me just below my neck, he traced his finger downwards until it rested where my cleavage was and leaning over and kissing me so gently, he started to unbutton my top slowly.

The champagne had gone; I had drunk a whole bottle.

Knowing I was drunk didn't seem to matter. I felt so relaxed and sexy and was now aware how turned on he was becoming, but I just kept on flirting with him, touching his face and hair while moving my head; knowing this was driving him crazy; while he continued to undo more buttons.

Closing my eyes for a moment, I heard him whisper my name.

As I looked up at him, he ran his hand through my hair, while undoing the last button. As he watched my top fall open looking at what was underneath, he said in a low voice, "Come to bed with me."

I couldn't believe how romantic he was acting; this wasn't how I had imagined it would be. Okay, this was what I had wanted from the beginning, but I hadn't expected the loving gestures he had made towards me. I thought he would have wanted sex as soon as we got into the room and then called me a taxi.

Sex as soon as we had arrived in the room would have been enough, but how he was acting was totally above my expectations, making my whole body long for him more than I had ever longed for anyone before.

Standing I held out my hand to him, standing up himself he took it in his he led me from the lounge. As we reached the bedroom, I began to panic.

I had no idea what to expect next; the quick sex I had anticipated hadn't happened, and now I feared making a fool of myself. My experience didn't stretch to this kind of romantic behaviour.

Standing facing him as he closed the bedroom door behind us, I wanted to cry. What did he expect me to do, he seemed so experienced, and I was worried that I wouldn't live up to his expectations?

As I closed my eyes, suddenly wishing I had not put myself in this situation, I heard him speak to me?

"What's wrong?" he said, so gently, pushing my hair away from my face, "Is this is your first time?" I could feel tears forming behind my eyes. "Please don't cry, we don't have to take this any further if you don't feel ready, we can lie on the bed together, and I promise I won't make you do anything you don't want to do." Putting his hands on my shoulders, he pulled me towards him and kissed me. Speaking again, I heard him say, "If you want to take it further, I promise I will be as gentle as I possibly can."

Stunned, I looked into his eyes and knew he meant every word that he had said.

But why? He took girls to his hotel for sex, not to lie next to them doing nothing more than kiss; worrying that they might be a virgin. Now

I was bewildered, and as I did no more than stare at him, he wrapped his arms around me and kissed me.

This was so beautiful. And although I still felt inadequate, I knew with all my heart I wanted to make love to this man kissing me so tenderly, experienced or not! Being here with him had been my whole goal from the beginning, and no way would I get this chance again, ever. I might appear useless to him once we got into bed, but at least I would have lived out my fantasy, achieving what I had wanted from the start.

Waiting until this wonderful kiss ended, I looked into his eyes, touching his face with my right hand, while running the fingers of my left hand up and down the front of his thigh.

"No, I am not a virgin, although I am in no way experienced, so please will you undress me?" I asked, "And then I would like you to make love to me." No way would I have said this if I had been sober – but I wasn't, I was drunk, and the smile it brought to his face was well worth it.

Closing my eyes, I felt his gentle hands push my top away from my body. Feeling much better now, I sighed, my body reacting to his hands brushing against my skin. As he started to unbutton my jeans, I responded by doing the same; undressing him, while touching him gently in the places I knew would affect him.

All I could do now was give it everything I had and hope I could please him enough; knowing that even though it would be quick sex and goodbye, I wanted the experience to be satisfying – for both of us.

Chapter 16

Gerry pulled away from the kerb and headed for the hotel.

Suddenly I had become unable to speak, I was so mesmerised by this girl's beauty, and that after my initial disappointment when she wasn't at the back of the arena, that she was now beside me. I just wanted to look at her, only I didn't want her thinking I was some kind of dumb, stupid pop star, and so I spoke, asking her where she wanted to go.

I don't think she knew what to say, as she just shrugged her shoulders at me, which made me laugh. Before she had time to answer me, I asked her if she wanted to come back to my hotel for a drink. Holding my breath, I expected her to say no, but instead I felt her take hold of my hand, look into my eyes and say, "Yes, I'd like that".

Was I dreaming or was the girl I had seen at the back of the arena and in the crowd tonight going to be with me, in my hotel? I just couldn't stop smiling.

Settling down in my seat, I put my arm around her and resting her head on my shoulder, I ran my hand through her beautiful blonde hair. As we travelled through the dark streets of London, although I had fantasised about having sex with her, now she was in my arms, I wanted to get to know her.

We fell silent for quite a while. Well, in all honesty, I didn't know what to say to her.

Never having had a problem chatting up the girls, somehow this felt different. I wanted this to be perfect and didn't want to open my mouth and ruin things, which I knew I was quite capable of doing. Although I realised that I would have to speak soon, as I was starting to make myself look like a fool.

As we crossed the Thames, I asked her what the name of the river was; although I knew it was the Thames, one of the most famous rivers in the world, I needed something to say. Asking this seemed to do the trick, and from there on, we started to talk; I also discovered to my relief that she was old enough to be here with me!

We arrived at the hotel, and before we left the car, I asked her if she was sure she wanted to come up to my room, telling her that if she had changed her mind, that I could get Gerry to give her a lift somewhere else. Why on earth was I behaving like this? This wasn't me at all! As where girls were concerned, I had never been considerate; just making sure I got them between the sheets and then losing interest as fast as it had appeared.

Although I wanted to make sure she was certain of what she had agreed to, as I said it, I was dreading her saying she wanted Gerry to take her somewhere. I had spent no more than thirty-minutes with her, now I wanted her by my side, in my room and my bed. Trying to rationalise my feelings to myself, I could only think it was loneliness making me act like this. I had not interacted with anyone in the last week or so, apart from Gerry and could only assume this was making me behave so strangely, being considerate and caring.

We made our way up to my room via the back entrance, and the courtesy of the night porter. As we had gone in through the back door, I had whispered to Gerry to order champagne from room service.

Going up in the lifts and through the hotel corridors, I kept hold of her hand. Although I knew she was old enough to be here with me and she had agreed to come up to my room, she was still young, and the last thing I wanted was for her to feel scared and uncomfortable. There it was again, the thoughtfulness that had suddenly gripped me; making me behave totally out of character.

As we arrived at my suite, I touched her face and thanked her for being here with me and then held her hand as we walked up the corridor to the lounge. What on earth had happened to me! I had turned into someone else. Someone who cared and treated girls with love and respect. Because this wasn't me. At all!

As we went into the lounge, I felt so sorry for her; she was stood in the middle of the room looking so lost and scared.

"What do you want me to do?" she suddenly blurted out.

I groaned to myself. She thought all I wanted was sex. But what could I expect when I had displayed my manhood to her; and mouthed the words 'yours tonight' to her?

I needed to make her realise that I wasn't about to drag her straight through to the bedroom. Walking towards her, I held her waist and asked her if I could kiss her and although she said "yes," I was scared that she wouldn't return my kiss, as I now knew I wanted her to do.

As I kissed her, there was no response, and then it happened! Her body pushed against me and her sudden incensed kiss made me want to rip her clothes off, throw her onto the nearest sofa and have what I wanted, like I would have done with any other girl. But no! Wanting sex straight away wasn't how I wanted to play this. Confused at my feelings, I continued to kiss her, although I wanted so much more. Feeling her arms wrap around my neck, and her body press even closer to mine was mind-blowing; this was the best, and I just wanted it to go on forever.

All too soon into this amazing kiss the champagne arrived, and as I reluctantly stopped, I asked her to wait.

Returning, I poured us a glass each and handed one of them to her.

Groaning to myself I knew this was making me look as if I was superior to her and realised what an utter and complete mess, I was making of this. As I passed her the glass of champagne, she looked at it as if I had given her a glass of poison! It was then I realised I should have asked her what she wanted to drink. Now it looked like I was just trying to get her drunk so that she would have sex with me.

I was behaving like an absolute fool, and as we sat side by side on the sofa, it became a little awkward with neither of us knowing what to say to each other.

Any minute I expected her to say she was leaving and had all but given up hope of the wonderful night I had anticipated, when she had first got into the car. Why would she want to be here with me when I was treating her as if I cared nothing for her feelings.

Finishing her drink, she got up from the sofa. "So, this is it," I thought to myself, my heart plummeting, but amazingly she poured herself another drink, turned to me and said, "This is lovely; I've never had champagne before". I felt like crying, "yes," she was staying, and I felt so incredibly happy. So happy that I jumped up off the sofa, pulled her into my arms and kissed her.

She started to talk to me then and asked about my life at home and about when I was a kid, seeming interested in me as a person and not the icon I had become.

Telling her that other girl's I had met while on tours of my country had always wanted me to sing my songs for them, which annoyed me. I knew the drink was starting to take effect when she looked towards my guitar and asked me sexily to sing, "Whatever I wanted".

Singing three songs that I always enjoyed singing, making sure they were all love songs which I hoped she would appreciate; she sat there and listened, properly.

After putting my guitar to one side, we settled down on the sofa again and talked to each other without any awkwardness, kissing every few minutes.

Knowing how much I wanted her, I tried my best to keep my hands to myself, going no further than kissing her neck, which I had to stop doing due to the thoughts racing through my head. Yes, I wanted her like mad, but much to my astonishment I wanted to act romantic; something I wasn't very good at.

On other occasions with girls I had picked up for a one-night stand, sex would be over by now, and I would be packing her off, either in a taxi or by courtesy of my driver. My feelings were confusing me; why was I acting in this way.

After finishing the champagne, she started to get very giggly and very touchy, sending shivers through my body. She had drunk a whole bottle, I knew she was drunk, and her closeness was turning me on so much.

She was now lay on the sofa with her head on my knee, and every time she wriggled, it made me want to touch her more than ever. Running my hand across her lower neck, I started to unbutton her top; wondering if her hand would suddenly grab mine, asking me to stop me. But no! I had undone four buttons, and the only response she had given was a deep sigh as she closed her eyes. And so, unfastening more buttons I bent over and kissed her, knowing I couldn't wait much longer; I had to do something and quick. So, whispering her name softly, she looked up at me.

Running my fingers through her hair and opening the last button, I gasped as her top fell open, revealing what was beneath. She was so beautiful, and I wanted her – now! Holding my breath, I whispered, "Come to bed with me."

Looking into my eyes, she smiled, got up from the sofa, and held out her hand to me. I took that as a yes and wondered how I had got so lucky.

Taking her hand, I led her from the room. I couldn't wait to make love to her, but as we reached the bedroom, I was shocked at the look on her face. She looked like she was ready to cry.

This wasn't what she wanted, and I was scared she would want to leave if I pressured her into sex. And as I thought of this, I realised that I didn't want her to go, and not because I wanted sex! I wanted her to stay whether we had sex or not.

As I looked at the scared expression on her face, I realised that she could well be a virgin. No, I couldn't do this to her. If she were, and wanted to stay that way, I would have to accept it, and so pulling her into my arms, I spoke as gently as possible. "Is this your first time?" Telling her I was happy just to lie on the bed, and that I wouldn't expect anything more if that was what she wanted, her look turned to one of confusion.

My reputation painted me as some kind of sex maniac, who had no real feelings and used girls only for sex. At that moment, I hated the image I had created for myself. I was lost here; how did I make her believe how differently I felt, and that having her here was more important than having sex with her. Whoa! More important than sex! What had happened to me?

I wanted to make love to her, but only if it was what she wanted too.

Not knowing how to handle this, I took hold of her hands and pulled her towards me, then wrapping my arms around her, I kissed her as gently as I could.

Not knowing how I was going to handle this; I eventually pulled my lips away. Before I could worry any more, she started to speak and what she said astounded me!

Looking into my eyes and touching my face with her right hand; her other running up and down my thigh, driving me crazy, she asked me to undress her and make love to her, assuring me that she was not a virgin.

Was she telling me the truth, or did she think I wouldn't want her if I felt she had no experience? The fact was I wanted her whatever her experience, and in a way, I wished she had said she was a virgin. The thoughts of me being her first was a wonderful feeling, making my protective instincts surface.

Now I was baffled by my emotions. Why did I care; she was a girl to have sex with and then throw out. But even as I thought this, I knew how wrong it sounded.

I didn't want "just sex," I wanted to make love to her.

Although I was still concerned about how she felt, no way was I passing up this chance. This beautiful girl standing in front of me was asking me to make love to her, so this was what I intended to do.

Starting to remove her top, she seemed to relax; sighing as I touched her.

Somehow, I knew without a doubt that I was about to experience the most amazing sex of my life, hoping that I would be able to satisfy her as I knew I wanted to.

Chapter 17

Sex had been amazing.

After I had let him know that I wanted him to undress me and make love to me, he had gently held me in his arms and then undressed me slowly, before turning back the covers of the bed and pulling me down beside him.

As my body lay by his, I realised that the bedsheets were pure silk. What on earth was happening here; I was in a bed with silk sheets next to the man of my dreams. Tonight, would live in my memory forever.

Once he lay facing me, he seemed to be holding back, and I was beginning to wonder again if he had changed his mind.

Worrying that he still thought I was a virgin, I started to panic. However, before I could worry more, he wrapped his arm around me and started running his fingers up and down my spine, driving me crazy.

Sod it, girl, I thought to myself. You're here now just make the most of it. If he doesn't enjoy sex with you because of your inexperience, then so be it. I'll be dressed and out of the door before I know it.

So, starting to touch the inside of his thigh with one finger, his breathing grew heavier, and this seemed to kickstart him. As he pushed me onto my back, he kissed me with so much passion my whole body came alive with desire.

Pure ecstasy!

He was gentle, caring and yet dynamic all at the same time! Doing everything he wanted, I tried to turn him on in ways I hoped he was enjoying. After touching and kissing me for what seemed like forever, he finally climbed onto me.

Waiting for him to push himself inside me, he stopped and spoke to me. "Are you sure this is what you want?" he said gently, "if you want me to stop, I will do. I'll do whatever you want."

Although still confused by his attitude towards me, by now I wanted this so much the only answer I could give was, "Yes, I want you, now," and pulling him towards me I kissed him.

As he pushed himself inside me so gently, my body came alive with passion; and at that moment, my inexperience seemed to vanish as I gave this incredible love making everything I had. This was so different from what I had experienced with boys back home, and the feelings it was creating were amazing.

As we both exploded with ecstasy together, and our bodies slowed down, I wanted to cry. This was it; it was over! I would be leaving in the next few minutes, leaving this perfect experience, and this caring, loving man behind, forever.

Waiting for him to get off me, and say the inevitable, "I'll call you a taxi," he did the complete opposite!

Lifting himself off me, he lay down by my side, faced me and stroked my hair. "Was I good enough for you?" he whispered.

Back came the confusion.

Was he good enough; should I not have been saying that to him? And although I didn't understand why he had asked me this, I knew I had to try and act mature and so kissing him first, I said, "Yes, not just good, you were amazing."

Did I imagine it or at that moment did I hear a sigh of relief? Lying by his side was beautiful. I knew, without a doubt, I didn't want to leave. But on the other hand, I didn't want him thinking I was some clingy female that he couldn't get rid of. What I had wished for had happened. He had asked me back to his hotel; we had made love, and now it was time for me to go.

Preparing what I was going to say, which was something along the lines of, "Thank you, I'll get dressed now," he suddenly jumped up, while muttering, "Need the bathroom, won't be long," making a dive towards the bedroom door.

Lying in this big beautiful bed, I gazed at my surroundings. The curtains had been left open, and the moon was casting a glow over the whole room. Feeling warm, comfortable and extremely satisfied, I wanted nothing more than to cuddle up to him when he got back into bed and drift off to sleep.

But I knew, that wasn't what this was about. It was sex and then goodbye, and so I swung my legs over the edge of the bed and sat up.

Finding my clothes, which had been scattered around the room, I started to dress. After putting on my top and pants, I was pulling on my jeans when the door opened, and he came back into the room.

Stopping dead, he stared at me, and the look on his face seemed to change to one of anguish. Crossing the room in an instant, he knelt at my feet and took hold of my hands, stopping me from pulling my jeans on.

Speaking so quietly, he said, "Why are you getting dressed?" He looked as though he wanted to cry, which of course confused me even more.

Before I could launch into my rehearsed line of, "Thank you, I'll be going now," my eyes looked down to the lower half of his body.

Realising I now knew what he wanted, panic seemed to cross his face. But before I could speak, he kissed me for what seemed like forever and then started to unbutton my top again, while saying tenderly, "Please don't go yet, I would like to make love to you again."

Staring back at him, I could only think, this is unbelievable. He wants me to stay longer, to have sex again. Standing up, I wrapped my arms around him, as he removed my pants, running his hands over my body.

Pushing me back onto the bed, our hands were everywhere and feeling much more confident my imagination took over.

This was fantastic and feeling so honoured that he wanted me again, I gave it everything I possibly could, wanting to please him even more than I had done the first time.

Eventually, after making love for much longer than we had done the first time and satisfying me yet again, he flopped onto his back, and as he lay there, I heard him yawn.

Taking this as a hint that he was tired and would now want me to leave, I prepared to say my goodbyes. However, before I could speak, I felt his arm wrap around my waist and his lips on mine.

This was nothing more than a goodbye kiss, and as I lay there loving every moment of what I knew was my last ever kiss from this wonderful man, I waited for it to end before speaking.

As his lips moved away from mine, I was astounded when he pulled me towards him, slid his arm underneath me, holding me in his arms with my head on his shoulder.

Although he had sat and sung love songs to me and waited for over an hour before he asked me to go to bed with him, then offering to 'lie on the bed', I was still convinced that I would be getting dressed and into a taxi fifteen minutes later.

This was the reputation he had, sex then a quick kiss goodbye.

Lay there in his arms with my arm around him; I couldn't help but smile to myself, thinking of the last twelve hours and just what had happened in this short time.

As we lay face to face, he was running his fingers lovingly up and down my arm.

Why hadn't he asked me to leave? Why was he still being so loving when he had got what he wanted?

Thoroughly exhausted after the trials of the day, I felt happy and satisfied and what he was doing was making me feel sleepy. Thoughts of getting dressed and into a taxi slipped from my mind and very soon, I was asleep.

I don't know how long I had been asleep, but suddenly found myself sitting up in bed, sobbing and shaking; thoughts of walking the streets of London alone in the dark going through my head.

Tears were pouring down my cheeks, making my eyes sting, as my mascara ran into them. Rubbing at my face and trying to calm myself, I hoped I hadn't woken him.

Too late. A voice by my side spoke to me softly, "What's wrong," he said, but I couldn't answer, I felt like such an idiot with mascara and snot all over my face—crying like one of his stupid little girl fans!

Suddenly, he jumped up, making me flinch. This is it, I thought, I could almost hear him saying it, "Right get dressed, I'll call a taxi."

Yet again, what he did was entirely different. Instead of asking me to leave, he knelt in front of me on the bed and took my hands in his. "Please tell me what's wrong," he said sadly, "regrets?"

Looking up at his face, full of concern, I sighed; knowing I had to explain just what had made me behave like a hysterical fool. He deserved to know that I regretted nothing!

Was he now thinking he had pressurised me into sleeping with him? What we had done I had wanted as much as he had and had done willingly. I would never, ever regret it!

If this ruined everything and he did ask me to leave, it was better if we had no physical contact. Pulling my hands away from his, I shuffled back and sat on the pillow, my back against the headboard. As I did, he grabbed my hand, while saying, "What have I done to you, why don't you want to be near me?" He looked so distressed and had tears in his eyes.

The look on his face was too much, and instead of sitting on the pillow, I fell into his arms. As he stroked my hair, I sobbed like my heart was breaking.

Although I wanted to stay here with him more than anything in the world, I knew at that moment whether he asked me to leave or not; I was going to end up with a broken heart.

Still struggling not to cry, somehow between the sniffles and hiccups, I started to tell him why I had become so distraught.

When I explained that I had expected him to ask me to leave, he sighed and held me even tighter in his arms.

Oh, my God! How good it felt, except that I was now covering his shoulder in mascara and snot.

Eventually he lifted my head and looking into my eyes, he said the most beautiful thing of the whole night. "The only place I want you to go is back to bed with me," he whispered.

Looking at me with a worried look on his face, I knew. We had now moved on from a night of casual sex and fun. The look on his face wasn't desire or lust anymore. It was caring and full of deep concern. This was no longer about getting into his hotel room and bedding him. I had got to know the real person, not the big star.

He was no longer my idol. He was now the man I was falling for, completely.

This wasn't supposed to happen.

Chapter 18

I had never experienced sex like this! She was so full of energy and aroused feelings in me that I didn't even know existed.

All the girls I had slept with before had been one-night stands whom I had fancied but didn't care about, just wanting sex with them. If I managed twenty-minutes, it was a bloody miracle. I knew I wasn't much good in the sack, but frankly, I had never really cared.; just as long as I got what I wanted.

This was different though; I wanted to get this right; I really cared what she thought of me. I wanted to make sure she enjoyed it with no concern for myself. Also knowing I wasn't much of a performer in bed, I was worried I wouldn't live up to her expectations.

Trying to take things slowly, I held her in my arms before I started to undress her. She was amazing when we finally got in bed, touching me in ways I was unused to, and responding to how I was exploring her body, giving small moans and sighs. This was incredible!

Although I wanted nothing more than to climb on top of her and go for it, I was experiencing feelings that were entirely new for me, holding me back.

Eventually, I could wait no longer. I had to have her, and although she had asked me to make love to her before I did, I asked her if she was sure it was what she wanted.

Half expecting her to ask me to stop, her response surprised me, when she said, "Yes, I want you, now." Pulling me down by the back of my head, kissing me, driving me wild.

As I pushed myself inside her, I was confused at the feelings inside me. Although this was what I had done many times with other girls, this felt different. It was *beautiful*; a word I never had in my life associated with sex. Usually, it was just about venting my frustration. I had never cared how long it lasted, or whether I had satisfied the girl who I had been banging away with.

Trying to take it slowly, I knew that I was rough some of the time, but at the same time I tried to be romantic; kissing her neck and stroking her hair, just hoping that I hadn't put her off by being too rough. And, as the thought shocked me, I was concerned that I had managed to satisfy her; being prepared to go for longer until I did!

Not knowing how long I could hold on for, she suddenly screamed out and thrust against me so forcefully I could hold back no longer, and as her body slowed, mine matched it, perfectly.

After what had been the best sex I had ever experienced, I asked her if I had been good enough; to which she replied I had been amazing. Was she being polite, or had she enjoyed it? I wanted her to understand that this meant something more than casual sex to me.

With previous girls, at this point, I would be saying goodbye to them, ready to get some sleep! But at this moment the last thing I wanted to do was sleep. I wanted to look at her, hold her, and as the thought shocked me, make love to her again. Where had these feeling come from?

Needing to visit the bathroom, I apologised and went to answer my call of nature.

Returning to the bedroom, intending to be as romantic as possible before I asked her if I could make love to her again, I was devastated to find her half-dressed, preparing to leave.

No, she couldn't leave me now and not because I wanted sex; this made no difference. If she said no to sex, I would still want her to stay.

Panicking, I almost ran across the room and knelt before her, asking why she was getting dressed.

Before she answered me, I saw her eyes look down. Now she knew what I wanted and looking at the confusion on her face just made me want to cry. She had thought that all I had wanted was sex when we first got to the hotel, and now, I was proving her right.

Backing up my reputation!

Not having a clue what to do next I kissed her, making me feel instantly better as she returned my kiss so beautifully and so sexily. The only problem was, kissing her like this was making me want her even more. Feeling suddenly brave, I pulled away, and starting to undo the buttons on her top, I spoke to her.

If she said no and left, then it would be down to me. "Please don't go yet. I would like to make love to you again." I said, in a shaky voice. As she stared at me, I had the feeling she was going to say she was leaving, then without warning, she wrapped her arms around me, leaving me to remove the rest of her clothes.

The sex I had already experienced with this amazing girl had been incredible, but nothing to compare to what happened next! This was mind-blowing. Not wanting it to end, I eventually rolled onto my back, knowing tiredness was catching up with me.

Making sure I had satisfied her enough, I lay there, totally exhausted. All I wanted now was one beautiful kiss, and to hold her in my arms. Running my fingers up and down her arm, after I had pulled her closer to me, her head resting on my shoulder, I was still scared that she would say she wanted to leave.

Trying my best not to fall asleep – partly, because it seemed rude - but also because I was so worried that when I awoke, she would be gone. It was impossible, the more I tried to stay awake, the more my eyes closed.

After a two-hour concert, drinking a bottle of champagne and then the fantastic sex I had experienced, (twice), I was sound asleep in seconds.

I'm quite a heavy sleeper, nothing much wakes me and so awakening to the sound of someone sobbing beside me, I thought I must be dreaming.   As I tried to make sense of what I was hearing, memories of what had happened earlier flooding through my mind.

Looking up, she was sat by my side, sobbing uncontrollably. No! What had I done to make her cry like this? "What's wrong?" I asked her quietly, not wanting to distress her any more than she already was.

When she didn't answer, I jumped up, knelt in front of her and took hold of her hands, and as I did, I felt her flinch. Pain shot through me at the thought of her not wanting me to touch her.

I had to know what was wrong, however bad the answer turned out to be, so I asked her what I thought was the obvious question, if she regretted sleeping with me? After all, she was younger than me and had been drunk, so was she now regretting what we had done? Had she been a virgin after all? Had she thought she couldn't say no to having sex with me because I had invited her here?

No, what had I done to her? My heart breaking at the sound of her sobbing.

As she gave another loud sob, she shuffled back on the bed so that she was sat on the pillow with her back against the headboard. Grabbing her hand and trying not to cry myself, I asked her why she didn't want to be near me.

Before I knew it, she was falling into my arms, still sobbing uncontrollably. Holding her in my arms as she cried, I stroked her hair.

When she had calmed down, she started to tell me what had made her freak out and become so upset. What she said, astounded me!

First, she assured me that she didn't regret any of what had happened; that she had wanted me as much as I had wanted her. She then went on to say that she was expecting me to ask her to leave at any moment.

She was still wrapped in my arms as she told me and thinking that I hadn't a clue where she had got that idea from, I realised it couldn't be further from the truth. If I could stay in this hotel room forever with her by my side, I would be the happiest man alive. Something about my feelings for this girl were different than anything I had ever felt.

I could feel her tears on my shoulder, but I didn't care, it felt beautiful.

Needing to reassure her that she had got this completely wrong I lifted her head away from my shoulder, saying quietly, "The only place I want you to go is back to bed with me".

At that moment I thought back to one of the songs I had sung to her earlier that evening, *"Will you still love me tomorrow"* and realised that I now meant every word of that song, *"But will my heart be broken, when the night meets the morning sun."*

I hoped not; I wanted her to love me. Not just tonight but forever.

Suddenly I knew, I had fallen for her completely, the thought scaring the hell out of me. What if she didn't feel the same, what if I was nothing but a night of fun to her? She had to feel the same: the thought of her feelings for me not being serious tortured me.

I had wanted a girl to love, and now I had found her.

Chapter 19

We stayed sitting on the bed for quite a while, still wrapped in each other's arms.

This was heaven.

Now that we had talked through my insecurities, I was starting to feel better. If possible, my feelings for him had grown; even though I knew how complicated this had become.

Realising that this was going to cause me total heartbreak, I knew there was nothing I could do about it? Nothing at all except love him for as long as he wanted me here. Although he had said he wanted me to stay, I assumed that he would still ask me to leave at some point. The only explanation I could think of was, that out of consideration he would wait until the morning when it was light; not wanting to throw me out in the dead of night.

Deep in thought, his voice broke through them, suddenly saying, "Let's go for a walk."

Turning to look at him as though he had completely lost the plot, I couldn't help laughing. "It's pouring down with rain, and this is South London," I replied, "it's a pretty rough area."

But by this time, he had stopped listening and was hunting for my clothes.

As I watched him getting dressed and throwing items of clothing to me, I realised I would agree to anything to be here by his side. If he had asked me to abseil down the side of the hotel, I would have agreed. Nothing seemed to matter except being here with him!

When he had dressed, he threw me the Basque top I had worn for the concert. I caught it and looking at it, shook my head and said, "No, I don't think so, South London in the middle of the night, not a good idea". Going through to the lounge with the clothes he had thrown to me, I found my bag and retrieved the bra and vest top, that I had worn to travel down to London earlier that day.

Once I was ready, I went back through to the bedroom. As we smiled at each other, he started to say something, then stopped.

"What?" I said, but he just grabbed my hand, kissed me and headed towards the door.

Walking down the corridor hand in hand, we made a reverse journey through the hotel until we found the back door that we had entered through earlier that night.

Looking at the door, I groaned. "And how are we going to get back in here," I asked. It was one of those doors that slammed shut behind you.

He looked totally clueless and just giggled. Too practical a question for a man I thought!

Sighing I started to look around the storeroom that the back door led out from, eventually finding a flattened cardboard box. Opening the door, I pushed him out, and then wedged the door open with the box.

As we stepped outside, we realised just how hard it was raining; it was bucketing down. Real British weather!

"Still want to go?" I asked, as he turned to me and held me in his arms.

Smiling at me and nodding, he took hold of my hand, as we walked out of the yard onto the narrow street that the hotel led out onto.

Walking to the main road, he told me he would like to walk to the river but didn't know in which direction to walk. Luckily, my sense of direction is relatively good, and so I led him through the streets, in what I hoped was the correct direction

As we walked along the rain-sodden streets with our arms around each other's waists, he stopped, turned to me, and kissed me.

Although every kiss had been romantic, this by far outweighed them all.

Standing there so close to each other, sharing this beautiful kiss, I started to realise he was becoming aroused again. Although I wasn't completely naïve, I didn't understand why this was happening.

When I had slept with boys back home, it had been once, and that had been enough for them. Back at the hotel, he had already made love to me more than once, which had astounded me; so why did I feel like he wanted me again, so soon?

By this time, the rain was soaking through my clothes and dripping off my hair. We were both soaked through, but I wouldn't have traded this for the world. I was walking through the streets of London in the rain with the man of my dreams; nothing could compare to how I felt at that moment.

Turning a corner by a large warehouse building, the Thames came into view, making me feel quite pleased with myself. He certainly looked impressed that I had found my way there without any problems, and turning to face me he held my face with his soft, gentle hands and said, with such a loving look on his face, "You're amazing, do you know that. I've never met anyone who makes me smile so much," and kissing me again he took my hand and together we walked towards the river.

Walking up to the barrier, we stood looking down at the grey, murky water.

By now I was shivering, it was freezing, neither of us had thought to wear a jacket.

I could now feel the water soaking through my underwear and into my skin, making my body tingle, as it created such a sensual feeling flood through me. Knowing how he had been feeling only a few moments ago made me want him too; right here, and I would have taken things further, only I was scared that I had mistaken his feelings and was scared of looking like a fool.

As we stood there looking into the water, my mind began to question what it was that he wanted now. We had slept together, twice, so what was it he wanted from me now?

Okay, he had been romantic and caring but all the same, he had got what he had wanted, so why was I still here walking in the rain with him in the middle of the night? Not asking me to leave while it was still dark outside was considerate. But this, why?

Not that I was unhappy about any of it. When I had dreamed of meeting him, I would never in a million years have expected this!

Glancing sideways at him, I could see he was also deep in thought. How I would have loved to know what was going through his mind at that moment.

As I was about to suggest we headed back, he turned towards me and put his arms around my waist. Standing there looking into my eyes, he was silent for a moment; then out of the blue, he just came out with it. Lifting his right hand, he stroked my wet hair, "I love you" he said, so quietly, I could hardly hear him, yet I knew exactly what he had said.

As I had stood here with him only a moment ago, wondering why I was still here with him, this wasn't anywhere near what I had expected. He was standing here in the pouring rain, in the middle of the night telling me he loved me!

A tear trickled down my cheek. No words could explain how I felt at that moment, as I knew at that moment how much my feelings for him had also changed in the last few hours.

Falling for him in this way wasn't supposed to happen. It was about getting him into bed and then walking away with good memories, boasting to my mates when I got back home. Now it had gone too far for that, and I knew I could never tell anyone. It would be hard enough getting friends to believe I had met him and had sex with him. But this, no one would believe a word of it.

Thinking that I loved him before I came to London, gazing at the posters of him on my bedroom wall and listening to his songs. I now realised that it had been nothing but infatuation.

This was love.

Pulling me into his arms, he nuzzled into my wet hair, saying, "Please don't cry. I was going to say it before we left the hotel, but I wanted to find a more romantic setting."

Although my heart was breaking, I couldn't help laughing. Romantic! Standing by the mucky Thames in the pouring rain; although when I looked around, I realised how romantic it really was. Tower Bridge was a dark shadow across the sky and moonlight glimmered across the water.

Turning back to look into the eyes I loved so much, I threw my arms around his neck and gave him a long passionate kiss. "I love you too," I answered.

Standing still taking in what we had just declared to each other, tears rolled down my face as he ran his hands through my wet hair.

Walking back to the hotel was the most magical experience ever as we stopped every few steps to kiss. Although I knew I had no more than a few hours left with him, I had never been happier in my life, and I was determined to make the most of every second left.

I also knew for sure that whatever happened to me in the future, I would never forget how I felt at this moment, and that I would love him until the day I died.

As we walked back into the hotel yard, we both needed to get out of our wet clothes. Fortunately, the cardboard was still in place, and as we made our way back up to the room, although we were soaked to the skin, I felt so incredibly happy.

Chapter 20

Feeling happy and content, I sat on the bed with my arm across her shoulder's, stroking her hair and wiping the last of her tears away with my other hand. I realised that my feelings for this girl by my side had grown unbelievably in the short time we had been together.

As I had gazed at her earlier, I had known how much I wanted to meet her; but at that time, it had been about getting her into bed. But now as I held her in my arms, her eyes still damp from the tears she had cried I knew how much this had changed. Now I wanted her in my life; to love her and be with her seemed more important than anything in my life.

How had this happened in such a short time? I had no idea but knew it was what I wanted, for sure; the thought of her walking out of my life was creating unbearable pain inside me.

Now that I had assured her how I felt, she was starting to calm down and had finally snuggled up to me.

Suddenly I knew I wanted to do something impulsive! Something that we would both remember well after today when we were miles apart.

"Let's go for a walk," I said and laughed when she turned her head and looked at me as though I had gone crazy.

Muttering something about the fact that it was raining and not being in a safe area of London to go walking, I had now stopped listening, and was getting dressed while at the same time, hunting for her clothes.

Sighing, she got off the bed and disappeared into the other room.

When she came back into the bedroom, she was dressed. Even though she was only wearing jeans and a vest top, she looked unbelievably beautiful and sexy. Wanting to tell her that I had fallen in love with her, I stopped myself, deciding instead to wait and see if I could find a more romantic setting out in London.

Holding her hand, we walked out of the room.

When we got down to the back of the hotel, she pointed out that we wouldn't be able to get back in through the backdoor, as it didn't open from the outside.

Staring at her and giggling I hadn't a clue how to get around this problem, but watched in amazement as she rummaged around, finally finding some cardboard which she used to prop the door open.

I was amazed at how intelligent and resourceful this girl was, and more so how it filled my heart with even more love for her.

Walking from the back of the hotel onto the streets, "Which way is the Thames, do you think?" I asked.

Although she said she was able to find her way, I wondered if she was bluffing, but still let her take my hand and lead me in what she thought was the right direction.

Kissing as we walked through the wet streets was so magical, and the fact that she was so close to me was starting to turn me on again, although I didn't want her to know.

She had been so upset back at the hotel. I didn't want her thinking that sex was the only thing I had on my mind.

Back home, my sex life had been good, plenty of girls to choose from - all of them more than willing to sleep with me. Knowing I was nothing more than a conquest because of who I was, I took sex as often as I could, but had no desire to see any of them again.

Being with this girl who had walked into my life tonight felt completely different. My feelings in the few hours we had been together had become so intense that I wanted to be with her forever. I had fallen in love with her, and although there was every chance that she would laugh in my face, I had to tell her.

As we walked on and turned a corner, the Thames came into view. Impressed, I hugged her. Was there no end to her talents!

Walking up to the barrier, we stood there looking at the river. It was beautiful, the moon was casting light across the water, and the scenery of London was stunning.

Gazing into the water holding each other, we fell silent, both locked in our own thoughts. Not wanting to wait any longer, I turned her towards me and held her waist.

Falling silent again for a moment, while she stared into my eyes, I started to speak. I was terrified of the reaction I was going to get, but I knew I had to tell her.

Running my hand down her wet hair, I said as quietly as possible, "I love you". A solitary tear ran down her cheek.

Wrapping my arms around her, I buried my head in her shoulder so she wouldn't see my tears.

We were both going to end up with broken hearts. What on earth had I done? I should have hidden my feeling from her, yet at the same time, I wanted her to know how deeply I felt for her

She was the girl of my dreams, and I thanked God I had found her and could try to make her happy, if only for a few hours.

Suddenly, she kissed me with so much passion. I thought I was going to scream.

When she stopped, she looked at me and simply said, "I love you too". Now there were buckets of tears pouring down her beautiful face, and all I could do was hold her and run my hands through her hair.

What a mess! Although there was nowhere, I would rather be, I knew for sure it would destroy me when I had to leave her.

Gerry II

One of the instructions I was given during my briefing for this job was, 'to get him anything he wanted.' And so, when he grabbed hold of my arm as we were ready to leave the arena and asked me to get a girl he had seen in the audience into the car, I had no alternative but to agree.

How I was going to get through hundreds of screaming girls to the one he wanted I had no idea!

I was also concerned about how old this girl was. Dragging an underage girl into the car didn't seem like the right thing to do, and when she wasn't at the back of the arena, I was quite relieved. Although as we drove away, I could see he had dropped his head into his hands and was starting to become upset.

When I spotted a girl standing by the traffic lights, I asked him if this was the girl who he had been looking for, and I was utterly amazed at the change in him, the smile and relief on his face was unmistakable.

Stopping the car at the spot where she was standing, he opened the door and asked her if she wanted a lift. As she got into the car, I saw to my relief, that she was quite a lot older than most of his fans.

Watching them for a few moments through the interior mirror, I smiled to myself, and all I can say is that if 'love at first sight' exists then I had just been a witness to it.

When we arrived at the hotel, I made sure they got safely up to his room.

He had whispered to me on the way up to order champagne, so after ringing room service, I lay on my bed fully clothed.

The rumour my colleagues had gleaned from somewhere was that after he had got what he wanted, he would ring my room, asking me to give the girl he had picked up a lift somewhere.

However, they had not met him and didn't know him. Something told me my phone wouldn't be ringing that night!

My room faced the back of the hotel, so when I woke during the night by a noise outside, I got up and looked through my window.

I couldn't help but smile. It was pouring with rain but what I saw was beautiful beyond words.

The two of them were walking hand in hand out of the hotel's back entrance. Silly sods, I thought, did they not realise that they couldn't get back in through that door.

Putting my shoes on, I went downstairs to the back door intending to prop it open for them when they returned. When I got to the door, all I could do was laugh; it was already propped open with a piece of cardboard.

It seems they didn't need my help after all.

Yawning I made my way back upstairs to get some sleep. Maybe not now, but I knew that I would be needed tomorrow.

What I had seen tonight was going to cause heartbreak, for sure!

Chapter 21

We got up to the room without encountering any problems, although how we didn't wake the rest of the hotel, I have no idea.

As we used the lifts and walked through the hotel corridors, we were like two naughty children; giggling, kissing and generally just being silly; even doing a mock waltz as we crossed the ballroom.

By this time, I was in heaven, feeling so happy and reckless, although my clothes were glued to my skin, and I was shaking with cold.

"Get undressed and have a hot shower" he advised, to which I could only nod, my teeth were chattering so severely all I could manage to say was "Can you help me undress please."

As he helped me to remove my wet clothes, his hands were continually brushing against my damp skin, sending shivers through my body until he helped me to pull off my jeans.

Suddenly the expression on his face turned to one of horror. "What's happened to your legs" he cried.

Looking down, I groaned. From the top of my legs down to my knees, my skin had turned black, with more black streaks running from my knees down to and covering my feet.

I looked back up at him, "It's okay" I said, laughing, "It's only the dye out of my jeans". He looked bemused, so I explained that we couldn't buy black denim in England, and that myself and my sister had dyed a pair of light blue jeans each in her washing machine, with industrial dye that someone had given her.

He couldn't stop laughing at my explanation and gave me a big hug. "In the shower now, I'll come in with you and help you get it off" he laughed, and then stripped off.

Somehow, I knew he had been looking for an excuse to join me in the shower and wondered why he hadn't just suggested it.

But I knew; it was because he was considerate and caring, which made me love him even more.

The black dye came off my legs quickly with a bit of soap, probably because it hadn't had time to dry on my skin. When my legs and feet were clean, he started to wash the rest of me, starting with my shoulders and arms and then moving to more intimate parts.

As he was washing me, he was kissing me repeatedly, each one becoming more demanding.

What he was doing to me was driving me crazy, and even though we had already had sex only a couple of hours ago I was so turned on, I tore the sponge out of his hand and putting my hands on his shoulders, I pushed him up against the wall of the shower.

His arms went around me and what happened next, took my breath away.

Pressing my body against him, I don't know what came over me. Straddling his legs, I pushed myself onto him, starting to tell him what I wanted him to do to me. I was aware of how I was talking yet didn't seem able to stop myself; even though I was expecting him to push me away at any second, telling me that I was disgusting.

But no! When I did manage to stop, all I heard was a whisper in my ear, "Don't stop talking dirty, it's amazing and so unexpected, and it turns me on even more, if that's possible."

Then kissing me so hard and demanding, we had fantastic sex, again.

Friends had told me in the past that sex standing up was uncomfortable and unfulfilling. Well, all I can say is they couldn't have been doing it right, or perhaps not with the right person.

Wanting him again so soon was worrying me, this had never happened with anyone else; so why did I feel this way. Also, I was afraid that he would think I was nothing but a slut, from how I had behaved in the shower; instigating sex with him and speaking to him as I had done.

When it was over, he held me close in his arms and thanked me. How had this happened in such a short time? Kissing me and smiling, he whispered, "I really have fallen in love with you." Looking into his eyes I knew it would be so much easier if I thought he was saying this to me so that I would agree to more sex, but I knew without a doubt that he meant it. The look on his face told me he was telling the truth.

Back in bed, after he had helped me dry, we lay there in each other's arms. I was still shivering and was wearing one of his t-shirts, as he lay naked beside me.

Lying facing each other, I could see how tired he was, and yet I knew he wanted to say something. Running my hand through his hair, I asked gently, "What is it?".

He had amazed me so much since I had got into the car, acting so romantic and finally telling me that he loved me, yet his next words were so unexpected I thought I was hearing things.

"Do you have a boyfriend at home," he asked, in what sounded like a scared voice.

Telling him that I had been seeing someone for a few weeks, but that it wasn't serious he pulled me into his arms and said, "Please save yourself for me, I want to spend the rest of my life with you. I can't bear the thought of you with anyone else. By the time I come back, I will have made arrangements for you to come home with me."

Sitting up and looking down at me, he continued, "I promise with all my heart, nobody else, even though sex is a big part of my life, I want to make love to nobody except you."

Wow, this was becoming a complete fairy tale. I believed him and knew I would do as he was asking, my smile and the one word "Promise," gave him my answer.

"Thank you," he said lovingly, as he lay down beside me.

Although I was feeling unbelievably happy, I needed to apologise for what had happened in the shower.

Telling him I felt like a slut for wanting sex again, and how I had talked, he pulled me into his arms, at the same time shouting, "No," startling me.

If it's any conciliation, I wanted to make love to you when we were out walking through the streets and would happily have found somewhere out in the rain. But I didn't take it any further as I didn't want you to think I only wanted you for sex.

Wanting someone so soon has never happened to me either. So no, you're not a slut, you're the girl I've fallen in love with who seems to want me as much as I want you."

Looking into my eyes, he smiled and continued to say, "And how you talked, I meant it when I said it turns me on even more…..so, as much dirty talk as you like; I love it."

Laughing now that he had told me how he felt, I kissed him and said, "You should have told me how you felt, I've never had sex in the rain."

This time we fell asleep together, our bodies entwined. There would be no waking with hysterics this time; I was much too happy and content.

Holding him and closing my eyes, I knew; I wanted this forever.

Chapter 22

When we got back, I ushered her straight into the bathroom, suggesting she had a hot shower to warm up.

I felt so guilty, she was physically shaking with cold, and a pool of water was forming at her feet, which strangely seemed to be black. It must be dirt from the streets, I thought, which had brushed up on the bottom of her jeans.

Her clothes had stuck to her they were so wet, prompting her to ask if I would help her undress.

Fantasising about being in the shower with her, but not wanting to suggest it I started to help her remove her top and bra making me want her again. Hiding the feelings that were surging through me as I helped her pull her jeans off, I stopped, staring in amazement.

Her legs were black from top to bottom. I must admit I started to panic, I had never seen anything like it, until she explained that she had dyed her jeans with industrial dye. I couldn't help but laugh and went to hug her; she looked so distressed.

I know it was naughty, but here was the excuse I needed to get into the shower with her.

After helping her to wash the black dye off her legs and feet, I started to wash other parts of her body; from her shoulders and arms to more intimate areas, while kissing her repeatedly, turning me on even more. As I was about to stop, feeling I was taking advantage of her, she suddenly ripped the sponge from my hand and forced me against the side of the shower, kissing me all over my face and neck.

Thinking I would be taking advantage by getting into the shower with her didn't matter, she seemed to want sex as much as I did and more so when she pulled my body lower, straddled my legs and pushed herself onto me.

Thinking how fantastic this was, she suddenly started to talk, amazing dirty talk which although surprised me, turned me on beyond belief; prompting me to ask her to keep talking, telling her what it was doing to me.

She was awakening every inch of my body, and it was so, so, fantastically astounding.

In the past, I would have sex which would be enough to satisfy me for a few days before I started to feel I needed it again.

Being with this girl was so different. She had managed to satisfy me more than any girl I had ever met, yet, within an hour, I wanted her again. I couldn't get enough of her and the fact that I now knew how much she loved it made me even worse.

After we had dried, we climbed into bed, exhausted.

Having told her that I loved her, something else was playing on my mind. I didn't know what reaction I was going to get, but I needed to ask her.

Starting to speak, I knew my voice was shaking as I asked her if she had a boyfriend at home. Telling me that she had been seeing someone for a few weeks, she went on to say that it wasn't serious.

Not thinking what I was going to say next was fair to her, but I knew I had to, the thought of someone else holding and kissing her and more importantly making love to her like I had made me feel physically sick.

So, asking her to wait for me, I promised that I would arrange to take her back home with me the next time I was in the UK, and that I would remain faithful to her.

She didn't need to give me an answer, her smile said 'yes' and the one word she did say, "Promise."

 As I started to relax with her in my arms, she suddenly started to say how sorry she was for what she had made me do in the shower and how she had behaved.

Made me do! She had astounded me wanting sex again. She hadn't made me do anything; she had given me the opportunity to do exactly what had been on my mind.

When she said, she felt like a slut for behaving this way I was horrified. We loved each other, so just what was wrong with wanting sex more often than was deemed normal.

I couldn't have her thinking like this, needing her to know it wasn't just her, so I explained,

"If it's any conciliation I wanted you when we were out walking through the streets and would happily have found somewhere to make love to you out in the rain. But I didn't want you to think that I only wanted you for sex.

Wanting to make love with someone so soon has never happened to me either. So no, you're not a slut, you're the girl I've fallen in love with who seems to want me as much as I want you.

And, the dirty talk - don't ever stop, I love it." Laughing, she kissed me and then said, "You should have told me how you felt, I've never had sex in the rain."

Knowing I had managed to reassure her how I felt made me feel so good, and now I knew; next time I wanted to love her, she would want me too.

This time I held her in my arms before she fell asleep.

Lying by her side looking at her, I could smell her perfume mixed with the soap she had used in the shower, a million different emotions running through my head. Satisfaction, gratitude, heartbreak, sadness, but most of all, the love I felt soared above everything.

Holding her as she slept in my arms and closing my eyes, I fell into a deep contented sleep.

Chapter 23

Awaking to the sound of wheels clattering outside the room and the sun streaming through the window, I lay in complete bliss wondering if the previous night had all been a dream.

I was here, in his bed and had not only lived out my fantasy, he had told me that he loved me, asked me to be faithful to him and to wait for him. He was the most caring, romantic man I had ever met and how I felt about him was overwhelming. Refusing to get upset by what I knew we had to face later that day I sighed and thought back to our lovemaking, how fantastic and satisfying it had been and that we both wanted each other so much. I was here with him. We had declared our love for each other; I trusted him one hundred per cent, and I was determined to have the most fantastic day of my life.

Laying there daydreaming of the future, I heard the door open, as the man I loved with all my heart walked in.

Smiling, he walked over to the bed, sat down by my side and kissed me. Being so loving now seemed like the most natural thing in the world. "Breakfast?" he said.

Knowing he loved me and trusting him had made me reckless, and so I replied, "Get in then" giving him an alluring smile.

He laughed and kissed me again, more passionately this time. "After breakfast," he said, "I need to build up some energy for what you have in mind". Thinking back to how awkward we had been with each other at first, I couldn't believe this was barely twelve hours ago.

Getting out of bed, I let him take my hand and lead me through to the other room. I didn't feel hungry until I saw the table full of food, only then realising that the last thing I had eaten was the bacon and egg sandwich the day before.

Eating a huge breakfast of bacon, pancakes, scrambled egg, toast and fruit, I began to enjoy myself. I also drank three cups of coffee, something I never touched at home. He didn't seem to realise that we drank tea in England

and had only ordered coffee. I didn't care though; I would have drunk dirty dishwater to be here with him.

All the time I was eating breakfast, he sat across from me and watched me eat, with a sad, confused look on his face. I knew he was thinking about saying goodbye later that day and that he was dreading it. Well, he wasn't on his own! I didn't even want to think about it.

He didn't seem to be eating much until I reminded him that he needed energy for later. "I want you as energetic as you were last night and I need satisfying again, like only you can do," I said huskily. I knew it sounded tarty, but as he had told me the night before that he liked dirty talk, I wanted to make sure I turned him on for what I had in mind later.

He just smiled his sexy smile and started to help himself to the food. As I sat watching him, I became lost in my thoughts, thinking how comfortable we had grown in each other's company – in twelve hours. Was this meant to be? That was still a dream.

Coming back down to earth, I was suddenly aware that he was pouring something onto a pancake with bacon on top. "What on earth are you pouring on your bacon," I spluttered, while laughing out loud.

He looked back at me as though I was the stupid one. "Syrup" he replied, through a large forkful of the concoction he had created on his plate.

I was English. We ate bacon with eggs and sausage, not syrup.

"Come here," he said to me and moved his chair away from the table. As I walked around to the other side of the table, he pulled me onto his knee and wrapping my arm around the back of his neck he then began feeding me with pancake, bacon and syrup. In between every mouthful he kissed me. We stayed like this until his plate was empty.

"Well?" he asked.

"It's good, delicious, I like it," I said, putting my other arm around him and laying my head on his shoulder. Sitting here with him was pure bliss, and I wanted so much more of it.

There had been a few boyfriends back home, but nothing serious. I also had limited sex experience, although this didn't amount to much. When I had planned to come to London, this didn't seem to matter as in my imagination it would have been quick sex and then goodbye, so my inexperience wouldn't have mattered.

But last night when he had romantically said 'come to bed with me', even though I had been drunk I had been so worried that he would be disappointed in me. The outcome though had been so entirely different. Once we were in bed, he had made it so easy, and it was then I realised, I was inexperienced because I had never wanted sex like this with anyone else.

He had instinctively known how to turn me on, which made me respond to him in a way I was unused to, but found I suddenly knew what to do, which just made it the most exciting and sensual experience I had ever had.

After breakfast, we walked out to stand on the balcony. Although it was still early in the year, it was a lovely bright morning. The view across the rooftops of south London was quite something. I could just about make out Tower Bridge in the distance.

Standing behind me with his arms around my waist and his face next to mine, I could sense there was something on his mind, and as he suddenly moved back, he said to me "Turn around, please."

Doing as he asked, I found him unfastening the chain from around his neck, the one I had admired the night before when we had been getting to know each other.

"Why are you taking it off"? I asked. But I found out why when his hands went around my neck, fastening the chain at the back.

Looking down at what he had just given me and then back up to his face, I was shocked to see tears swimming in his eyes.

As I held the small round pendant hanging from the chain in my hand, I asked, "Why?"

Stepping closer to me he ran his hand through my hair and kissed me tenderly, "Last night I asked you to wait for me and be faithful to me," he said quietly, " I want you to be my wife so that we can spend the rest of our lives together. If my life were normal you would now be wearing my ring to symbolise the love I feel for you, but" and with tears in his eyes, he added, "this is all I have to give you, so please take it to remind you of the commitment we made to each other."

As if I needed anything to remind me of the promise we had made, it would live in my heart every second of every day until I was back in his arms once more.

Holding each other, nothing else that needed to be said. Taking my hand, we walked back into the room.

As we went inside, I wondered to myself how I was going to get through the coming months without him. I should be back home now with the memory of getting my idol into bed. But no! I was still here, completely in love with him and facing total heartbreak. If someone had told me a few days ago that this was how it would be, I would have said they were mad.

But I knew one hundred per cent. I wanted it no other way.

Chapter 24

As I awoke and stretched, I wasn't immediately aware why I felt so happy and content until the memories of the previous night flooded into my mind. Turning over to face her, I lay there for a while, doing nothing more than look at her, as she slept beside me.

Sleeping, she looked more beautiful than ever. Tracing my finger down her face, I felt her stir and give a big satisfied sigh.   At that moment, I would have traded everything I owned to be with her, love her and never let her out of my sight. I groaned at the situation I had got us into, my heart aching.

Not wanting to wake her, I got out of bed quietly. She had been so upset last night and although what had happened after had been fantastic, I wanted her to sleep for as long as possible, feeling refreshed when she did wake. If I was right and she did want sex as much as me, she would need a decent amount of sleep before we started again, which brought a massive smile to my face.

Going through to the lounge, I opened the balcony doors and stepped outside. Waking over to the rail I looked out over the sights of London and not for the first time thought how hard it was going to be later that day, when it was time for us to say goodbye.

I would manage to handle my feelings of devastation, but the thought of leaving her heartbroken hurt me so much.

Not realising I was crying at first, I found I couldn't stop. Sitting on one of the chairs, I began to sob. How on earth was I going to get through today? On top of saying goodbye to her later, I had another concert tonight. It was going to be torture, smiling and singing for all those screaming little girls when from the same stage only a few hours ago, I had found the girl who was now asleep in my bed.

Pulling myself together as much as possible, I went back inside and rang room service to order breakfast. What I ordered I had no idea, rhyming off anything I thought she might like. At least I could make sure she had food inside her, I hadn't eaten since the morning before, and although I felt sick with worry, I knew we both needed to eat something.

Once room service had brought breakfast, unloaded the trolley and left, I decided to see if she was awake.

Visiting the bathroom first to wash my face, I plastered the same big smile on my face that I used when I went on stage. False. But as I opened the bedroom door, I knew my smile had changed from false to one that I knew was full of love and longing.

Lying in bed awake, she looked at me, her eyes full of love.

As I walked over to the bed, I sat down and kissed her. "Breakfast?" I asked, to which she replied, "Get in then" giving me the sexiest look.

Again, I thought about how I had been so worried about becoming turned on as often as I had when all the time it seemed she had felt the same. How good this made me feel; I no longer had to worry about wanting her and the day ahead seemed full of promise. The inevitable goodbye later that day now seemed a million years away.

Making her eat breakfast, telling her that we needed food inside us so that we would have the energy for what she had in mind had made me smile, thinking of what was to come. I even introduced her to pancakes with bacon and syrup, which she had found hilarious until she tried it.

As I watched her tuck into breakfast, I suddenly realised that love was not only about physical attraction but also caring unreservedly about the other person. I had never cared about any of the girls I had slept with before, only wanting sex and then moving on to the next one. But I cared now, so much it physically hurt inside.

I wanted to cry again—God, what had happened to me here in this room with this beautiful, perfect creature.

Deciding we both needed some fresh air, I suggested we go out onto the balcony.

We stood there looking over the rooftops of London, and as we did, I slid my arms around her waist from behind.

Standing together, I felt satisfied and happy, but one little thing was playing on my mind. Last night I had asked her to wait for me and be faithful to me; and that I would take her home with me the next time I was in the UK.

So, in effect, I had proposed to her, which meant she should now be wearing my ring. Going to buy her one, of course, was impossible, as we couldn't just walk out of the hotel to visit a jeweller's shop like I would if I had a normal life. I wanted her to believe I was serious about the promise I had asked her to make to me, and more so what I had promised her in return.

Impulsively I asked her to turn around, and as she did, I unfastened the chain I was wearing, the one she had admired the night before. Frowning she asked why I was taking it off. My answer to her question was to fasten it around her neck.

"Why?" she whispered, so softly it brought tears to my eyes.

Explaining how I felt, I told her I wanted her to take it as a symbol of our promise, that I wanted to marry her—spending the rest of my life with her by my side.

Although I didn't want her to suffer when we were no longer together, the thought of her not believing how serious I felt about her was too much to bear. I needed nothing to remind me of the promise I had made to her; I knew I would never love anyone like this again, ever. Although sex was important to me, the thought of being in bed with another girl made my skin crawl. I wanted no one else, ever!

She looked at me, her eyes full of love, took my hand and led me through to the bedroom.

Chapter 25

When does sex turn into love?

It was as fantastic as the night before, both in bed and in the shower, but so different. Gentle, more sensual with words of love murmured to each other. We now knew exactly how to turn each other on, which made it so beautiful I wanted it to go on forever.

When we were both completely satisfied, I was so full of emotion, I lay my head on his chest and cried. Without warning, he started to sing one of his songs to me. Lying there in the same position listening to him, I couldn't help thinking how beautiful his voice was. When he had finished singing, I lifted my head, and it was only then I realised that he too was crying, silently.

We held onto each other for a few minutes, until I broke the silence saying, "Right! Up now, I want to enjoy this afternoon with you and put what we have to face later out of our minds for a few hours".

As we got dressed, I asked him what he wanted to do, and although when he hesitated, I was sure he was going to suggest we get back in bed and start again, but then he suggested we order coffee and sit out on the balcony.

When it arrived, we sat together outside, completely at ease with each other. I guessed that this was the only fresh air he could get, not being able to leave the room.

Sitting there just talking for a while, laughing at different stories that we told each other was lovely.

I told him about my job, that I was a weaver in a cotton mill. At this he looked astounded, asking me why I didn't have a 'good job'. Laughing out loud I explained that I had worked in an office when I had left school, but that I earned more doing the job I was currently in as it was a job that had required months of training.

In turn, he told me about his life at home and what he got up to when he wasn't performing or recording.

One story that he seemed to find funny was when he had taken a girl to a celebrity party. Cringing, he told me that when he had gone to pick her up, she had been wearing long false eyelashes and a pair of earrings that reached down to her shoulders, which he had found horrendous; continuing to say that he had spent the whole evening trying not to look at her.

Speechless I could do nothing more than stare at him.

I was so thankful that my sister had talked me out of wearing false eyelashes, but what the lady at the market had said about the earrings I had bought. Somehow, she had known he wouldn't like them; making me believe that there was some truth in this, 'mumbo jumbo,'

He also brought up the subject of what he termed as 'his performance in bed; asking me if it was politeness that had made me say he had been amazing, as he knew he wasn't much good.

Moving my chair so that it was facing his, our knees touching I took hold of his hands and spoke gently, "No, I wasn't being polite, I meant it with all my heart. Nobody has ever made me feel the way you do, how you touched me made me come alive and how you satisfied me so much was truly wonderful."

Looking back at me a worried expression on his face, he lowered his head, saying, "I was so concerned that I wouldn't be good enough for you. Although you said you had no experience, I was scared that I wouldn't be able to satisfy you, leaving you disappointed in me. I know I'm not much good in bed because when I've had sex with other girls, it's lasted twenty minutes at the longest. By that time, I've had what I wanted and lost interest. Being with you is so different, and that's because I've never really made love, properly.

No! We needed to clear this up, and so I explained why I had looked so worried when we had first walked into the bedroom the previous night; telling him that I thought I wouldn't live up to his expectations, not the other way around.

Taking his hands in mine, I smiled and kissed him tenderly. What a pair of idiots we were. We had both been worried about letting each other down, but the reality was it had been beautiful, experienced or not, because we wanted each other so much.

Taking my hands in his, he looked at me quizzically. "Tell me the truth, please," he said, "Last night, when I asked you if you were a virgin." His grip on my hands seemed to grow tighter, "Did you tell me the truth?"

Not knowing where this conversation was going, I leant forward and kissed him again. "Yes, I did tell you the truth. Why?" Lowering his head, I had a feeling he didn't want to tell me. "Please tell me," I insisted.

Taking a deep breath, he sighed, saying. "Okay, but please don't laugh." Shaking my head and feeling confused, I replied, "Why would I laugh?" Then he started to talk, very quietly. "When I asked you if it was your first time, I wanted you to say it was. I wanted to be your first; I wanted to be the only man who had ever touched your body, to feel that you belonged to me, and only me."

By this time, I could see tears in his eyes and pulling him into my arms; I felt so special. Lifting his head with my hand, I answered with as much love in my voice as was humanly possible. "Why on earth would I laugh at what you have just told me? Do you not realise how special that makes me feel? If I could have seen into the future, I would have saved myself for you, without a doubt. But, none of my experiences have lasted very long, so last night was a first for both of us. The first time either of us had made love with someone." Kissing him long and sexily, I added, "So now I do belong to you, and only you."

When the sun went in, and it grew a little chilly, he wrapped his arms around me and suggested that we go back inside.

Once we were inside, he sat down on the sofa and pulled me onto his knee.

Kissing me tenderly, I noticed that he had a sheepish look on his face, like a naughty schoolboy, who had been caught out doing something he shouldn't.

Looking at him with a puzzled expression on my face, I said as I laughed, "Well spit it out then."

"Can I order some champagne?" he blurted out and then added quickly, "It's okay; you can say no if you want to."

I looked at him as though he had gone mad again. Coming out with strange requests was becoming quite a habit. "If you want to, of course, you can" I answered, "But would you like to tell me why you're looking so guilty?".

The look on his face now was one of total embarrassment, which made me laugh so much. He had backed himself into a corner and didn't seem to know how to get out.

Feeling sorry for him, I ran my fingers through his gorgeous shiny hair, and said gently "Come on, tell me."

Eventually, taking a deep breath, he spoke. "Okay," he paused took hold of my hand and looking at me said, "When you've had champagne you're like a wild animal in bed, and I want some more of it to remind me how fantastic you are when I'm back home, missing you". He then went on to say, "just now was so beautiful, making love like we did earlier is something I never thought possible. But how you behave in bed after a drink is mind-blowing, I've never had sex like that either, that's why I was worried about not being good enough for you".

Wow! Some speech. It seemed that he had enjoyed sex with me so much he wanted even more; well that suited me fine, I was more than happy to have more, the thought doing strange things to my insides. Looking at the expression on his face, I knew he thought I was going to say no. "Order it then" I said jumping up off his knee. Almost running to the phone, he rang room service before I had time to change my mind.

As I sat there, hugging my knees, listening to him order the champagne, I smiled to myself. He was in for the best sex of his life; I was going to wear him out completely. If he thought I was an animal last night, then today I was going to be the whole zoo.

Chapter 26

By the time we reached the bedroom I wanted her right there and then, just as I had been with any other girl and yet I just wanted to kiss her and hold her in my arms. The way I felt about this girl here with me was tearing at my emotions. Had I got it right? Did I love her, or was I just feeling lonely, mistaking my feelings of isolation for love?

Once she had let me know that she wanted me, I started to take things further and taking my time; I made it as beautiful as I could feeling my heart soar with love for her. When we were both completely satisfied, I lay on my back with her head on my chest. Why, I have no idea, but without really thinking, I started to sing one of my songs to her. Singing my songs off stage was a big no-no, but this wasn't normality, all the rules had gone out of the window. By the time I finished the song, silent tears were running down my cheeks.

Would I be in floods of tears if I didn't love her and even more so, would I be in such a state every time I thought about leaving her behind, later that day?

Looking up at me, we clung to each other, lost in our thoughts. Suddenly she sat up, "Right, up. Now" she said. She wanted to enjoy our last few hours together. I would have gladly stayed just where we were until it was time to go but knew I would do anything she wanted.

Spending the next hour sitting on the balcony, drinking coffee, talking and laughing was just what we both needed.

I was so grateful she had made me get up; this was lovely. We had just had the most fantastic night together but didn't know anything about each other except the unconditional love that we felt for each other.

We sat and told each other stories from our respective lives, laughing at most of them.

Falling silent, I had to ask her something, although I didn't know how I was going to approach the subject. Starting to speak, I asked her if it was politeness that had made her say I had been amazing in bed. Telling me no, she had meant it and went on to say how much I had satisfied her.

As I explained I had been worried about not being good enough for her as I knew I wasn't much good, she sighed and held my hands. It turned out that we had both been worried that we wouldn't be good enough for each other.

But what the hell, what had started as two people worrying about how they would perform turned into the most fantastic sex either of us had ever experienced.

Discussing the subject of our lovemaking, I had a question to ask her, and so taking her hands in mine; I started to speak. "Tell me the truth, please," I said, "Last night, when I asked you if you were a virgin." Gripping her hand even tighter, I continued, "Did you tell me the truth?"

Looking worried, she kissed me, saying, "Yes, I did tell you the truth, why?" I didn't know what to say next, and so lowering my head I hoped she would just leave it. But no, not a chance! "Please tell me," she demanded.

Taking a deep breath, I tried to smile and said. "Okay, but please don't laugh." Shaking her head, she looked anxious, "Why would I laugh?" I had to tell her now. I didn't want her to think it was a problem and so, I started to talk. "When I asked you if it was your first time, I wanted you to say it was. I wanted to be your first; I wanted to be the only man who had ever touched your body, to feel that you belonged to me, and only me."

Finishing my ''speech' I was near to tears. She now had tears in her eyes, and the thought that I had hurt her by what I had said distressed me. Pulling me into her arms, she lifted my head and answered with so much love in her voice. "Why on earth would I laugh at what you have just told me? Do you not realise how special that makes me feel? If I could have seen into the future, I would have saved myself for you, without a doubt. But, none of my experiences have lasted very long, so last night was a first for both of us. The first time either of us had made love with someone." Kissing me, she said sexily, "So now I do belong to you, and only you."

I can't begin to explain how this made me feel. Now I had no anxieties about her love for me. I had found the girl of my dreams, and as far as I was concerned, the rest of my life was mapped out for me.

When the temperature dropped, she started to shiver, and so holding her in my arms, I suggested we go inside.

Once inside, an idea was forming in my mind. Sitting down on the sofa, I pulled her onto my knee. She knew I wanted to ask her something I could tell by the puzzled look on her face.

Laughing, she said, "Well spit it out then".

Wishing I hadn't started this, I didn't know how I was going to put my idea to her. But, what the hell. "Can I order champagne?" I asked nervously, then quickly assured her that she could refuse if she wanted to.

She looked at me like I had completely lost the plot, before answering, "Yes, if you want to, but why are you looking so guilty?"

Now I didn't know what to say, and I think by now, she was feeling a bit sorry for me. As she ran her hands through my hair, she said gently,

"Come on, tell me". All I could do was be honest with her. If she thought it was a stupid idea, then I would forget all about it.

Taking a deep breath, I started to speak. "When you've had champagne you're like a wild animal in bed, and I want some more of it to remind me how fantastic you are when I'm back home, missing you", I went on to say, "Just now was so beautiful, making love like we did earlier is something I never thought possible. But how you behave in bed after drinking champagne is mind-blowing, I've never had sex like that either, that's why I was worried about not being good enough for you".

Sat there staring straight ahead, waiting for her reaction, I had a feeling she was going to refuse, and that I had just ruined everything we had built up in the last few hours. What a stupid idiot I was, why had I been so impulsive? Why on earth would she agree when, as usual, I was thinking of myself and not giving a damn about her feelings? Wanting something so ridiculous and crazy when I had the love of the girl who I wanted more than anyone I had ever met.

She looked at me for what seemed like forever, her next words astounding me "Order it then," she said and jumped off my knee.

Shooting to the phone, I rang room service, at the same time thinking about how she would do anything to please me, like walking in the rain in the middle of the night. Now she was prepared to do this for me; I had to make sure it was as good for her as I knew it was going to be for me.

As I turned back to her after ringing room service, she was sitting on the sofa with her knees under her chin, smiling at me, making me wonder just what she had in mind. Well, I had asked for this and knew whatever she had planned; it was going to be out of this world.

Chapter 27

The champagne arrived along with two glasses. While we had been waiting for room service to bring it up, I had sat and thought about what he had asked of me. I was sure of his love for me but still felt I had to please him in every way I could, which meant making this daring, exciting and fulfilling in every way.

As he opened one of the bottles and started to pour the first glass, I caught hold of his hand and shook my head. "Open the other bottle," I requested. He looked at me puzzled, shrugged his shoulders and did as I had asked.

When the second cork had popped, I walked over to him, kissed him and picked up the bottle before sitting down on the sofa. Watching his face as I raised the bottle to my lips and took a big gulp, I wanted to laugh.

He looked astounded.

"What!" he said in a shocked voice, although he was laughing.

"No point in wasting time," I replied, "I don't want to wait even if you do," I then took another massive gulp, and rubbing my hand between the top of my legs I moaned softly. He stood and stared at me in disbelief, then walked towards me. "No!" I laughed, "Not a chance!"

Time to go and get ready, I thought.

"Stay there and have a drink" I ordered, "and don't follow me; I won't be long," kissing him long and hard and then walking out of the room. If he wanted it like this so badly, I wanted to look the part, not just act it.

Going into the bedroom, I picked up my bag and shoes then looked around on the floor, among his scattered clothes. Finding a black t-shirt with quite a low scoop neck, I stuffed it into my bag. Yes! Just what I need.

Next, I went into the bathroom and started to apply make-up. I usually made sure I applied my make-up tastefully, but on this occasion, I wanted to look like a tart. So, this meant lots more mascara and eyeliner than I usually wore, also some olive-green eyeshadow, finishing the look with bright red lipstick.

Looking in the mirror, I smiled. I looked so slutty. Finding the hair tie in my bag that I had used to travel down to London, I stood in front of the mirror, only instead of just tying my hair behind my neck, I bent over until my hair hung below me, tied it as tightly as I could and then lifted my head. The tie was on the top of my head, with the rest of my hair hanging down the sides of my face. It looked anything but tidy.

Perfect, just the image I was wanted.

Lastly, I stripped off, leaving just my pants on, then pulled on the t-shirt I had found in the bedroom. Bringing it halfway up my body, I pulled it around me and tied it just under my bust, pulling it down as far as possible, so that there would be a good view of my cleavage.

After putting on my shoes, I checked out my appearance. Laughing to myself, I hoped he realised what he had let himself in for, and that I was going to completely wear him out.

While I had been getting ready, I had been singing happily, thinking about what I was going to do to him. I couldn't wait to see his face when I walked back into the lounge. A generous squirt of perfume and I was more than ready. Throwing my bag over my shoulder, I made my way back to the lounge.

Opening the door to the lounge, I deliberately stopped in the doorway for effect.

Standing in the middle of the room, he looked like a lost little boy, although his face when he saw me was well worth the effort.

As he walked over to me his eyes full of longing, he tried to kiss me. Putting my hand on his chest, I pushed him back and said as sexily as I could, "No, sit down, you can wait until I'm ready" turned and picked up my bottle.

The look on his face was what I wanted, lust, and as he sat at one end of the sofa, I sat at the other end and put my feet on his legs, moving my feet about in between the top of his thighs, while I drank the rest of my champagne.

I looked over at him. His head was laid back on the sofa, his eyes closed, his breathing becoming heavier and desperate, a look of pure agony on his face.

Knowing what effect I was having on him, I felt that I was being cruel and finishing the last dregs of my bottle I stood up, wanting this as much as he did now that I was full of champagne.

Opening his eyes, I walked over to the other end of the sofa and sitting on his knee, with my knees at either side of him, I took hold of his arms, wrapping them around me.

Asking him what he wanted I was shocked when he said breathlessly, "Stand up and undress me," and so standing and pulling him up from the sofa I removed his clothes as he had asked me to, while at the same time kissing him and pushing my body against him. I then made him sit back on the sofa.

Climbing back onto him and pulling my pants to one side, I lowered myself onto him, pushing down hard, moving with the rhythm of his body. Planning to stop after a few seconds became impossible as I realised what was happening inside me. As usual, he was managing to satisfy me completely, which made my thrusts harder and faster as his body match mine. Screaming in ecstasy, I waited until I had recovered slightly, kissed him and stood up.

Turning away, I walked towards the bedroom, saying to him as I got to the door "You want more, then come and get me. I'm more than ready."

Diving onto the bed and facing the door, I knelt with my legs apart. Placing my left hand just inside the top of my pants, and the middle finger of my right hand seductively in between my lips, I waited.

As the door opened, and he walked into the room, I heard him gasp.

When he was standing in front of me, he stopped and looked at me, taking in my pose. "How do you do this?" he said, with so much longing in his voice. "I've never wanted anyone like this before, it's like you're a drug that I'm addicted to, the more I get of you, the more I want."

Removing my hands, I pulled him onto the bed so that he too was kneeling, facing me. Brushing my lips against his I said as lovingly as possible, "I feel the same, I want you constantly," then pulling away slightly I untied the t-shirt I was wearing and pulled it over my head. Pushing my body against him I placed my right leg between his, moving it against him, whispering in his ear, "Do you want to feed your addiction now, because my addiction is only just beginning."

Dragging him back on the bed, I climbed on top of him.

To say the next two hours were fantastic was an understatement. Doing what I knew turned him on the most, I held nothing back, making him do everything the way I wanted, although I knew he was loving every minute of it.

Aware that on several occasions he thought I had finished, but after giving him no more than a minute to recover, I would then start touching him again until he was ready to carry on.

Knowing that men don't like silent sex, I made sure I was as noisy as possible. Making noises that demonstrated how much he was satisfying me, and at one point, I screamed louder than any of his fans, although it was all completely genuine. The more I demanded, the more he seemed to want.

Having quite long fingernails, I was aware that I was digging them into his back and ripping them down his skin. I just hoped he was wearing black for his concert later that day.

After just over two hours, he begged me to stop and let him rest. I must admit I was tiring but would have kept going as long as he wanted. He had asked for this, and I was making damned sure he didn't regret it.

I wanted him to remember this for the rest of his life.

Lying there for a while afterwards, side by side, sticky and wet with sweat, he lifted his head, looked at me and said, "Let's have a shower". I looked at him like I didn't believe what I was hearing, "No! to freshen up" he laughed, saying "Is sex all you ever think about", then kissing me, he added in his beautiful sexy voice, "I hope it is".

Chapter 28

My stupid idea was now making me so nervous, feeling like I was pushing the boundaries too far, even though she had agreed. If I thought she had agreed to my crazy idea just to please me, I would regret it so much.

Wanting today to be special was so crucial before our painful goodbye later. After my concert tonight I was flying straight back home, so when I left the hotel, it would be time to say goodbye.

My heart ached at the thought.

Once the champagne was on the table in front of me, I started to pour two glasses. As I went to pour the second glass, her hand grabbed mine and stopped me, asking me to open the second bottle. Looking at her, with confusion, I opened it just as she had asked me to do.

Taking the bottle from my hands, she sat on the sofa, raised it to her lips and took a long drink.

I couldn't help laughing. "No point in wasting time", she said and then took another long drink. It seemed I had nothing to worry about after all, what I had suggested she seemed to want as much as me, which I knew for sure when she told me she 'didn't want to wait,' rubbing her hand between the top of her legs. Watching her do this turned me on so much, and I hoped her 'not wanting to wait' really wouldn't be that long.

I was having trouble waiting at all.

After downing half of the bottle in two gulps, she stood up and walked over to me, kissing me while brushing her hand across the front of my jeans. Walking to the door, she turned to me and ordered me to 'stay there, and don't follow me'. Having no idea where she was going or for what reason, I did as she asked, knowing whatever she did it would be wonderful.

After a while, as I sat drinking my champagne, I began to worry. Where had she disappeared to, had she not wanted this and done a runner on me? The thought that she had gone crucified me, and although I promised to stay where I was, I knew I couldn't sit here not knowing where she was.

So, creeping from the room, I crossed the corridor and slowly opened the bedroom door. As I looked around, I noticed that her bag and shoes had gone from beside the bed.

Sinking to the floor, my head in my hands, my worst fears were confirmed, she had gone. Why had she agreed if it wasn't what she wanted? She should have told me. I loved her and would never make her do anything that made her feel uncomfortable.

Sitting on the floor as sobs wracked my body, I realised what a mess I had managed to make of everything.

How long I stayed there I didn't know, but eventually I got to my feet, deciding to go and down the rest of the champagne to dull the aching in my heart. I should have known how this would end, when would I learn.

As I came out of the bedroom to return to the lounge, something caught my attention. She was in the bathroom, singing.

As quickly as possible, I went back into the lounge and closed the door quietly behind me. Standing in the middle of the room, feeling drained after the emotions I had just gone through; I sank on one of the sofas.

Now I was one hundred per cent sure that I loved her. When I had walked into the bedroom a few moments ago, thinking she had gone, I had wanted to curl up and die; the thought of never seeing her again was soul-destroying.

I was fine though, she was still here, and if she had changed her mind it didn't matter one bit, I would do anything she asked. I loved her so much.

Getting up from the sofa I walked around the room when suddenly I was aware of the door opening. Turning, I stared as she walked in and stopped in the doorway, making my eyes widen in amazement.

She had put on loads of make-up and done something to her hair which made her look so sexy I just wanted to rip what little she was wearing off, right there and then.

As I walked up to her and tried to kiss her, she pushed me back and told me to sit down. So, she was making me wait even longer; I was okay with that. She was still here, and I would have agreed to anything.

Sitting down on the sofa, I watched her as she sat at the other end with her feet on my legs. Starting to drink more champagne from the bottle, she was wriggling her feet about near the top of my legs. Closing my eyes, I lay my head back wondering how long I could stand what she was doing to me. Yes, I wanted this to be her performance, but if she didn't make a move soon, I would have to drag her through to the bedroom and start it off myself.

Being seconds from jumping up and dragging her through to the bedroom, she suddenly swung her legs off me and stood up. Opening my eyes, I looked at her walking towards me, as she sat across my legs with her knees on either side of me. Thinking how hot she looked, I wanted to grab her and have sex right here; thinking I couldn't wait any longer.

Asking me what I wanted, I realised I was still fully clothed. Although I knew how much I wanted her, I was powerless to remove my clothes, and so asking her to undress me; I let her take my hands and pull me up.

As she removed my clothes as I had asked her to do, she kissed me and pushed her body against me. Being seconds from throwing her onto the sofa, she pushed me back onto it and sat astride me, pushing herself onto me.

How she was acting was mind-blowing, as the animal that I wanted started to appear. As she screamed out with pleasure, my whole body exploded.

Seconds later she jumped off me and walked away, leaving me thinking that was it until she got to the door and said, "You want more, then come and get me. I'm more than ready."

Having just been completely satisfied, I walked into the bedroom thinking I could hold her in my arms for a while before we continued, but no. Opening the door, the sight of her faced me, knelt on the bed in such a seductive pose. Thoughts of holding her in my arms vanished in an instant; I wanted her again; right now.

Dragging me onto the bed, knelt facing her, she rubbed against me with her leg. Letting out a massive groan I couldn't hold back no longer, but, before I could do anything more, she dragged me back on the bed; closing my eyes I lay there ready to let her do whatever she wanted to me.

She had been wild the previous night, but it was nothing compared to the next two hours. She took the lead entirely, and I willingly did everything she wanted. Sex in this way was astounding; I couldn't believe how wonderful she was. At times I was completely worn out, but I had asked her to do this for me, so I didn't want to stop her.

On several occasions, I had thought she was ready to give up, only for her to start touching me again and asking for more, using language that she knew would make me ready.

She was also incredibly noisy. Since I had been in the UK, I had grown to hate the sound of screaming, I had heard far too much of it, but her screams were pure ecstasy. Even when I knew she was ripping my back apart, I still wanted more.

After two hours of none stop wild sex, I needed to rest and pleaded with her to stop. She didn't seem tired at all, which made me wonder just how long she would have gone on.

As I lay there by her side, I realised how hot and sweaty we had become, so I suggested we had a shower. She looked at me in amazement, thinking I wanted a repeat performance. "No! to freshen up," I said laughing, "Is sex all you ever think about?" then I kissed her, adding, "I hope it is."

Chapter 29

We stood in the shower under the jets of hot water facing each other, his arms around my waist and mine around his neck. There was no longer any need for words; time was running out.

It was now less than two hours before he had to leave. When I had first met him the day before his eyes had a sad, lonely look in them, this look had disappeared as we had got to know each other and fallen in love. Now, as I looked at him, I could see traces of the same look returning. We were both thinking the same thoughts, dreading saying goodbye.

I remember thinking this must be what a condemned prisoner feels like waiting for the hangman to come for them.

We dried each other gently and then lay on the top of the bed; resting my head on his shoulder, we lay there in silence. Suddenly, "I can't do this," he said, turning to face me. I stroked his face, "What?" I replied, although I knew what was going through his mind. I felt the same. This time yesterday, we had never met, and now we were so deeply in love that the thought of parting was devastating beyond belief.

Without warning, he jumped up and sat on the edge of the bed with his head in his hands, while making a noise like a wounded animal which then turned into loud sobs.

My heart was breaking as I lay there, listening to him. Having no idea how to console him, I knew I had to try. Sitting beside him, I put my arm around him with my head on his shoulder. "Please don't torture yourself", I said, "Somehow, we will find a way to be together, if not now then sometime in the future. I'll come and find you the next time you're in the UK,".

He lifted his head, looked at me and whispered "Promise?", I looked into his eyes, "With all my heart, nothing could stop me wanting to be with you".

Chapter 30

Standing under the hot shower with her was beautiful; just holding each other was enough. The sex had been out of this world, but time was now running out, and all I wanted was to feel her in my arms, look at her, and most of all tell her how much I loved her.

The loneliness that I had felt before she had got into the car had vanished overnight, but I could feel it returning, drowning me.

It was less than two hours before I had to leave for my concert. Trying to push it to the back of my mind, I buried my head in her neck. I could smell her perfume and her hair and could quite easily have taken her back to bed, instead I just let the tears pour down my cheeks.

After our shower, we lay on the bed together. As I held her in my arms, I could think of nothing else apart from saying goodbye. My stomach was in knots, and I felt sick with worry.

Knowing how I would feel after we had parted, even though I had a concert to do, I would find the strength to get through it somehow. But I was far more worried about how she was going to feel. How I would have loved to be able to take her to the train station myself, knowing she was safely on her way back north. But of course, that was out of the question.

At that moment, I hated my life so much.

She had told me earlier that day how she planned on getting back home. I was dumbstruck that she had travelled to London that way, but no way on earth was she hitchhiking back. More than anything I wanted her to be safe, so I had planned for Gerry to take her to the train station, buy her a ticket and see her safely onto her train.

The thoughts of leaving her were going around in my head, making me feel nauseous, and I knew I was near to tears. Impulsively I jumped up and sat on the edge of the bed, not wanting her to see me cry again, it was only distressing her even more. But, instead of silent tears, I was suddenly sobbing like a baby. She got up, sat beside me and held me in her arms. Telling me she would come to find me when I was next in the UK, I made her promise, not because I didn't believe her but so that I had something to hold onto.

Something to believe in until we were together again. To get me through the lonely months ahead.

Chapter 31

When he had calmed down, we moved into the lounge and sat on the sofa side by side. "Can you pass me my bag, please" I said to him, needing to brush my hair which had become tangled while lying on the bed. As he reached down to the side of the sofa to get it for me, I started to panic, realising that when he lifted it, he would see what was on it, on the side that would be facing him.

As he reached down and lifted it level with his face, he stared at it in shock.

My football team badge and their name was on one side which he had seen the night before, however, on the other side, there was three words embroidered on it, insinuating that I wanted him to have sex with me. Looking at it in total shock, he slowly turned his head to face me. The look of devastation on his face was horrible, and all I could say was, "Well, you did."

Passing it to me slowly, he said, sadly, "Why?" I knew he was referring to what he had just seen. At that moment, I had never regretted anything as much in my life as I did those words on my bag.

Putting my head down, I tried not to cry, not wanting him to think I was crying just to get out of this awful situation I had created for myself. "Please just tell me why, you're too classy for this?" He sounded so sad. No, I couldn't stop them; the tears came, but I kept my head down hoping he wouldn't see. But of course, he knew and lifted my head with his hand. "I'm so sorry, I didn't mean to upset you," he said softly, "I love you and this doesn't change a thing, I just want to understand why you would do this," he said so softly.

Again, I had to explain, I owed it to him, to be honest. "I like to shock," I said, "I'm not the sweet little innocent girl you seem to think I am. And what it says on there had been my goal in life for the last two years."

He looked back at me and then smiled. Oh no! How well I had come to know that smile, it wasn't just a loving smile, it was the smile that said, 'Sex please'. "If you like to shock, then go ahead, shock me," now he was laughing, knowing I couldn't refuse.

What was I supposed to do next? I had told him I liked to shock, and he had thrown me a challenge. I knew by the smile he had given me that although we seemed to have done nothing much more than have sex, he wanted more. He certainly had a massive sexual appetite, which, of course, didn't bother me one bit.

Loving it just as much now that I had found someone who could turn me on as much as he did; but this was the ultimate challenge, and I certainly needed to think on my feet, needing to do something that would shock him completely. If I failed, I would feel like I was letting him down. Although I had become more experienced in the last few hours than I had ever been, he seemed to think my sexual knowledge was never-ending.

Kissing him passionately, I picked up my bag and left the room.

Once outside, I dug out the hair tie, that I had used earlier. Hoping this would work I dropped my bag in the hall and then turned to go back to the lounge, then smiling, I picked my bag up again, retrieving the scarf the lady at the market had given to me the day before.

Stuffing the hair tie in the front of my jeans, I folded the scarf and placed it in my back pocket.

As I walked back into the room, I found him pacing the floor, looking scared.

Laughing, I asked, "Want to forget it?" He looked at me with an expression on his face that I was unfamiliar with, so walking over to him, I wrapped my arms around his neck and kissed him. "This has got out of hand now," I whispered in his ear. "I'm so sorry you saw what you did, I do like to shock but feel I don't have to while I'm here with you. I love you so much I just want to be with you and be whatever you want me to be." I could feel the tears threatening again, and when he unwound my arms from his neck and held me at arm's length, I knew; he wanted this now. "Oh no," he answered, smiling the sexy smile I loved so much. "You're not getting out of it so easily.

Grabbing my hair and pulling my head back, he kissed me so hard I could taste blood on my tongue and then stopping, he pushed me away and said forcefully. So! Shock me"

Staring at him, I hoped this was going to work. Loving him so desperately I couldn't face doing what I had planned if it didn't turn him on enough. If this went wrong, it would be ultimately down to me. I had got myself into this and knew I had to shock him as much as I possibly could.

Taking a deep breath, I looked at him again and said shakily, "Okay, strip off... everything." He grinned and started to remove his clothes until he was completely naked.

I turned and went to get one of the chairs from the table, which I placed in the middle of the room. "Sit," I demanded. He looked confused but did as I had asked and sat on the chair. "Hands behind," I said as I went behind him.

Taking hold of his wrists as forcefully as possible, I pulled the tie from my pocket. As I bound his wrists together, I heard him moan softly. "Good," I thought to myself relieved, this seems to be having the desired effect.

Standing facing him, I smiled, knowing he was quite happy to be tied to a chair naked. What I did next was the shock I wanted.

Removing the scarf from my back pocket, I threw it around his neck while I kissed him softly until his moans had become much louder. "Please, do something," he said breathlessly.

So, I did, I wound the scarf around his eyes and tied it at the back. Standing away from him and laughing seductively, "Shocked enough?" I asked. He laughed, "Depends what happens next."

During the next thirty minutes, I touched him seductively, both with my hands and my mouth until he was almost screaming with longing and begging me to go further. Every time he begged, I stopped, laughed and spoke to him, using lots of foul language and taunting him, asking how it felt to be completely powerless.

Where this new experience had suddenly come from, I had no idea. It was as though I instinctively knew what to do to him, that would drive him crazy.

Every time I stopped touching, I stepped back and removed some of my clothes. I had been fully dressed when I had put the blindfold on; now I too was naked.

I was enjoying what I was doing to him, so much that I hadn't noticed that his begging had become more frantic, and he was starting to shake.

Suddenly I realised I was taking this too far and began to panic, my only thought being, "Shit!" I need to finish this. And so, sitting across him, I kissed him and left him finish off. He was still shaking as I put my hands behind his head and untied the scarf, letting it fall between us.

This time he was the one who screamed, until his screams turned into sobs. No, I was mortified! What I had done was meant to be the ultimate turn-on, not leave him in tears.

Reaching behind him, I untied his hands, expecting him to push me off and yell at me for what I had done.

But as I should have come to expect, he didn't, he put his arms tightly around me and buried his head in my hair. When his breathing had returned to normal, he lifted his head, looked at me with so much love in his eyes and said just two words. "Thank you."

He then pushed me off, dragged me over to the sofa, lay me down and climbed on top of me, forcing my legs apart with his knee. As he made love to me again, so forcefully and rough it hurt, I knew how much I needed this, begging him 'harder', putting everything I had into what was most definitely the best of the whole weekend.

Staying where he was, on top of me, he kissed me tenderly. I felt so satisfied and could easily have fallen to sleep like this. He was stroking my hair, and my arms were around his waist. Returning his kiss, I whispered to him, "Gerry will be here soon, we need to get dressed, he'll have a bloody heart attack if he walks in now."

Reluctantly we got up off the sofa and dressed.

"When we were ready, he stood before me and held my waist. "Can I ask you something?" he asked me with a worried look on his face. "Have you done all that stuff with anyone else." Now he looked scared, as if he was dreading my answer. Smiling, I touched his face and said gently, "No, that was for you, and only you, no one else, ever."

He looked so relieved.

I know all men have a jealous streak, and the fact that he felt this way made me feel like a million dollars. What was it that made him feel this way about me? I didn't have a clue, but oh, it made me so happy.

Chapter 32

Moving from the bedroom to the lounge, we sat side by side on the sofa. Lost in thoughts of how the next few hours were going to make me feel, I suddenly heard her say, "Pass me my bag please." Automatically I reached down to my side of the sofa I lifted it.

What I saw sewn on the outside of it made me so angry. She had put 'three words' on in stitching, insinuating that she wanted me to have sex with her. Doing this was all wrong; she was too perfect to behave in this way.

When I insisted that she tell me why she had done this, she started to cry. Immediately I regretted asking her; I loved her, this made no difference to my feelings.

Although I would have left it there, she went on to explain. She liked to shock, and as she had wanted to meet me for the last two years, she had decided to stitch those words onto her bag. "Fair enough," I thought. I quite fancied her trying to shock me, although what she could do, I couldn't imagine. We had spent two hours having sex earlier, and as far as I was concerned, there was nothing she could do to shock me.

How wrong could I be!

I told her "If you like to shock, then go ahead, shock me," having no idea what to expect when she left the room and was back within a minute.

She tried to get out of it at this point, but that wasn't going to happen. I had geared myself up to what she was going to do to me and already become turned on. Laughing, I said, "No way, you're not getting out of it so easily.

As I kissed her, my senses seemed to take over, and I became far too rough, pulling her head back with her hair and kissing her so hard I drew blood from one of us.

Stopping, I told her. So! Shock me"

The next half hour or so astounded me. Her imagination was beyond belief. Ordering me to strip off, she tied my hands behind my back on the chair she had placed in the middle of the room, and if that wasn't enough, she then blindfolded me.

Behaviour like this is every man's sexual fantasy. However, I was still completely shocked.

She then touched me, using both her hands and her mouth but stopped if she thought I was too close. Every time she did this, she laughed and said things to me that I can only describe as disgusting but oh so sexy.

Needing her to go further I started begging, which seemed to make her behaviour even worse, which in turn made me so desperate to have her that my begging became more intense and I started to shake.

She must have noticed as suddenly she sat astride me and undid the blindfold. I made a hell of a lot of noise, and as I slowed down, I became so emotional, my screams turned to sobs.

She must have panicked then as she undid the ties on my hands. As I held her tight, all I could manage to say was thank you. I felt I had been selfish in throwing her a challenge to please me, but she had risen to it and as usual, astounded me completely.

What I had just experienced should have been more than enough to satisfy me, but no, what this girl did to me was beyond anything I had ever experienced and once she had freed my hand's I dragged her over to the sofa and went for it again. I knew I was being far too rough and was about to slow down when she screamed to me 'harder'.

Not for the first time, I thought how wonderful she was and how I was going to live without her.

While I was getting dressed, I was starting to wonder where she had learned to behave like she had just done. I had to ask and dreaded her saying it was what she had done with other boyfriends; the thought of this made me feel so insanely jealous. "No, that was for you, and only you, no one else, ever." She told me.

I wanted to be with her forever; no, I needed to be with her forever.

Chapter 33

When Gerry came to say it was time to go, we had dressed and were back on the sofa—lying with my head on his knee, just as I had been the night before; as he sang softly to me.

I had wanted to go home with good memories. Quick sex and a kiss goodbye was how I thought it would have been.

But what had happened here in this hotel room was as far from what I had expected as it could be. The memories I would take with me would break my heart repeatedly, but what had happened had happened, there was no going back.

We had decided that I would wait in Gerry's room while he took him to the arena. Gerry would then come back to the hotel to collect me, take me to the train station and buy me a ticket for my journey back up North.

When we had been sat on the balcony earlier that day, he had asked about my transport home, and I had told him how I had travelled to London. He had looked horrified. "And how do you plan on getting home?" he asked. "Same way" I replied. "No way", he said, "I don't want you standing at the side of the motorway in the dark, I would be worried sick." I went on to explain that I didn't have enough money to buy a train ticket, so I had no choice. "No, no way" he shook his head, his face full of panic. "Wait there," he said, went back into the room and picked up the phone. I could hear him talking to someone but couldn't hear what he was saying.

When he came back, he told me what he had arranged and added "No arguments, the girl I love is not hitch-hiking back to the north of England". Only when I agreed did he relax and lose the worried look on his face.

As we got up from the sofa, we walked into the hall, where he picked up his bag and guitar. Leaving his suite, we walked across the corridor to Gerry's room. "I'll wait near the lift mate," Gerry said, taking his bag and guitar from him.

As we went into Gerry's room and turned to each other, we both had tears in our eyes.

Time seemed to stand still until he said softly "Kiss me" with so much love in his eyes.

Holding his hands between us, I did as he had asked. I don't know how to explain that kiss; it was soft, loving and yet so full of passion I could have made it last forever.

Eventually we pulled apart, "Go", I said, "I love you with all my heart". Taking my hands from his, I stepped back and pushed him towards the door. I knew he didn't trust himself to speak, so the fact that he hadn't told me he loved me too was okay.

It didn't need to be said; it was there in his eyes.

As he started to walk to the door, he stopped and walked back to me. Touching my face tenderly, he said, "Please do something for me." "What?" I asked. "Close your eyes, let me kiss you one more time, then keep them closed until I've gone. I don't want you to see me go. I know how much you're hurting, and it will make it easier for you". No, it won't, I thought, there was nothing that could make this any easier for me, but I did as he had asked.

As I closed my eyes, I felt his hand slide down my hair, and his lips meet mine for a few seconds, then I heard three simple words, "I love you".

Feeling him move away from me, he turned and walked to the door. As he did, I heard a sob, then the door close.

He was gone.

Chapter 34

Once we had dressed, we sat down on the sofa together, "Lie with your head across my knees", I asked. Doing as I had asked, without question, she closed her eyes. I looked down at her face and ran my fingers through her beautiful blonde hair.

How had I come to feel like this in less than twenty-four hours? Yes, I had fancied her like mad when I had seen her in the crowd and thought that she was something special to the point where getting to meet her was the most important thing in the world, but never did I anticipate these feelings that were making me hurt so much.

I started to sing softly.

Singing had always made me feel better; only now it wasn't working, so I stopped and bent over to kiss her. She clung so tightly to me that she took my breath away.

Eventually, she lay back down and asked me to sing again.

I wanted to stay like this forever, I was so happy and yet, at the same time, my heart was breaking.

Still in the same position on the sofa, was how we were later when Gerry came to collect me. Feeling so distraught I thought I was going to throw up.

Getting up from the sofa, I knew we were both trying to be brave, so I took her hand, collected my belongings, and we walked out of the room. Gerry said he would wait by the lift for me, so after passing him my bag and guitar, we walked to his room.

Standing facing each other, we were both close to crying. I didn't want to hurt her or make her feel any worse than I knew she already did, yet however painful this parting was, I wanted it to be special. "Kiss me," I asked her with all the feeling I had inside.

She looked at me, held my hands and gave me the most tender, sensual kiss ever, that made my body go weak with longing. How on earth did this girl manage to awaken my senses so easily?

Eventually, she pulled away, well one of us had to, and I would have gone on forever, it was doing such beautiful things to me. "Go, I love you with all my heart," she said and pushed me towards the door.

Turning away from her, I started to walk to the door without speaking. I hated not being able to tell her how much I loved her too but knew if I spoke, I would break down again, and the last thing she needed was for me to start blubbering.

Saying goodbye was hard enough for her despite her trying to put on a brave face, so I turned and walked back. I asked her to close her eyes, let me kiss her one last time and keep them closed until I had gone, telling her that it would make it easier. She looked at me with the look I had become so accustomed to in the last few hours, the one that said "Okay, but you're talking complete rubbish," but she did as I had asked and closed her eyes.

Running my hands through her hair, something else I had got so used to doing, I kissed her. Still not feeling that I could speak without crying I just about managed to whisper the words "I love you".

As I felt the tears starting, I turned and made for the door, as I went through it, I think a sob escaped.

I hoped she hadn't heard it.

Chapter 35

Opening my eyes, I stared at the door, feeling completely numb inside until the enormity of what had just happened hit me, like a bolt of lightning. It was then the tears began to roll down my face. "Noooooooooo" I screamed out, feeling my legs give way I collapsed onto the floor. Lying with my head on the carpet, I wailed in agony, the pain inside me so intense I couldn't breathe.

At that moment, I just wanted to die, anything to stop these unbearable feelings of desolation that were making my insides hurt so much.

How long I lay on the floor, I have no idea, but eventually the wracking sobs stopped. Having no more tears left I just lay there wondering how I was going to go on living without him.

As I stood up, my head hurting from all the crying, I walked across the room and flopped into a chair. It felt that he had left me hours ago, when in fact it was probably only about thirty minutes. I felt lonely, lost, and so desperately sad.

When Gerry returned, I was still sitting in the same chair sniffling. I had cried more and wondered if I would cry forever if I never saw him again. Gerry took one look at me, came over and sat on the arm of the chair. "Can I get you anything", he asked kindly, "Brandy". I shook my head; the last thing I wanted was alcohol, knowing it would make me feel worse. "Tea" I blurted out, and despite how distraught I felt I smiled, "I've spent the last twenty-four hours drinking coffee," I said, "I'm English, we drink tea."

When room service had brought my tea, he poured me a cup then sat talking to me about his family. He was married to a girl he adored and was the father of three-year-old twin girls. Knowing he was trying to take my mind off what I had just gone through, I thought what a kind and considerate man he was.

After three cups of tea, he said it was time to leave for the journey to the train station.

Going to the bathroom, I looked through the mirror. What a mess, I was thankful he couldn't see me like this. My eyes were puffy and red, and my hair looked like rat's tails from lying on the floor. Taking my hairbrush from my bag, I brushed my hair thoroughly and washed my face in cold water.

Luckily, I was wearing no make-up. After our crazy lovemaking session, he had asked me to wash my make-up off, telling me I didn't need to wear it. Thinking back to this threatened more tears. Not for the first time, I wondered how I was going to get through the months ahead, after the love that had grown between us.

I'm not a religious person, although I went to church when I was younger but at that moment all I could do was pray to God that he wasn't going through the same agony as me, he had a concert to endure and then a long flight home. I didn't want him suffering, yet I knew wherever he was, he was feeling as miserable as I was.

I didn't doubt the love he felt for me and knew every word he had said to me was how he felt.

The thought that he was feeling as bad me just made me feel worse, if that was even possible.

Chapter 36

Closing the door behind me, I ran down the corridor to the lift, where Gerry was waiting for me. He took one look at me, shook his head and said, "Oh mate, how on earth are you going to get through tonight?" By now, I was sobbing uncontrollably, tears pouring down my face.

Standing there just staring at him, I had a million different thoughts going around in my head. I had known saying goodbye would be difficult but never thought it would make me feel like this. I felt so desperately lonely, even though we had only parted a few minutes ago. Feeling like I had nothing to live for, I knew, however hard I tried, and wherever I went, I would never love anyone as much as the beautiful girl I had met last night.

The only thing that consoled me was that she had promised me she would come back the next time I was in the UK.

We had got into the car, travelling through the streets of London, even though I knew none of this. Gerry had led me all the way. I remember wondering what I would have done without him, he had been brilliant, looked after me and been a mate at the same time.

Eventually, I had made myself stop crying, knowing what a mess I would look on stage. As usual, I was to throw white roses to the crowd, while I sang the same song that I had sat and opened my legs for her, only last night. The thought of this was horrendous, throwing flowers to a bunch of screaming brats.

Knowing it was wrong to think of my fans like that, but right at that moment I didn't care, I just wanted to remove myself from my life, go back, get my girl and get a job anywhere, a shop or a factory. Knowing if we were together, it wouldn't matter where, we would be happy.

As we continued to drive through London, I asked Gerry if he had some paper and a pen. "Yes mate, in the boot," he said, and explained that he always wrote letters to his wife, when he was away from home for any length of time.

Thinking what a nice person he was, I knew she would be in safe hands with Gerry and that he would do as he had promised me, getting her safely on a train.

A minute later, Gerry pulled into a pub car park, got out and went around to the back of the car. Returning he handed me a pad and pen. "Try not to cry anymore while you're writing that" he said with a crooked smile. Nodding I tried to smile back at him.

As he set off again, I opened the pad and started to write; pouring out everything I felt in that letter. Although I knew it would make her cry, I wanted her to know even though we had said goodbye, that I had meant everything I had said, and I was still thinking of her, and of course how much I loved her.

Although Gerry had jokingly told me not to cry, I couldn't stop my tears from falling and landing on the paper I was writing on.

Finishing my letter, I handed it to Gerry to give to her, then wiped away my tears. Closing my eyes, I was dreading the next three hours.

Chapter 37

Leaving the room, we went down in the lift to the car. Like the gentleman Gerry was he held the back door open for me, but as I looked at the back seat in horror, all I saw was the two of us sat there together, the previous evening. Taking a step back, I looked at Gerry and shook my head "I can't", I said as tears filled my eyes. "Sorry", he said, "I didn't think".

Again, I thought what a kind man he was. "Sit in the front with me then", he suggested, opening the front passenger door. Getting in, Gerry got in the other side, and we drove away, from the place where I had spent the most wonderful night of my life.

Nothing could ever replace last night and today.

Parking in a side street near to Euston station, we walked the short distance to the station building. After he had settled me down in the café with yet another cup of tea, he went off to buy my ticket.

Sitting there sipping my tea, I felt more unhappy and miserable than I had ever felt in my life. The emptiness inside me was killing me. Going over what had happened inside the hotel, I had smiled at some of it, but I was still completely numb inside.

Being lost in thought, I hadn't noticed Gerry sitting down opposite me. "You okay," he asked. Staring at him, I realised how worried he looked. "There's a bit of a problem he continued, fidgeting with a teaspoon, "There are no trains to the North tonight, it seems the Sunday service finishes earlier than on other days".

I shrugged, "It's okay, I'll sit in the waiting room till morning" I answered in an uninterested voice. Nothing mattered anymore; I didn't care about anything. I felt dead inside. "No" Gerry looked at me and shook his head, then said, "I can't leave you here till morning, he would never forgive me. You know he's going to ask if I put you safely on your train when I pick him up later, and I don't want to lie to him". I shrugged again, "I'll hitchhike then," I said, getting up, "Can you give me a lift to the motorway please."

As I started to walk away from the table, he caught hold of my sleeve. "Look" he said, "There is a solution, there's another bed in my room, you can stay till morning and then get a train home". He looked so embarrassed at offering me a bed in his room that I felt quite sorry for him. I sat back down and tried to smile at him. "Okay, I'm fine with that" I answered, "Thank-you."

He went on to explain that although he was taking him to the airport after the concert, he was staying in the hotel tonight, as he was minding some boxer or other for the next three days, here in London. He would check out tomorrow morning, moving into another hotel, which the boxer's management company would provide for him.

What Gerry had said made sense and I had no problem being in the same room as him, he was a complete gentleman and totally in love with his wife. When I agreed to his suggestion, he looked relieved and went to get us another drink.

Sitting there, staring at my cup of tea, I looked up to see him pulling something from his coat pocket. "I was going to give you this as you were getting on the train, but I should give it to you now", he said, "I know he'll ask me when I pick him up.

I opened it, read it and fell apart.

> My darling,
>
> Last night I met the most beautiful girl in the world. She was at my concert, and like the intelligent, wonderful person she is she made sure she got to meet me. I am so utterly thankful for this, as, within hours of her getting into my car, I was totally and completely in love with her. I said goodbye to her about 30 minutes ago, yet this seems like forever.
>
> Take care of yourself, my beautiful angel. I will not be happy until I am back in the UK and you are standing in front of me at

> my concert. This time I
> will make sure it is forever,
> I promise.
>
> I love you more than life
> itself. Wait for me.
> Please.
>
> Love you forever.

Gerry sat and held my hand, watching me read the letter he had given me. There was nothing he could say or do that could stop my tears. People stared at me as though the man sitting across from me had done this, but I didn't care.

Thinking of him writing the words I had just read broke my heart into a million pieces. I could even see where his tears had fallen onto the paper.

Eventually I was down to sniffing into a napkin. "Come on, and I'll take you back to the hotel before I go to pick him up", Gerry sighed "Or" ……, he didn't finish his sentence, he didn't need to. The only alternative to going back to the hotel was for me to go with Gerry to pick him up from the arena, to take him to the airport.

My whole face lit up.

My head said no, we had gone through one agonising goodbye, and the sensible option was to go back to the hotel, but oh, my heart soared at the thought of seeing him one last time. Even though I knew it was the wrong decision and at the end of it, we would both be worse than ever.

My heart won.

Chapter 38

Eventually, I had made myself stop crying as we made our way across London. The traffic was moving slowly, giving me more time to pull myself together; being ready to smile and wave to the crowd outside the arena.

I didn't want to do this concert one little bit and even thought of asking Gerry to stop the car, so that I could get out and go to the north of England to find my girl. But, I didn't know England that well, and I couldn't even remember the name of the town, where she had said she lived.

Being so deep in thought, I didn't realise we had arrived at the back of the arena, until the sound of chanting and screaming broke through my thoughts. I tried my best to smile as we got nearer, but knew it must have appeared false, waving no more than two or three times.

I just couldn't summon up the enthusiasm to do any more.

Luckily, we got into the caged area quickly. The screams faded to the back of my mind. I got out of the car, almost running through the door. Once inside, I leant my head on the wall. That part of the evening had been bad enough, how on earth was I going to sing for two hours.

Gerry's voice cut into my thoughts. "I'm going now, mate," he said. "I'll see you later". Becoming alert for a moment, I turned to him, wanting to go through the arrangements I had made with him. More than anything, I needed her to be safe and on her train home, needing Gerry to confirm everything. Thanking him, I headed down the corridor to get ready.

Standing in the wings, waiting to be announced I thought back to this time yesterday. I had felt great then! I enjoyed performing (even though most of the audience didn't listen). But now I just wanted to get this over with and get out of here. I felt like I was going to cry again. Just what had happened to me in the last twenty-four hours?

I had fallen in love; that's what had happened.

Walking onto the stage, I waved and started to sing. The tears were still threatening to fall, but somehow, I managed to hold them back, going through my playlist in a trance and thanking the crowd at the end of each song.

There would be no house lights or talking to the audience tonight; I just wanted to get through this as quickly as possible and get out.

Then, the part of the concert I had been dreading, the slow ballad where I sat on the edge of the stage. A member of the stage crew brought on the flowers and lay them near the front of the stage. Sitting down, I began to sing. I was on the right side and knew this is where I would be staying; the thought of moving over to the left was out of the question.

If I did, then I knew for sure the tears would start again.

Every few seconds, I threw a flower into the crowd, laughing in between the lines of the song, but with every flower, my laugh became more hysterical until it started to sound quite eerie. I was losing it now, and so looking down, I counted four flowers. Sod it, I thought. Picking them all up in my left hand, I threw them as far as I could, jumped to my feet and finished the song standing up.

I knew I was going to be in trouble for this, but hell, it was either that or I would have burst into tears right there on the stage. In my mind, I chose the best option.

At last, it was my final song. Letting my mind wander at the thought of being able to get out of here, I didn't realise that I had walked to precisely the place where she had been standing the night before. I looked down, but of course she wasn't there.

Too late, I could feel the tears rolling down my cheeks. I was becoming so choked up, it was starting to affect my voice. I couldn't go on any longer, I cut the song short and ran from the stage.

Once I was out of sight, I collapsed onto the steps leading from the stage, burying my head in my hands.

Aware of someone standing over me, I looked up. "What the hell was all that about, have you lost your senses?" my manager bellowed.

I just looked at him, with a look that said, "Yes, I think I have".

He went on about professionalism, what the fans expect and other rubbish that I didn't want to hear. Eventually I jumped up and screamed, "Shut up", pushed past him and headed to my dressing room.

As he followed me down the passage, his voice exploded behind me, screaming, "Is that blood on the back of your suit, what slapper did you pick up last night?" I stopped so suddenly he crashed into me. "She wasn't a slapper, she's beautiful and wonderful, and I love her," I yelled in his face, I just wanted to punch him I was that angry.

So, I had blood on my suit. The thought made me smile, as I thought back to earlier that day and our fantastic lovemaking.

He must have decided I was better being left alone, and I spent the next fifteen minutes alone, cooling down, although my body felt chilled to the bone. There had been a pair of loving arms around me for the last day and night, and without them, I felt like ice inside.

I got dressed slowly, hoping the crowd outside had given up and gone home.

On impulse, I picked up my guitar and started to sing "Will you still love me tomorrow", or as much of it as I could manage, through my sobs.

Chapter 39

As we walked from the train station, back to the car, Gerry spoke to me, "Are you sure you're doing the right thing?" he said with a worried look on his face. Looking up at him I answered, "Of course, I'm not doing the right thing, but I am still sure this is what I want to do." He just looked back at me with a confused look on his face. "I'll be here to look after you after he's gone, you know that." I was so grateful to have such a nice person by my side. I squeezed his arm affectionately.

It was too early to go to the arena, so we stopped off at a pub about ten minutes away. Gerry had a half pint of beer, while I ordered an orange juice; not wanting to smell of alcohol in the car when he hadn't had anything to drink.

We sat down in the corner of the bar, and Gerry explained that the airport that he was flying from was yet another decoy. It was a smaller airport about an hour away from London, where he would meet just one of the crew. The rest of the gang would leave from

Heathrow. They would meet at an airport in Paris and fly on from there.

Soon it was time to go to the arena. As I couldn't go into the arena with Gerry, we had decided I would wait by the traffic lights where I had stood last night, and that he would pick me up there on the way out. We left the pub and drove towards the arena.

When we came up to the traffic lights, Gerry stopped the car, and getting out, I walked across the road, to the same spot that I had stood in after last night's concert.

Was it only one day since I had been standing here? I felt I had lived a lifetime in that day. This time yesterday I had been so carefree, standing here hoping to meet my idol. Now, I was in love with him and felt the weight of the world on my shoulders, wondering how I was going to get through the coming weeks and months without him.

Taking my mirror from my bag, I looked at the reflection staring back at me. I looked awful, nothing like the night before. My eyes were red and puffy from crying, and I just looked so incredibly sad. I shouldn't have come to the arena. I should have left it as it was, for both our sake's.

But the chance of being near him even for even a short time was impossible to resist.

Listening to the crowd chanting his name and the usual screams, I waited until I heard them become louder.

Right on cue, the noise grew in volume, which meant a few minutes of negotiating through the multitude of girls and then he would be here. Excitement coursed through me at the thought of being in his arms again, even for a short time.

The noise was deafening, much louder than last night. The emotions I was feeling at that moment were a mixture of knowing how wrong it was of me, coming here with Gerry, and exciting anticipation at the thoughts of his lips on mine.

Lost in thought, I realised it had been over ten minutes since the screams had increased in volume. Why was it taking so long to get out?

Another fifteen minutes went by making me worry like hell. What had happened, it shouldn't be taking so long to get out of the cage? He had told me security helped to pull the girls back so that Gerry could inch forward through them. The screams continued, and I panicked more and more.

Something was wrong. It had to be.

It was now thirty-five minutes since the noise outside the arena had grown louder. The panic inside me had become so unbearable, that without thinking what I was doing, I set off walking down the road, towards the back of the arena.

As I rounded the bend in the road, I stopped dead. There must have been five thousand girls; they were halfway up the road. I was struck dumb at the sheer amount of them.

Suddenly the car appeared through the girls that were closest to me, only about fifty yards away. Shit, if Gerry put his foot down, he would drive straight past me, thinking I was one of them. As I saw the car approaching me, I closed my eyes and standing in the middle of the road, I hoped and prayed Gerry would see me and stop before he hit me.

Hearing the roar of the engine and then the screech of the brakes, I held my breath. As I opened my eyes, a voice shouted out to me from the driver's window. "Get in quick." Running around the side of the car, I jumped in the back door that he had opened for me, slamming it shut behind me.

By this time, girls were running up the road behind the car. As I launched myself onto the seat, I fell into his arms. Holding me, he stroked my hair, "You're shaking," he said, "Why didn't you wait at the top of the road?"

Starting to explain, I told him how worried I had become at how long it was taking them to get out of the arena, compared to the night before; and that I had thought that something was wrong. "I'm so sorry," he murmured into my hair, kissing my face and neck. "I'm okay now that I'm here with you," I answered, lifting his head so that I could look at him properly.

I was so shocked by his appearance. His eyes were red, his usually beautiful hair was all over the place, and his face was wreathed in sadness. All I wanted to do was hold him, kiss him and make his pain go away. As we clung to each other like two drowning people, we were both close to tears.

We were so wrapped up in each other we didn't notice the crowd of girls suddenly appear around the car, until they started hammering on the windows. Looking up, we both groaned.

A girl was lying across the bonnet of the car with no pants on, her skirt around her waist.

The traffic lights had been on red, which had given them time to catch up to the car. Gerry couldn't go while the girl was still lying on the bonnet. They could see through the car windows and would know there was someone with him; they had probably even seen me get into the car. Knowing I was in the car with him, however, didn't stop them screaming his name.

We tried to ignore them, hoping this would make them give up and go away.

Asking me why I had gone to his concert when I knew his fans were much younger than me, I just told him the truth. I was determined to meet him, whatever it took. He laughed and told me he believed me, as he had seen me kick the girl in the crowd the night before. So, I went on to explain what that had been about, even telling him that I had told her 'What was on show up there was mine tonight', he laughed and hugged me tight.

Eventually, Gerry got out, lifted the girl off the bonnet, walked over to the pavement and laid her on the ground. He then jumped back into the driver's seat and quickly sped through the lights, even though they were on red.

All this had at least stopped the tears from falling. As we looked at each other, we started to laugh. The whole experience had been so bizarre. "Thank you for coming," he said, with a solemn look on his face.

God, how I loved him; the only place I wanted to be was by his side, now, next week, forever. "I thought you might be mad at me," I said, looking down at our hands clasped together between us. "Mad at you," he frowned, "What for?" I gave a loud shuddering sigh, "For making things harder than they already are." He smiled at me, that gorgeous smile that melted my heart. Then held me so tight that I could hardly breathe and whispered in my ear. "This is a bonus. Just a pity Gerry can see everything we're doing." He ran his hand down my back and gave me one hell of a sexy kiss.

When he stopped, I looked at him with an amused look on my face. "Just who thinks about sex all the time then?" but couldn't resist running my fingers up the inside of his thigh. I knew this turned him on, but couldn't help myself, running his hand down my back had the same effect on me. Looking down, I realised just how much I had turned him on. He knew too and putting his hand over mine; he moved it onto the seat beside him.

It took him a few minutes to recover, but by this time, I had snuggled up to him with my head on his shoulder.

As he started to tell me about the concert and how much of a mess he had made of it, he began to laugh and said that his manager had bawled him out when he had come off stage.

When I asked him what was so funny, he told me that his manager had gone ballistic because there was blood on the back of his 'white' stage clothes. My hand flew to my mouth. "I'm so sorry," I said, I shouldn't have done that to you." He ran his hand down my face, looked at me with so much love and said, "No, I wouldn't change what happened in that hotel room for the world, the memory of our lovemaking is what will keep me going until I see you again".

We held each other and sat in silence until Gerry's voice broke through our thoughts. "Ten minutes to the airport," he said.

His arms tightened around me, and he buried his head against my chest. Nothing I could say would change how we both felt at that moment; we had gone through this once a few hours ago.

Oh, why had I done this to him? I felt so guilty.

Yet I was so glad I had done, being here holding him was worth the heartbreak inside, and I knew he felt the same.

Chapter 40

The door opened; it was Gerry. "Come on, mate," he said, "time to go". I jumped up, wanting to get the hell out of here, past the screams outside and away. I wanted to be alone to re-live the last twenty-four hours in my mind. Re-living our time together was all I had left now until I came back to the UK.

As I went to pass Gerry in the doorway, he grabbed my arm. I stopped and looked at him, "What?" I said puzzled. He fidgeted and had a worried look on his face. "There was a bit of a problem mate," he stuttered, "no trains back up north tonight." I didn't give him the chance to explain further. "Where is she?" I screamed, thinking of her alone somewhere in London and starting to panic. "It's okay, she's okay," he went on to reassure me, "she's waiting at the traffic lights at the top of the road. I stared at him in disbelief. "Really!" I answered. A huge smile broke through my worried look. Okay, it would be another agonising goodbye but knowing I was five minutes away from seeing her again was the best feeling ever. I ran down the corridor with Gerry trying to catch up with me.

Now I really couldn't wait to get out; I had a good reason.

Opening the door, I stopped dead and stared in disbelief. All I could see were girls everywhere. Halfway up the road, all around the cage and on the grass verges at either side.

There were thousands of them and about six security to control them. They had no chance.

Any other time this would have made me laugh, but not tonight. What usually took about five to ten minutes was going to take forever. Getting into the car as fast as possible, I kept my head down. There were no waves or kisses blown. My only thought was getting to the top of the road as quickly as possible, which now seemed impossible.

Security opened the gates, and the crowd swamped the car, girls on the bonnet and the roof. As fast as the guards were pulling them off more were climbing back on. "Think you would have been safer walking out the front door and catching the tube," Gerry laughed, although it didn't sound like all this amused him. I put my head in my hands, thinking if I didn't look at them, then perhaps they would go away. No such luck! It was taking forever, and all I could think about was my girl waiting at the top of the road; knowing how worried she would be.

She would know when the screams got louder, I had come out, and it was now over thirty minutes later.

Eventually, after some of the security from inside the building had joined the ones outside, we emerged through. "Foot down, Gerry," I said, then the next second, I screamed out "STOP!" She was stood right in the middle of the road. The car screeched to a halt, inches away from where she stood. I didn't have to tell Gerry, he shouted for her to get in and I opened the door.

Once she was safely in the car, Gerry drove on. She had thrown herself at me the moment she had got in the car, and as I held her, I realised how much she was shaking.

She had thought that something was wrong because of how long it had taken for us to get out. This was one of the reasons I loved her - she had felt there was a problem and was coming to find out what was happening. I knew that no number of screaming girls would have stopped her.

We held on to each other, so happy to be together if only for an hour or so.

Suddenly there was a loud banging on the window, my name being chanted from all around the car. The traffic lights had been on red, giving a gang of girl's time to catch up with the vehicle.

I looked up and groaned. A girl lay across the bonnet of the car, her skirt pulled up around her waist, waving her pants in the air. Why on earth did I have to put up with this? Yes, I wanted to entertain people with my music, but not at this expense.

Ignoring what was happening, I turned to her asking a question that had been bugging me, ever since I had seen her in the crowd the previous night. "Why did you come to my concert when you knew how immature my fans are? Why did you want to be associated with a bunch of stupid kids?" She looked at me and laughed, "You" she replied, kissed me and went on to explain, "I had to meet you, not doing wasn't an option. And if it meant putting up with crazy young fans, then so be it. Nothing would have stopped me from trying to meet you." "I know that," I replied laughing, "I saw you kick that girl standing at the side of you last night, the one that kept shouting 'He wants me'." I looked at her and laughed, then continued talking. "You were so determined to get what you wanted; it made me want you even more."

She looked down, and I realised I shouldn't have mentioned the 'kicking' incident, but now I had I was curious and wanted to know why she had done it. Asking her, she replied, "I spent two hours during the day working out how to get to this spot after the concert," she waved her arm to explain that she meant next to these traffic lights, "no way was that girl standing in front of me when you had started blowing kisses and displaying everything you had." Then she laughed, "I even told her that what you had put on display was mine later that night."

He looked at me with an amused look on his face, saying cheekily, "Well, you got that right, didn't you?"

Looking up as Gerry got out of the car, we watched in amazement as he lifted the girl off the bonnet, walked over to the pavement and left her there. When he got back in, he revved the engine as loud as he could, scattering girls everywhere and shot off through a red light.

As soon as we had settled down with our arms around each other, she started to apologise for coming with Gerry to the arena, saying that she thought I would be mad at her. How could I be mad at her? I had another hour with my beautiful girl.

Holding her tight, I said, "This is a bonus, just a pity Gerry can see everything we're doing." She had laughed and accused me of being the one who thought about sex all the time. I had started to run my fingers up and down her back knowing how it turned her on. Although my heart was breaking, I still wanted to make love to her, and more so when she retaliated, starting to run her hand up the inside of my thigh.

This girl could turn me on in seconds. Moving her hand onto the seat next to me, it was either that or I wouldn't care if Gerry was there or not.

We spent the rest of the journey talking to each other, and I told her about my disastrous performance. When I mentioned the bit about me having blood on my suit, she had looked distraught and had said how sorry she was. I had assured her it didn't matter, that it was a reminder of our beautiful afternoon together.

When Gerry informed us that we were ten minutes away from the airport, we both became silent seeming to hold each other even tighter. Nothing I could say could change how we both felt at that moment; we had gone through this once a few hours ago.

But I was so happy that she was here.

Chapter 41

Gerry turned into the airport and found a space to park.

He lifted his head, and the look on his face made me gasp. He looked so vulnerable, like a lost little boy. The same thoughts ran through my mind, how stupid and self-indulgent I had been. Why couldn't I have been stronger and gone to the hotel, if not for me then for him?

He clung to me like his life depended on it. I would have to stay in the car, so this was our final goodbye. Gerry got out and walked round to the back of the car, to get his bags from the boot.

Looking at him for what I knew was the last time, I kissed him. "Go," I said, "Keep safe, it won't be long; I love you." At that moment Gerry opened the door. "Time to go, mate." He kissed me again, turned and got out of the car. As Gerry closed the door, he turned and looked at me, blew a kiss and mouthed the words 'Love you forever'. Then he walked away with Gerry by his side.

I had told Gerry I would stay in the car but have never been much good at following orders, so opening the door I followed the steps the two of them had taken a few minutes ago.

As I approached the airport terminal building and stepped through the main door, I saw him, walking down the departure hall with Gerry at his side. All I wanted was to watch him walk out of sight; knowing one last glimpse of him would be enough. Instinctively he stopped walking, turned where he stood and looked at me.

No, what had I done, again? He started to run down the hall towards me, and there was nothing I could do; I was rooted to the spot.

He flew at me and grabbed the back of my arms so hard I screamed out. "I can't do this," he said through his sobs. "Take me with you, nothing matters except being with you, I don't want to go home, I don't want to sing, I want to be with you. His fingers were digging so hard into the backs of my arms my fingers had started to go numb.

I couldn't believe this was happening and all because I couldn't let go, the man I loved with all my heart was standing in front of me begging me to take him away with me. Running away with him at this moment, was the biggest temptation I had ever faced, but I couldn't do it. How could I take him away from the life he had made for himself? His singing, his music, his home.

Shaking my head slowly, the look on his face very nearly made me grab his hand and run.

He dropped his hands from my arms, his eyes full of disbelief. "Why? We love each other, that's all we need." I knew if I told him the real reason, he would say all those things didn't matter, so I said the only thing that I knew would make him go. How I managed to get the words out, I will never know? "I'm so sorry, it's not what I want right now, I've loved the time we've had together, but what your asking isn't what I want." I looked at him and saw the unbelievable pain in his eyes. "No, I don't believe you. I know you feel the same as I do; I can see it in your eyes" he screamed, making everyone in the vicinity stop and stare.

Not that it mattered to me. The only thing that I cared about was the man I knew I would love forever standing there in such a mess that it was destroying me.

By this time Gerry was hovering behind him. I looked up at him for the help I knew I needed, and thankfully he understood. "Come on, mate," Gerry said, taking hold of both of his arms from behind he started to pull him away from me. Stepping closer, I kissed him gently and whispered, "Go now, I'll see you next time, I promise."

He had been holding onto both of my hands when Gerry had pulled him away. Closing my eyes, I felt my fingers slide away from his. I didn't want to watch him walk away; I was too scared that I would run after him and drag him back. Standing there, rooted to the spot with my eyes closed until I knew he would no longer be in sight, I opened them and sank to my knees.

I don't know how I had managed not to cry, while he had been in pieces, but now the tears came and staying knelt on the floor, I cried like

I would never stop, until I felt Gerry's strong hands under my arms, lifting me to my feet.

When I was standing, he lifted me across his arms, and I lay my head on his shoulder, still crying uncontrollably. He walked out of the building and over to the car like I weighed nothing, opened the door and put me in the front passenger seat.

Walking to the other side of the car he got in and took hold of my hand.

Chapter 42

We arrived at the airport and parked up. I wasn't at all sure I could say goodbye for a second time that day, feeling physically sick at the thought of being without her and worried about how she would be when I was no longer there to love her and take care of her. I knew my expression was giving my thoughts away. I could see it reflected in her face as I held her as tightly as I dared without hurting her.

Gerry opened the door, "Time to go, mate," he said. Looking at her one last time, I kissed her and climbed out of the car. I wanted to walk away but couldn't help but look back. Blowing a kiss, I mouthed the words 'Love you forever' and then turned and walked with Gerry, I didn't trust myself not to cry again and didn't want that to be her last memory of me.

Walking silently by Gerry's side with my head down, I wanted nothing more than to get away from here yet wanted more than anything to run back to the car and hold her in my arms. I had left her two minutes ago, and yet it seemed like days, weeks. I just knew that my life suddenly felt so empty and unbearably lonely.

We walked into the airport building and along the long departure hall. Not knowing why, I had a sudden urge to stop and turn around. At the other end of the room, she was standing with her arms hanging loosely by her side and the saddest expression ever.

Without thinking, I started to run back, tears rolling down my cheeks until I was standing facing her. I needed to tell her the truth, how I felt, that I couldn't leave her whatever the consequences. As I reached her, I grabbed the backs of her arms. She screamed out in pain, and even though I knew I was hurting her, I couldn't let go, I had to make her understand. "I can't do this," I sobbed. "Take me with you, nothing matters except being with you, I don't want to go home, I don't want to sing, I want to be with you. How I expected her to react, I had no idea, but no way did I expect her to say what she said back to me.

Shaking her head, she took hold of my hands and said, "I'm so sorry, it's not what I want right now, I've loved the time we've had together, but what your asking isn't what I want." I didn't believe a word she said. I could see in her eyes that she was making it all up. But why? Why didn't she want us to be together? I just wanted to grab her and run from this place, together as we should be.

I wanted to say so much more, trying to convince her that what I was saying made sense, to stay with her now and forever. I knew she didn't trust herself to say anything else. I saw her look behind me, and the next thing I knew Gerry was taking hold of my arms and pulling me away.

She took a step closer, promising that she would come back next time I was in the UK. Our hands slipped apart as Gerry pulled me away turning me around.

I walked through the hall for the second time. This time I didn't turn around. She had made her decision, and I loved her too much to hurt her anymore. Whatever her reasons were, I had to respect them.

Hoping and praying with all my heart that she would come back the next time I was in the UK, and that she wouldn't forget me.

Because now my heart belonged to her, forever.

Chapter 43

We sat in the car for quite some time. As I cried, Gerry just sat next to me, holding my hand. Eventually, I stopped crying; I felt as though I had no tears left to cry. "You feeling any better now?" he asked kindly. "No," I replied, "Can we go back to the hotel now please, my head hurts, and I think I want to lie down?" "Anything," he said, "I promised him I would look after you, so that's what I intend to do."

My reply to this was to burst into tears again.

We set off for the long drive back to London. Gerry occasionally spoke, although my replies were either one word, or I just didn't speak at all. Eventually, he left me to my thoughts. I was so exhausted from crying I drifted into a fitful doze, dreaming of him singing to me and holding me in his arms.

Gerry's voice broke my dreams. "We're back, come on let's get you up to the room, you look done in."

Gerry opened the door to the room and held it for me. As soon as I went inside, I could see the two of us stood there, saying goodbye, and the tears started again. How was I ever going to get through this? Every time I heard one of his songs, saw a picture of him or something reminded me of this beautiful weekend I would be as bad as ever, and what haunted me more was that I knew he would be suffering too.

One thing I was one hundred per cent sure of was his love for me. Having no idea how long it would be before his next tour of the UK, I had no way of knowing how long it would be before we could be together again.

Walking over to the single bed, I threw myself onto it and buried my head in the pillow. Lying there, I wailed, sobbed and shouted out all the hurt I was feeling inside.

Anything to try and get rid of this pain that was eating away at me.

Chapter 44

We met the crew member who was taking over from Gerry in a private room close to the departure gate. As we walked into the room, he jumped up, introduced himself as Don and held out his hand. I'm not usually a rude person, but I couldn't drum up the enthusiasm to even shake his hand. I stared at him blankly, walked past him and sat down.

Ignoring him didn't put him off, however, and he sat down beside me and began going over the arrangements. I didn't want to listen, and his voice was starting to annoy me. Jumping up, I yelled, "Shut up, leave me alone; I'll just follow you shall I, will that do?" He looked astounded and stopped talking.

I needed to talk to Gerry, privately, "Go get yourself a coffee or something," I said to Don. "I'm good," he replied cheerfully, "Well don't get coffee then," I said impatiently, "I don't care where you go, just disappear, I need to speak to my driver, alone."

He took one look at my face and must have realised I was serious. He moved back towards the door and went through it.

Sitting down beside Gerry, I put my head in my hands. Over the past few days, I had come to think of him as my friend. There was no one other than Gerry that I would be happy leaving her with tonight, I trusted him and knew he would look after her until she got on her train tomorrow.

As if reading my mind, Gerry put his hand on my shoulder and said, "I will look after her if that's what's bothering you." I won't let her out of my sight until she's safely on that train tomorrow.

I looked up at him, so grateful for this. "Please tell her" I stopped for a moment, no words could explain how I felt, but I had to send a message to her, "I will love her forever, please come back next time. And I meant what I said about being faithful to each other; I want no other girls." I paused for breath then added, "I don't understand what her reasons were for not wanting me to go away with her, but whatever they were I know she must have thought it was for the best."

By the time I had finished speaking I had tears running down my face, but managed to say through them "And I know she loves me just as much as I love her. What she said to me didn't fool me one little bit". I had to get that back to her as I knew how bad she would be feeling about what she had said to me.

I wiped away my tears just as Don came back into the room. He looked at me and said, "Time to get on the plane."

Chapter 45

Still lying there with my face in the pillow, now sobbing quietly, I felt Gerry's hand on my shoulder. "Here, drink this and no arguments this time," he said in as stern a voice as he could probably manage. As I lifted my head and looked at him sat on a chair by the side of the bed, I lifted myself into a sitting position.

Despite how devastated I felt; I couldn't help but smile. In one hand there was a glass of liquid which I took to be brandy and in the other a box of tissues.

Sitting up properly, I took the box and kscooped out a handful of tissues, blew my nose noisily and dried my eyes. Throwing the box down, I took hold of the glass with both hands and took a big gulp. The golden liquid burned my throat as it went down and made me start to cough. It felt good though, so I raised the glass to my lips again and emptied the glass. "You were only supposed to sip it," Gerry laughed. I held the glass out to him, "Another, please," I requested with a pleading look. I knew getting drunk was not the answer, but anything to numb the pain.

He must have been expecting me to say this because he got up, went over to the other side of the room and came back with another glass. I knew he was going to tell me to sip it, so before he had a chance to speak, I downed the whole drink, burped and then giggled.

The pain and hurt was still there, but the drink had helped to numb it. We talked for a little while longer and then decided to get our heads down for the night. Asking if he had a spare t-shirt I could use to sleep in and after getting one for me, he went into the bathroom while I got undressed and into bed.

I was still desperately unhappy, but it was late, and two exceptionally large brandies drunk in less than two minutes had taken their toll on me. I was asleep in seconds.

For the second time that day, my dreams were of his face looking into mine, and his body lay next to me. Was this how it was going to be until he came back.

Chapter 46

The short plane journey was so boring; I was in no mood to talk, so I just sat staring out of the window, torturing myself with the fact that with every minute that passed, I was moving further away from her. Somehow, I had managed to stop crying; I had to as I knew it would cause more problems when I got to Paris and met with my manager.

Finally, we got to the departure lounge in the Paris airport. "What's wrong with your face?" my manager asked. Looking through a mirror on the back of the door, my hands flew to my face. My eyes were all puffed up, and my skin was red and blotchy and my usually tidy hair, well I don't know how but it was everywhere. I looked a complete and utter mess.

I decided to tell him the truth, hoping it would make him leave me alone with my misery. "I've just said goodbye to the girl I've fallen in love with," I said. "Oh, the slapper who made your back bleed, you'll soon forget her," he laughed, "Girls like that are ten a penny, she'll be in bed with someone else before your back in your bed."

I couldn't help my next action. I punched him so hard he hit the floor. I walked away before doing anything else to him.

Once on the plane home, I sat alone and got blind drunk, thoughts torturing me of her finding someone else and forgetting me.

I didn't know how I was going to face the coming months, but I knew for sure she was the only girl I would ever love.

She had said she would be faithful to me. I had to hang on to this or I was finished.

Chapter 47

I awoke with the hangover from hell. From two brandies!

Gerry ordered me strong coffee from downstairs. I wanted tea but didn't have the heart to tell him when he was looking after me so wonderfully. My mouth was like sandpaper, partly from the brandy but also from the amount of crying I had done the previous day.

Gulping the coffee, I ran to the bathroom and was violently sick.

As I sat on the bathroom floor with my head over the toilet, a thought struck me. We had made love like it was going out of fashion in the last few hours. I was currently using no contraceptive. My previous birth control pill hadn't agreed with me, so my doctor had advised me to stay off it for six months and then try a different one. That was five months ago. I was due a visit to see my doctor in a couple of weeks.

Leaning back on the bathroom wall my hand instinctively going to my stomach, I realised that I could well be pregnant. I couldn't help but smile even though the thought scared me to hell. Wanting to be with him but trapping him this way was not the answer. I pulled myself up off the floor and told myself, 'worry about it if it happens'. But the thought wouldn't go away.

Gerry ordered breakfast for us both. He loved his food and wolfed down a big hearty breakfast, although all I could manage was a piece of toast and a banana. Feeling sick and empty, I was constantly worrying about how he was coping on his own.

Gerry knew how upset I was, and after we had eaten breakfast, he sat with me and talked through how I felt. I knew he didn't want to hurt me anymore, but as always if he promised something, he carried it out. "He asked me to give you a message" he muttered.

He took a scrap of paper out of his pocket and looked down at it, before starting to speak. He told me everything he had said when he had left him at the airport. By the time he had finished, silent tears had slid down my cheeks, but I was so gratified that he had managed to send his feelings to me through Gerry. I had told him I didn't want to be with him, which was the biggest lie I could have ever told.

I missed him so much already and loved him unconditionally, and even though I had become tearful again, I felt a little more content knowing he knew I loved him.

Soon it was once again time for Gerry to take me to Euston station. After washing my face and brushing my hair, I looked a little more presentable.

Sat by Gerry's side in the car as we travelled through London my heart felt as heavy as an anvil. Somehow leaving London felt as though I was leaving him all over again. London had been where we had met and fallen in love, even though he would be hundreds of miles away by now. Going home felt like I was leaving our love behind. I just had to get through the time left until he was back in the UK.

Sitting in the same café with yet another cup of tea, Gerry went to buy my ticket. This time when he came back, he was holding my train ticket in the air as though he had achieved the impossible. "Forty-five minutes," he said "I'll get us another drink.

When he returned, he placed the drinks on the table, sat opposite me and took hold of both my hands. He looked at me with a grave look on his face. "When he said he wanted to get you in the car, although it didn't seem possible, I was more than prepared to help; I could see how much it meant to him," he said, "You two were destined to be together, and I'm so happy that I was able to play a part in it. He meant it when he said he would be faithful, I know he did, but can you do the same?" "Yes," I answered, "Without a doubt, I don't want anyone else." I needed to go home and end it with the boy I had been seeing.

I belonged to someone else now, and that's how it would stay.

When it was time for my train, Gerry walked me onto the platform. I stopped at the train door and turned to him. I felt quite emotional, leaving him. He had been an absolute rock in the last two days, and I know he would think the same if he had been here. I gave him a big hug and kissed his cheek. He looked quite embarrassed, but all the same, he hugged me back and told me to take care.

Finding an empty compartment, I leaned out of the window and waved to Gerry as the train pulled away from the station. He waved back and then disappeared as the train rounded a bend.

Sitting down, I leaned my head on the window and watched the sights of London pass by. It was forty-eight hours since I had arrived here. Thinking back to how I had felt when I had climbed down from the driver's cab, how excited I had been, I couldn't believe how drastically my life had changed in that time.

The feelings I had for him now were nothing like what I felt before I came to London. He had been my idol then, now he was the man I would love forever.

I was crying again. Is that all I would do until his arms were once more holding me?

Yes, it probably was.

Chapter 48

A car was waiting to take me home. My manager had wanted to go for coffee in the airport lounge to discuss some of the forthcoming arrangements, interviews, photoshoots and what he classed as 'other' pressing issues. No way could I try to pretend everything was normal.

When he suggested coffee, I had pushed past him and told him to call me the day after. As I walked away, I could still hear him, shouting after me about it being important and needing to be attended to, now. His voice faded away as I kept walking, got into the waiting car and dropped my head into my hands.

It was my regular driver, and as I am usually quite chatty, he was continually firing questions at me, asking me all about the UK tour. Trying to be as polite as possible, I answered his questions; however, I think he knew I wasn't in the mood to talk, and after a while, he became quiet.

I wanted to think about her and what had happened between us during the last two days. To dream how I would feel when I returned, and she was once again standing in front of me, smiling her beautiful smile with her head on one side.

Groaning, it seemed so far away. I had no dates yet for when I would be returning to the UK, so I would just have to get on with my life as best I could; that and arrange to bring her back with me, so that we could be together.

One thing for sure, there would be no girls in my life. I had no interest in anyone but my beautiful English girl, and I knew for sure she would feel the same.

Eventually, I was home. Letting myself in, I threw my bags on the floor and headed for my bedroom. Lay on my bed, alone; I let the tears fall.

Gerry III

I got up late, having a feeling that today was going to be difficult.

This job had been easy, so one day of helping him out wasn't a problem. I had got to like him and the girl from last night, (who I presumed was still with him;) seemed like a nice girl.

It was confirmed when my room phone rang. He sounded upset and explained to me how the girl he was with had travelled down to London. I wasn't as surprised as he was, I lived in England and saw many hitchhikers while I was driving around the country.

He asked if I would take her to the train station after I had taken him to the arena, and make sure that she was safely on a train. I told him that I would look after her, and after running through the details, he hung up. He had sounded much happier once I had said that I would do this for him.

I thought back to what I had seen through my window during the night. There was going to be tears later.

When it was time to take him to the arena, I went over to his room, making as much noise as I could as I went up the hall, just in case they were doing anything they didn't want me to see. What I walked in to, took my breath away. She was lying on the sofa with her head on his knee, and he was singing quietly. They were so lost in each other I don't even think they had heard me come in.

I waited by the lift, while they went to my room to say goodbye. When he came out, he was in floods of tears. Not having seen him cry up to now as he had always been cheerful and happy, I just wanted to do what I could for him. He had another concert to do tonight and needed to be in a better frame of mind than he was now.

He had managed to stop the tears as we drove across London, then suddenly asked me if I had paper and a pen. I watched through my mirror as he wrote a letter to her, which I presumed he was going to ask me to deliver, I also watched his tears dripping onto the paper as he was writing.

When we got into the arena, he wanted to go over the arrangements we had made, so I assured him again that I would look after her. I didn't envy him having to sing for two hours while he was in this state.

Walking back into my room, I found her huddled in the chair crying into a tissue. Although I didn't know her, I felt sorry for her, understanding their feelings for each other had gone way beyond what he had expected when he had asked me to get her into the car. As I offered to get her a brandy she asked for tea, and after ordering from room service, I sat and talked, telling her about my family, trying to take her mind off how bad she felt.

Soon it was time to take her to the train station. Stupidly I held the back door of the car open for her to get in, not realising that this would distress her; as the last time she had been in the car she had been in the back with him. Apologising I suggested she sat in the front.

Once we got to Euston, I settled her down in a café and went to get her ticket. Asking the guy in the ticket office for a single ticket, he looked down at some timetables. "Nothing tonight, mate," he said, "It's Sunday, services finish earlier on a Sunday." I thanked him, wondering what I was going to tell her. Worse still what I was going to say to him when I went back to the arena later that evening.

As I walked back to the café an idea formed in my mind, I was staying at the hotel tonight as I was going straight onto another job tomorrow and my room had an additional bed; but would it be ethical to ask her to stay in the same room as me? I would have to put it to her, and more importantly, I would have to make sure he was happy with the arrangement.

When I told her that there were no train's, she had said she would sit in the waiting room until the morning. When I had said no, she had asked me to run her to the motorway so that she could hitch-hike home. No way were either of those realistic suggestions; he would ask if she had got her train when I picked him up later and I couldn't possibly tell him I had left her sat in the station or worse still that I had dropped her on the motorway. To my relief, she was okay to stay in my room.

At this point, I remembered about the letter he had written to her. I decided to give it to her now so that I could tell him later that she had read it. Holding her hand as she read it, I could feel the agony she was going through. Ten minutes later I said I would take her back to the hotel and then did a stupid thing, I said 'or'. Her whole face lit up. Yes! Although she knew it was the wrong decision, she wanted to come with me to pick him up and take him to the airport.

When I got to the arena, after dropping her at the traffic lights, I found him in his dressing room waiting for me. "Let's go," he said. Grabbing his sleeve, I had to stop him and tell him about the train situation and where I had suggested she stay until tomorrow. Her staying in my room wasn't a problem. He went on to tell me that he trusted me and was grateful that I was looking after her. When I said she was waiting at the traffic lights, he couldn't get out fast enough. These two really knew how to make things difficult for themselves.

We had a situation at the back of the arena. There were a lot more girl's than on the previous nights, and it took me more time to edge my way through them. After finally getting through, I started to drive up the road only to find her standing in the middle of the road, halfway up. It seems she had been worried that something was wrong because of the time it had taken us to get out.

Then to top it all, we had another situation at the traffic lights with a gang of girls who had ran after the car. This alone wouldn't have been a problem; only one girl lay across the car bonnet with her skirt pulled up and her pants in her hand. I thought I was a man of the world but didn't know where to put my face.

Looking through the interior mirror, I saw them in each other's arms, oblivious to what was happening.

I needed to do something, or we would be here all night, so I got out and walked to the front of the car, picking the girl up in my arms, I took her over to the pavement and lay her down on the ground. The other girls who were still chanting his name and banging on the windows stared in amazement. I jumped back in the car as quick as I could, put my foot on the accelerator and shot through a red light.

We got to the airport, which was the worst part of the whole day. He was in such a state he ran back, wanting to go with her and leave his life behind. Amazingly, she said no, although I know how much she wanted to be with him.

After taking him to meet the crew member and promising I would pass on his message, I managed to get her to the hotel. Two large brandies later she eventually went to sleep.

The following morning was so hard for her. I could feel her pain and tried my best to make her feel better. We sat and talked for a while, going over what she felt and even though I could see how much it was hurting her, in a way, I think it helped.

I was quite sad to say goodbye to her when I walked her to the train. I had got to like this girl with whom he had fallen in love. She hugged me, kissed my cheek and waved from the window of the train. Waving back, I hoped and prayed she would come back to him when he returned to the UK.

Chapter 49

The train journey seemed to take forever, and as I got off at the station in my hometown, I just wanted to lie down and sleep. I had gone through the whole weekend in my mind during the last few hours, leaving me feeling drained and thoroughly exhausted. Luckily, it hadn't been a busy service, and I had managed to remain on my own in the carriage.

Some of my reminiscing had made me smile, but it had mostly made me cry even more. I was shattered.

I didn't want to go home and face my parents. I had been missing for three days, and they had no idea where I had been. I know this sounds irresponsible, but they refused to accept I was grown up still thinking I was a little girl who should be in every night by 9 pm.

Quite often disappearing for days on end, I turned up when I wanted, so I knew that if I went home, I would have to face the endless questions and lectures.

I decided instead to go to my sisters, at least she knew where I had been and would understand how I felt.

Letting myself into my sister's house, I could hear the girls playing in the lounge. Running towards me as I came through the door, they threw themselves at me. Putting on a brave face, I hugged them and gave them both a kiss. "Where's mum?" I said, at the same time as my sister appeared in the doorway to the kitchen. "Oh, the wanderer returns," she said, smiling, "Come on tell me, how did it go? I take it from the length of time you've been away the plan worked."

I looked up at her and tried my best to smile, but somehow knew how false it must have looked. In place of the smile, the tears started again. She came over to me and put her arms around me, instantly knowing what was wrong. "Oh love, this wasn't supposed to happen," she said sadly, "You were supposed to enjoy the experience and then walk away smiling." Managing a weak smile, I said "I did enjoy it, probably too much, put the kettle on and I'll tell you all about it.

In between getting the kids to bed and going out to buy some beers from the local shop, I told her everything that had happened, holding nothing back. She was my sister, and we had no secrets from each other. "And you're going to be faithful to him," she exclaimed, "It's a big thing to commit to."

She knew how much I loved my life, a boyfriend for a few weeks before becoming bored and moving on to the next one. "One hundred per cent," I replied, "I don't want anyone else, and before you say it, this is not because he's a big star; I love him so much, the real person, not his image."

She laughed then and went on to say, "I should have been in London with you to drag you out of his room after you had bedded him." I looked at her with such determination and responded by saying, "You could have tried, but I wouldn't have listened to you, I was where I wanted to be, nothing could have made me walk away."

Staying the night, I had breakfast and took the kids to school on my way to the bus. I had to face my parents some time, and I was back at work the day after.

Listening to the tirade of shouting and accusations for two hours, I couldn't stand any more. "Okay, you've made your point, now leave me alone I'm going to my room" I screamed.

Remembering that I had a bottle of rum at the back of the wardrobe, which I had bought to take to a party a couple of weeks before, and never used. Making myself two large glasses of orange cordial, I took them upstairs to my room. I would use this to mix with the rum.

Once in my room, I retrieved the bottle, drunk half of one of the glasses of orange and filled it to the top with rum. Having mixed my drink, I took a massive gulp and lay down on my bed and closed my eyes.

For what seemed like the hundredth time I went through my time in London, tears pouring down my face. Sitting up, I downed the rest of my drink, then realised I was staring at my posters of him on my bedroom wall.

Having posters of various bands and singers on my walls, my posters of him had always been on the wall where I could look at them while lying in bed, dreaming of meeting him one day.

Looking at them, I felt the tears start to fall again, wailed and then ripped every one of them from the wall. Staring at his face on my wall wasn't what it was about anymore. I was no longer one of his many fans, and he was no longer my idol. He was the man I loved with all my heart who I couldn't live without.

 By the time I had finished, I was sobbing.

Within an hour of opening the rum, I had drunk it all, drinking it neat when I had used up all the orange. Falling asleep crying to myself, I clung to the pendant he had given to me in London.

Although I went to work every day, the rest of my time I stayed in my bedroom drinking. Buying a bottle of rum or gin on my way home from work, and for the first few days something to mix it with, coke or lemonade. I would hide it in my work bag and take it straight up to my room. Eventually I was buying the bottle and no mixer.

At the weekend I would go to my sisters and spend time with the kids, getting drunk when they had gone to bed, either looking after them if my sister was going out or we would have a drink together.

I had stopped going out, having no interest in having a good time. All I wanted was to hear when he was back in the UK.

It was all I was living for.

Chapter 50

It was two weeks since I had arrived home from the UK.

Due to my recent concerts, I had some time off from recording and other engagements, but had just moped about, hardly eating and drinking far too much.

Even picking my guitar up and singing made me miserable, reminding me of singing to her when I was in London. I knew I was a mess, but as much as I tried to climb out of my misery, nothing worked.

Deciding to try and write some new songs while I had time on my hands, I found the only subject I was writing about was my love for the amazing girl I had left behind; making me feel even more miserable than ever.

An awards ceremony and a film premiere were coming up which I would be attending. The problem was that I didn't have anyone to accompany me.

Finding someone to take had never been a problem in the past. I would pick a girl, take her with me to whatever event I had been invited to, usually ending up in bed with her afterwards. Having a reputation for doing this, the girls I knew had come to expect it. I had no idea who to ask without having to fend them off at the end of the night.

How I wished I had a sister who I could take along.

My brother was dating a girl, from one of the wealthy families in the area, and suggested that I take a friend of his girlfriends. He would explain that I needed someone to accompany me on a 'no strings' basis. I didn't like the idea; rich girls annoyed me as they thought they could have anything they wanted. However, I agreed, I had no other option.

On the day of the awards ceremony, he rang me, giving me a name, phone number and the address where I was to pick her up. I looked at the details I had written down, 'Simone De Vallier' she was three years younger than me and the address he had given me, well, I knew the properties in that area of town. My house would probably fit into their garage.

Having got myself ready, I waited for my driver to pick me up, wishing for the hundredth time that my beautiful girl was here to accompany me and how proud I would be, having her by my side.

How uncomplicated our time had been, being together with nothing to worry about except when we next wanted sex.

Smiling, I could feel the tears forming at the back of my eyes.

As we turned into the driveway of the De Vallier's house, I stared in amazement. House? More like a mansion. A set of stone steps led up to a large oak door with colossal marble columns at each side. I counted the windows on the front of the house as we approached. Twenty-six and that was only at the front.

My brother had informed me that Simone was an only child, so that meant that three people lived in this house. Why would anyone want all these rooms for three people?

As we stopped, my driver got out of the car and stood beside the back door of the vehicle. Someone inside must have been watching, waiting for us to arrive, as within a minute the front door opened, and a woman stepped out. I frowned; this couldn't be Simone surely. This woman looked to be in her thirties. However, as she approached, I realised her older appearance was her clothes and make-up, which looked like it had been slapped on with a trowel. She was hideous.

My driver opened the door for Simone to get in and she slid into the seat beside me, smiled at me with a set of teeth so white and shiny it looked like someone had put a coat of gloss paint on them. She leant forward and held her cheek out for me to kiss.

Looking at her my face full of dread, I wanted to be sick, or run, or maybe just die.

The evening was awful. I made no attempt to have any physical contact with Simone at all, while she took every opportunity to hold onto my arm and paw at me, stroking my hair and continuously calling me *'darling'*.

Somehow, I got through the ceremony quietly, while she talked, none stop. At the after-ceremony party she had insisted I dance with her, not once but twice.

She must have realised I didn't want to, as it took all my will to put my arms around her; I was completely rigid, while she was running her hands up and down my back, leaning her face close to mine.

At one point, I felt her hand move to the inside of my thigh. No! This part of my anatomy was where my girl touched me and was definitely out of bounds to anyone; especially this unbearable girl who didn't understand the term 'no strings'.

As we left, reporters flashed their cameras at anyone they thought was interesting enough to photograph. If she saw a camera pointing in our direction, she immediately grabbed my arm and put her face close to mine.

Luckily, I had explained to my girl in England that I was often invited to various functions, and that I would need to be accompanied by a girl. So, if she saw any pictures in newspapers or celebrity magazines that they meant nothing.

She had smiled sadly, saying, "That's okay, but please don't fall in love." I had assured her that there was no chance, the girl I loved was standing right in front of me."

Thinking back to this made me want to cry.

The minute we got into the car at the end of the night Simone ordered my driver to go straight to my place. I groaned aloud, "Not a chance Simone," I said, "You knew this was a 'no strings' arrangement." She turned to me trying to look alluring and sexy and said in a loud, vulgar voice, "That doesn't mean you can't fuck me, what's up with you, don't you fancy me?" she then went on to say, "I'm the best fuck you'll ever get, believe me."

Smiling to myself, I thought, 'I don't think so; I've had the best, that's why I'm not interested in you'.

Luckily for me, she was the type of girl who sulked if things didn't go her way, and as she turned her back to me, I sighed with relief. Tapping my driver on the shoulder, I asked him to take Simone home first. As I leant back in my seat, closing my eyes, my mind took me back to London and the arms of the girl I loved.

We arrived at Simone's. Before my driver had time to get out and hold the door open for her, she had shot out of the car and slammed the door so violently the whole vehicle shook.

I dropped my head into my hands. How on earth was I going to cope with all this? Events I didn't want to be at, spoilt girls and being away from the one I so desperately wanted by my side.

When I got home, I poured myself a large drink, took it outside and lay on the garden swing. The glasses of brandy I had downed earlier at the ceremony and the large one I was now drinking tipped me completely over the edge.

Soon I was asleep and dreaming of being back in London, a beautiful face looking up at me from the front of the crowd.

Awaking to my phone ringing, I jumped up and went through to the kitchen. It was 7 am, who on earth was ringing me at this unearthly hour? I picked up the receiver and said "Hello." Annoyed that I had answered the call, I heard Simone's squeaky voice simpering to me. Sinking onto the tiled floor, I wondered what I had done to deserve this. Although I wasn't listening, I caught snatches of her ramblings. Hearing 'respect me' and 'better next time'. I didn't want or need this and suddenly heard myself saying, "I'm busy right now, I'll call you later," then slammed the phone back in its holder.

It turned out her mother had told her she had behaved badly the previous evening and that she should ring me and apologise. After thinking it through, I decided to let her accompany me to the next event, which was the film premiere. At least then I didn't have to go through all this with another girl who I didn't know.

Ringing her later that day as I had said I would, I regretted as soon as she answered the phone. Assuming I was keen, she suggested we go out to dinner that evening. God no! An instant lie came out of my mouth. "Sorry I've got studio rehearsals, recordings and interviews over the next two weeks, I'm just too busy to socialise," I then went on to invite her to the premiere.

I could hear the excitement in her voice as she told me how envious her friends were going to be now that she was dating a superstar.

Again, I groaned. I'm not dating you, I thought to myself, I'm enduring you.

What was happening to me? My life seemed to belong to someone else. I wanted to be in England with my girl not here with a spoilt brat I couldn't stand.

I had to get out of this situation before it took me over.

Chapter 51

I knew I was bordering on being an alcoholic, but it was the only way I could get through each day and the loneliness that was swamping me.

My sister knew how much I was drinking and badgered me constantly to get help. I just shrugged her off, saying I was okay, and that I knew what I was doing.

My parents hadn't noticed anything. If I went to work, tipped up my keep at the end of each week and came home every night, they didn't seem to care what I did. That suited me fine, the less they complained at what I did, the better.

The last week I had found it harder to get up in the morning, feeling sick when I got to work and had put it down to how much I was drinking, having gone from a bottle, to one and a half bottles a day.

I had even had to run to the toilet on one occasion and vomited.

The time I had been back home from London had passed in a blur, every week being the same routine and the fact that I was drinking made it harder to keep track of time.

As I looked over at the calendar on the wall above my machine, I started to work out how many weeks had passed since I had been in London. Suddenly I realised that I hadn't given a second thought to the visit I was supposed to be making, to see my doctor for my contraceptive pill.

It was nearly four weeks since I had been in London. My monthly period was almost two weeks late.

Staring at the dates on the calendar, I was willing them to be wrong and yet as my hand moved down to my stomach, I knew. I was pregnant, I was having his baby, and I was deliriously happy.

How this was going to play out, I had no idea. Would he be happy and want us to get married, or would he be mad at me for being irresponsible? It was something we hadn't discussed during my time with him, which I supposed made it both our responsibilities.

It didn't mean he would welcome a baby; he had his career and maybe didn't want this in his life.

That evening when I left work, I made straight for my doctor's surgery.

Sitting in the waiting room until it was my turn to see the doctor, I fantasised about telling him I was expecting his child. In my dreams, he would hold me in his arms, tell me how happy he was and want us to get married as soon as possible.

But was this how it would be? As I came down to earth, I could hear him saying to me that he didn't want a child in is life, and how did I know it was his? One crucial fact I hadn't told him was, although I had said I had been seeing someone before I went to London, I hadn't thought to mention that we hadn't slept together.

So, this baby I was expecting had been conceived in London. However he felt about the situation; he was about to become a father.

When my turn came to see the doctor, I entered the surgery and sat down. I was nervous as hell but came straight out with it, "I think I'm pregnant," I blurted out. Seeing his disapproving look, he asked me a few questions and then handed me a small pot to provide a urine sample. "Fill this tomorrow morning and bring it back," he said, "come back in three days for the results." By this time, he had turned back to the papers on his desk.

Leaving the surgery, I felt thoroughly sickened by his attitude. I was a pregnant woman, not a mass murderer.

Walking home from the doctor's surgery, I passed the off licence for the first time in four weeks. I needed a drink more than ever but knew I couldn't, not with a new life growing inside me.

We had made this baby during our weekend together, and this made me smile more than anything. When he came back to the UK, he would see me standing in front of him heavily pregnant, either that or I would be breaking the news to him after the concert that he was a father.

The morning after, I quickly did my urine sample, dressed and left the house to walk to work. That way if I felt sick, it would either be on the way to work or when I arrived there.

But I had only been out of the house for two or three minutes when I vomited on the pavement. My head swam, and I held on to the wall to steady myself. The sickness seemed to be getting worse by the day. After sitting on a step for a while, I finally made it to work, only having to rush to the toilet to vomit again the minute I got into the building.

I must have looked terrible as my supervisor gave me easier work for the morning.

By lunchtime, I felt a little better and managed to take my sample to the doctor's surgery, before returning to my usual work in the afternoon.

However, I had an immediate problem; my sister was away for the weekend. She and a friend were taking their collective children to a caravan park for two nights, which meant I was at home for Saturday and Sunday morning.

While there was no one around on Friday evening, I had found an old plastic bowl in the outside shed, took it up to my room and hid it under the bed. When I got up the following morning, I would stay in my bedroom, so that if I felt sick, I would have something to use. I could then wash it out in the bathroom later that day.

Using the bowl I had found sounded like an excellent plan to me, but, the following morning while throwing up into the bowl, I was making so much noise, that looking up, my mother was standing in the doorway, a disapproving look on her face. "What's wrong with you?" she said in disgust. I knew I looked terrible; I was dripping with sweat and could see myself through the mirror on my wardrobe door; I was as white as a sheet. "Don't know," I mumbled, "think I must have eaten something." She snorted, walked out and slammed my door. I burst into tears. I knew that I was pregnant for sure, and all I wanted at that moment was for him to be by my side with his arms around me, telling me everything would be okay.

Because at that moment in time, I had no idea what my future held.

I stayed in bed for most of the day. The sickness had passed, but I felt so miserable, missing him more than ever and wishing he knew what I was going through.

Only in my darkest moments did I believe he wouldn't want me because I was pregnant. In my heart I knew he would be as happy as I was, this was his baby too, the one we had made together.

Sunday morning came, and I decided to stay in bed to see if it would help keep the sickness at bay. Doing this seemed to work, and after about an hour, I got up slowly and sat on the edge of the bed.

So far so good I thought, still not feeling sick, but as I stood up, the nausea came. Feeling under the bed for the bowl, I realised it had gone. My mother must have come into the room the day before and taken it while I was asleep.

As I tried to make a run for the bathroom, my door swung open and instead of throwing up in the toilet, it splattered all down the front of my mother's dress. Pushing past her as I felt more coming up, I dived to the bathroom and knelt on the floor with my head over the toilet, vomiting until I was doing nothing more than retch. My head was splitting, and my chest hurt like hell.

Staying where I was for how long, I had no idea, but eventually standing up, I made my way back to my bedroom only to find my mother blocking my way on the landing. "Move," I said, "I'm not well."

She followed me into my room, "You're pregnant, did you know," she said, like she was telling a small child it was raining outside. I glared at her; did she think I was completely stupid. "Tell me something I don't know, why don't you," I answered her in an uninterested voice.

Saying this made her explode and call me all the names she could think of, 'whore, tart, slag, dirty cow and a whole lot more. I looked at her with an amused look on my face. I knew I was unreasonable, but frankly, I didn't care. "I didn't know you even knew words like that," I said back to her, got into bed and turned my back to her. Again, I heard my bedroom door slam.

Feeling worse than ever, I lay there, crying silently, clutching my pendant. It made me feel close to him even though he was thousands of miles away.

Finally slipping into a fitful sleep, my mother's voice woke me. She didn't wait for me to wake up properly before she started talking to me. "I'll take you to the doctor's in the morning," she said, and then "We can arrange for you to get rid of it." Jumping to my feet so quickly, I nearly overbalanced and had to grab the edge of my drawers to stop myself falling.

I was speechless. It was my life and my baby, but she was talking to me as though we were discussing throwing out some old shoes. "Not a chance," I said, shaking my head, "No abortion, I'm having this baby, so just get out and leave me alone."

As I sat back down, I dropped my head in my hands, but not before I saw that she was looking at my bedroom wall where I had ripped down his pictures.

Starting to speak again, I heard, "And just whose is this baby anyway?" she sneered. As I looked up at her, I saw her look up at the wall again and then say in a nasty tone. "You silly little cow, so that's where you disappeared to for three days. You went to open your legs for your popstar idol. How could you do that with someone who doesn't give two hoots about you? You do know if you go ahead and have this baby, it will grow up without a father, because nobody else will want you with a child."

By this time, I had heard enough and screaming, I picked up my hairbrush from my dressing table and launched it at her. "My baby won't grow up without a father," I yelled, "He loves me, and I love him. When he comes back to the UK, I'm going back with him."

Stopping at my bedroom door, she turned back to me and laughed, "And you believe him do you, you stupid girl. Why on earth would he want someone like you, your living in fantasy land? Get rid of it and try to keep your legs shut in future." Her parting words were, *'And don't think you're bringing your bastard into this house.*

I got up slower this time, looked at her and said, "I'll pack and get out then, that's what you want isn't it?"

Twenty minutes later, still sobbing, I was walking out of the door with my suitcase. Being too heavy to carry on and off buses, I walked to the nearest phone box and rang the local taxi company. When it arrived, I gave the driver my sister's address, got in the back of the car, closed my eyes and carried on sobbing.

Did he love me? Or had it just been the fun of a romantic weekend with someone who enjoyed sex as much as he did? What my mother had said was going around and around in my head. I had grown up believing everything she had said to me, so was she right, had he been stringing me along to amuse himself?

Paying the taxi driver and assuring him I would be fine waiting for my sister to come home I sat down on the doorstep and sobbed some more.

Deep in thought, I was startled by a voice speaking to me, "What on earths wrong love." It was Andy from next door. Looking up, I sniffed and said, "I'm okay." Picking up my suitcase, he answered, "Well, you don't look okay to me. Come on, and I'll get Cath to put the kettle on."

Following him into their house, still sobbing Cath took one look at me and held open her arms. The look on her face was too much, and falling into her embrace, I wailed like a child. Sitting down on the sofa with Cath by my side, she held me, rocking me until I had no tears left.

Wiping my eyes and blowing my nose on a big cotton handkerchief that Andy had passed to me, I took a big gulp of the hot sweet tea in front of me.

After making the tea, Andy had kindly disappeared into the kitchen. "Right," Cath said, "Tell me what's made you cry like this. I know you well, and this isn't like you at all, your tough, nothing usually bothers you." And so, I told her everything.

She knew I had been to London but didn't know the details. My sister had told them both that I had managed to meet him. Andy, of course, had got my ticket for me and given me a lift on the morning I had gone to London, so he was curious to know if my plan had worked.

After going through what had happened in London and the feelings that I thought we had for each other, I told her I was pregnant and what my mother had said to me.

Hugging me again, she started to speak, "And why wouldn't he want you, he's just a man, and you're just a woman. It doesn't matter where you come from or what you are in life; you're still entitled to fall in love with each other. I've listened to everything you've told me, and I've got a few things to point out."

Putting my cup into one hand, she took a deep breath and took hold of my other one. "Okay, if he hadn't fallen in love with you, would he have behaved like he did at the airport; he would have just kissed you goodbye and got on the plane, and would he have been bothered about how you planned to get back home." Stopping to take another breath she continued, "Would he have been so upset at leaving you and more than anything would he have adopted the 'love you forever' phrase if that's not what he wanted to do." Then quietly, she said, "Your mother doesn't know any of what happened. She thinks you're a starstruck fan who managed to have five-minute sex with him. So yes, he does love you as much as he has told you he does, so don't doubt that love for a minute. It's real, and you know it is."

By this time, I had tears pouring down my face, but knew how right Cath was. He did love me; he did want me, and I knew everything he had said to me was one hundred per cent true. Hugging Cath and thanking her I felt so much better.

When my sister and the kids arrived home from their weekend away, Andy carried my suitcase to her house. Giving me a peck on the cheek, he left me to explain what had happened.

Telling her everything; what my mother had thrown at me and then what Cath had said, she listened and then added, "Would he have talked about taking you back with him the when he comes back if he didn't love you?" Smiling, I answered, "Cath missed that one."

Knowing I was welcome here anytime and under any circumstances, I felt that at that moment I wouldn't belong anywhere, until he was back by my side.

I had never felt so lost and lonely in my life.

Chapter 52

The film premiere had been every bit as bad if not worse than the awards ceremony. Simone acted as though we were a couple and introduced me to anyone she knew as her 'new boyfriend'.

After the third time she had done this, I pulled her to one side. "What part of 'no strings'," didn't you understand I said to her. She looked back at me, pouted and said in a menacing voice, "If I want something, I get it, and I want you, so get used to it." She walked away laughing, leaving me scared to hell.

I needed to get out of this before something happened that would affect my life in a way I couldn't control.

At that time, I didn't realise how close to the truth I was.

Feigning a migraine at the premiere we left before the party started, and after dropping Simone off, I made my way home.

I had driven her there myself in my car, lying that my driver had a prior engagement. I hadn't had anything to drink and was in full control of my senses; it also stopped her from pawing at me on the way home.

Before getting out of my car, as I pulled up on her drive, she had leant across and tried to kiss me. Pushing her away, she had asked why I didn't want to sleep with her. She had asked me this question several times; my reply was that I didn't want to be in a relationship at that time.

But this time she was persistent and even went on to say that she wasn't bothered about being in a relationship with me and that she just wanted sex; using the term 'I just want you up me', which made me feel like vomiting. The only time my girl would ever use expressions like that was during sex when she was tarty to turn me on.

Quite suddenly, she said, "Are you a puff? Is that why you won't come near me?" and then continued in a sneering voice, "Just wait till I tell everyone, the big star with thousands of female fans who doesn't like girls."

Looking at her, I started to laugh, "Do your worst Simone," I said, still smiling. "I think you'll find quite a few girls around here who will discount that theory," and then banging my hand on the steering wheel, I shouted, "Now get out of my car, I never want to see you again." Leaning over her, I opened her door and unbuckled her seatbelt then stared straight ahead.

Getting out without saying another word, she once again slammed the car door. She was one spoilt, rude brat.

"As far as I was concerned that was the end of our 'arrangement'. There were no more events coming up in the next few months that I needed to be accompanied to, meaning I had time to find someone else, who would be more suitable.

Taking a drink to bed, my first one of that evening, I lay down and thought about my girl. Still having no news about any UK concerts was making me long for her even more.

I fell asleep, longing to feel her in my arms, to my usual dreams, us together forever.

Chapter 53

My parents had been to visit me twice at my sister's house. My mother assumed when I had calmed down and seen sense, I would then arrange to have my pregnancy terminated.

Sitting on the edge of the sofa, she threw the question at me, "So who is the real father then?" Having decided I couldn't possibly attract the attention of a famous pop star, and I had concocted this 'lie' so that I didn't have to tell her who the real father was.

The more I told her who's baby it was, the more she laughed at me until I screamed at them to get out and leave me alone. Standing at the door, she turned to me before she left saying. "Just grow up you silly bitch and get shut of it." My father had, as usual, said nothing, just sitting there with a sad look on his face.

Sinking onto the sofa, I sobbed. I needed him by my side; this was too much to handle on my own. But I didn't have a choice, I had to face it alone, until I was back by his side.

Two weeks later, they were back; this time to tell me they had made an appointment for me at the local hospital to discuss a termination.

When would she listen to me? I was having this baby - it wasn't her decision. Being as calm as I could and with my sister sat by my side, I started to explain that he did love me and that I was going back with him when he was next in the UK.

Interrupting me, she laughed nastily as she said, "What do you think he will say when you tell him he has a child, well I'll tell you shall I?" Leaning forward and raising her voice, she continued to say, "He'll have you thrown out of wherever you are and deny it's his. You dropped your knickers for him, so he'll know you would do the same for anybody."

At this I ran upstairs in tears. That he might not believe the baby was his was the worst possible thing she could have said to me. Although I knew how much he loved me, I had told him I had been seeing someone before I went to London; but hadn't mentioned that I hadn't slept with him. I just hoped his love was strong enough to believe in me and understand that I wouldn't saddle him with a child that could possibly be someone else's.

Sitting on the bed, I could hear my sister's raised voice, and then the door slammed. She had thrown them out, telling them that they were distressing me.

Later that evening, as I was using the toilet, I discovered a large patch of blood in my pants. Screaming, I yelled for my sister and yelling back, asking me what was wrong, she ran upstairs to me. Helping me downstairs she lay me on the sofa, while she went next door to phone for an ambulance.

By the time she returned, I was hysterical as I was sure I was miscarrying. Climbing in the ambulance beside me, she held my hand as I cried for the baby that I was sure I had lost. Although I knew it would be less complicated if there were no baby, I knew it wasn't what I wanted. I had grown to love our baby and deep down in my heart, I knew that he would feel the same way.

Arriving at the hospital, I was wheeled into a cubicle and examined by a doctor a few minutes later. He had a stern look on his face which did nothing but filled me with dread. Suddenly he smiled and said, "There doesn't seem to be anything wrong with your baby; you seem to be about fourteen weeks."

Crying with relief, I thanked him; I was so sure I had lost our baby, and the news that he had given me had made me emotional. After being informed I was being kept in overnight as a precaution, I thanked my sister, giving her a big hug before she left for home.

Lying in my hospital bed, one hand clutching my pendant and the other across my bump, I spoke to the man I loved. "Please come back soon, I need you so much, and I'm not sure I can do this without you."

But even though I was missing him desperately, I was happy and content. Our baby was healthy and still growing inside me.

Waking from a deep sleep, I thought I must be dreaming when I heard my mother's voice droning on beside me. Did this woman not realise that I needed to be awake before she started to talk to me?

Opening my eyes, I was just about to say hello when she launched into one of her rants. "So, you've lost it have you, well it's for the best? Now you can get on with your life and try to keep your legs shut. Oh, and keep away from his concerts, or he'll only end up getting his own way again."

Sitting there smiling, thinking everything had gone her way I also smiled; I'll soon wipe that look of your face, I thought to myself.

Pushing myself up, I gave a little chuckle. "What are you laughing at you stupid girl," she sneered. Becoming a little more serious, I started to speak. "No, I have not lost our baby, (seeing her bristle at the word 'our') it's strong and healthy, and I'm fourteen weeks, so sorry - too late for an abortion. And whether you believe it or not, he does love me, and I will be going back with him when he comes back to the UK. This baby growing inside me is your grandchild, but because of how you feel you will never see it. But that doesn't bother me one bit, as it will have two parents to love it. And by the way, he did not get 'his own way'. Sex with him was fantastic, and I wanted him as much as he wanted me.

I had purposely said this as I knew my mother thought sex was disgusting and dirty. "Now leave me alone I want to sleep, so JUST GET OUT;" screaming the last three words as loud as I could.

Just as she was about to answer me, a nurse appeared; having heard me shouting from the other end of the ward. Seeing my parents, she informed them that they had no right to be on the ward at this time, as it wasn't official visiting time. She then told them to leave immediately, as I was by this time crying and shaking.

Storming off my mother walked down the ward, shouting out to anyone who could hear her that I was nothing but a trollop, and that I was under the illusion that my baby's father was a famous singer.

Hugging me and kissing me on my cheek, my father left, waving to me when he was at the door to the ward. I felt so sorry for him. He did everything my mother wanted and knew if it was up to him, that he would have me back home in a heartbeat.

Wiping my eyes, I sank back on my pillow and closed my eyes.

Hearing the nurse appear by my bedside, I opened my eyes and smiled at her. "You feel any better now?" she said as she prepared to take my blood pressure. "Yes," I answered, "I just wish she would learn to keep her opinions to herself."

As she put the blood pressure cuff on my arm, she looked at me quizzically. Laughing at her expression, I couldn't help but say, "Go on, then, ask me, I've done nothing I'm ashamed of." Trying to look professional, she went on to say that it would help if I unburdened myself to her.

More like being nosey, I thought! But I told her anyway.

Starting by telling her about London, I went through the whole story as she sat on the edge of my bed. Watching the expression on her face when I told her who he was made me laugh so much. She wasn't much older than me, so she would be aware of his music; maybe she even had a crush on him.

Even so, she squeezed my hand and said, "You lucky girl, I hope it all works out for you."

Chapter 54

Hearing nothing from Simone in the next few weeks surprised me. When she had said she 'wanted me' it had scared me; I don't know why, she just seemed the type of girl to do anything to get her way. I had started to breathe a sigh of relief, thinking she had given up; realising I wasn't interested in her.

As I sat watching TV one evening a few days later, the phone rang. Answering it to a voice that I didn't recognise, the voice introduced herself as Grace, Simone's mother.

She went on to invite me to a 'little house party' at their place. When I asked her what the occasion was, she laughed, a silly tinkly laugh and said, "You'll find out." She then said goodbye and hung up. I stood there with the telephone receiver in my hand, puzzled. What was that about, I hadn't even said I would be there. Okay I would attend, a house party was safe enough, especially as my brother would be there; it also seemed churlish to refuse an invitation from her mother.

How naïve could I have been?

A few days after the phone call, I had received a formal invitation in the mail. Looking at it, I tried to find out the reason for this 'party', but all it said was an 'informal gathering', dress code casual.

I decided to speak to my brother to see if he knew any more. He, however, was as clueless as me, going on to say that rich people had parties for no particular reason. But as there would be significant amounts of food and drink, he was quite happy to be there.

On the evening of the party, I arrived with my brother, to more food and drink than I've ever seen in my life.

There was also an eight-piece band playing and waiters dressed in black and white, serving champagne from silver trays. They seemed to have gone over the top for a 'little house party'.

I was beginning to feel uncomfortable about this, although I didn't quite know why.

A passing waiter offered me champagne, but I waved him away and poured myself an orange juice instead. I wanted to keep a clear head and knew what champagne did to me, smiling to myself, thinking how it also affected a certain someone else.

Thinking of her made me so sad, and I was standing in a corner lost in my thoughts when Simone found me, grabbing me by the arm. "Come and meet everyone," she said.

Being dragged around the room and introduced to so many people, their faces became a blur. Shaking hands and making appropriate comments and noises, I wanted to turn and run from this house and its bunch of pretentious people.

Eventually, after we had exhausted everyone in the room, Simone left me in my corner and went to find her mother.

Standing there nursing my orange juice, I started thinking about how my girl would act in this room full of snobs. I knew she would be out of her depth, but if I were here with her, it wouldn't matter, I would look after her, laughing out loud at that thought. If she were here in my country, we wouldn't be here at this stuffy snob's party. We would be at my place sitting in the garden or out walking in the woods with my dog.

The sadness inside of me was overwhelming and not for the first time tonight, I thought about walking out and going home. If my brother hadn't been here, I might have done, but it wasn't fair leaving him to explain.

When the party was around an hour old, Simone's father announced that the men were all going into the games room to play some pool and poker.

Following all the others I spotted my brother, "What's all this about," I said uncertainly. He shrugged and answered, "Who knows, the guys are going to play pool, the women are doing whatever they do when they're all together, come on, loosen up and have some fun."

He walked on ahead of me, leaving me thinking that this was not my idea of fun.

Once in the games room, the men divided themselves up. Some headed for the pool table, some to the card tables. There were even more waiters in here, but this time they were walking around with bottles of spirits. I still didn't want to drink; my stomach was in knots, making me feel nauseous and shaky.

Just as I was deciding how to put myself out of everyone else's way, one of the waiters thrust a glass of something in my hand; before I had the chance to refuse, he had gone. Sniffing the drink, I realised it was brandy; the smell of it made me feel even worse.

I decided that the best plan of action was to walk around the room, pretending to sip my drink, looking interested in what was happening on the tables. I set off, interweaving with the others.

As I walked about, I was suddenly conscious of someone walking behind me; realising that it was the same waiter who had given me the drink. Having no notion of what was going on here, an idea formed in my head. As soon as I saw him go to get a fresh bottle, I threw most of my drink into a large pot plant and then stood leaning on the edge of an ornamental table.

As soon as he appeared back with a full bottle, he made straight for where I was standing, filling my glass to the brim. Thanking him, I continued to wander around the room. Still not knowing why, I knew he was watching me; waiting for my glass to become empty, immediately filling it again.

The same happened three more times, the waiter filled my glass, I walked away to stand near a pot plant and when he was distracted, I would throw my drink into it. Was he that stupid? If I had drunk the amount of alcohol he had been pouring into my glass, I would be comatose by now.

It was also fortunate that Simone's mother liked pot plants.

After an hour or so, everyone started to drift out of the games room back to the room where we had left the women. Throwing the last of my drink in the nearest plant, I followed everyone out.

Having stood on my own all evening finding a seat in a corner suited me. I didn't feel like socialising. For some reason, I was missing my girl more than ever tonight and wondered if it was because I was feeling uneasy about this whole evening.

Looking around, I noticed that a champagne fountain had been set up on the tables at the other side of the room, surrounded by more bottles of the stuff. It was as if there was going to be some big announcement.

No! My stomach lurched. Surely Simone wouldn't do something so underhand.

Suddenly feeling like a trapped animal, I looked around for a way to escape from this room. As I was about to make a run for the door opposite, I felt someone grab my arm. Thinking it was Simone, I jumped violently, only to find it was my brother. "Outside now." he hissed in my ear, "I need to talk to you."

Looking back at him; I must have appeared so scared he pushed me through a door behind me that I didn't even know was there, which led to a passageway and then outside to a rockery garden.

"What?" I said to him knowing somehow, that I wasn't going to like what I was about to hear. "I've just heard Simone is about to announce your engagement, are you mad you haven't known her five minutes," he said to me in disbelief.

I stared at him in silence. "Speak to me," he yelled and shook me. Pulling myself away from him, I legged it over to one of the flowerbeds and threw up.

When I had finished and composed myself as much as was possible, I turned back to him. "No, I'm not mad." I said, "I know nothing about this fiasco, for God's sake, I haven't even kissed her, let alone proposed to the stupid bitch."

By this time, I was in tears, but managed to say to him, "Please, do me a favour. Go back inside and tell Simone I want to speak to her on the front terrace, near the ornamental pond. I'm not going back through that room; I'll walk around the outside of the house."

He nodded and gave me a brotherly hug. "Don't worry, we'll sort it out," he said, then disappeared back through the door.

I walked, as slowly as possible around the perimeter of the house to the front terrace, where I had asked to meet Simone.

As I approached, I saw her sitting on the edge of the pond. She hadn't seen me, and as I got closer, I saw that she was arranging her skirt so that she was showing the top of her stockings. "Just what's going on Simone?" I shouted.

As she heard my voice, she jumped up and came towards me, smiling, "Darling. There you are, I've been looking for you," she answered in a voice that sounded like it should belong to a small child. Trying to put her arms around my neck, I pushed her away, so forcefully she staggered backwards. I wouldn't usually treat any female in this way; however, while I had been walking around the outside of the house, I had become outraged at what my brother had told me.

She looked back at me and then said the most astounding thing imaginable. "In five minutes, our engagement is to be announced, and we will be married within a month. She then gave what I can only describe as an evil laugh, "Like I told you before, what I want, I get."

My first thought was to run, anywhere, as far away as possible.

But no, I needed to put a stop to this, as I knew, if I left, that she would go ahead with this ludicrous announcement without me there.

There was only one way to put a stop to this, and so ignoring her, I walked back into the house, to the other side of the room full of people. My heart was hammering in my chest. I didn't want to do what I was about to do, but in my mind, I could see the face of the girl I loved and knew I was doing this for her.

Walking to the top of the room, I pulled a chair from the corner and climbed onto it. Taking a deep breath, I started to speak as loudly as possible.

"Excuse me, everyone," I started with, "I have an announcement to make." I could see everyone looking at me with smiles on their faces, noticing that Simone had come back into the room, a smug look on her face. She thinks I'm going along with her crazy idea, I thought to myself. Well, she was in for one hell of a shock. "I'm not sure who was going to announce that Simone and I were about to become engaged, but that doesn't matter now as I am here to announce to you that this is not the case. She has accompanied me to two functions, and as a result of this, she seems to think that I belong to her; this is not the case either. I am in love with a girl in the UK, who hopefully I will be spending the rest of my life with. And, I wouldn't marry Simone if she was the last woman on earth."

I watched the faces in front of me change from smiles to horror. Simone screamed and ran from the room. The only person in the room smiling was my brother.

Making a hasty exit after my 'speech' in less than five minutes, I was walking across the field adjoining Simone's parent's property. It was miles to home, but I had no other choice than to walk. However, walking in the fresh air was making me feel a whole lot calmer. As far as I was concerned that was an end to this entire episode in my life.

It took me two and a half hours to reach my house, which seemed like no time at all, as I passed the time reminiscing about my time spent in London with my girl. The love, the sex but most of all the promise we had made to each other.

Chapter 55

My pregnancy wasn't going well. The sickness had if anything become worse and my back ached constantly. I had been to all of my hospital appointments, following all the advice that I had been given.

I wanted this baby so much; we had made it together during our wonderful weekend. Thinking about this brought me closer to him, although he was thousands of miles away and knew nothing of what I was going through.

Although I was still working, I knew this wouldn't be for long. As soon as I started to show, I would be asked to leave. Unmarried pregnant women were not welcome in the workplace. However, I had managed to save as much money as possible to see me through the time I wasn't able to work.

The following Friday afternoon towards the end of my shift, I was asked to go to the manager's office. Asking me to sit down, he then asked me outright if I was pregnant. I didn't try to deny it; he was a thoroughly decent boss who I respected. He treated all his workforce with upmost decency, always being pleasant and courteous.

He looked sad and went on to say he would be sorry to lose me, and that he would give me an additional week's pay. I left that day, saying goodbye to the few people I had got to know.

As I got off the bus near my sister's house, I decided to treat myself to a magazine. Truth was I went into the newsagents quite often and looked through the teen magazines to see if there were any pictures of him in them.

As I walked through the door, the bell above tinkled alerting the owner Paul. "Hi, Paul," I greeted him. "Thought you might call in today," he said, through a mouthful of the sandwich he was eating. Smiling, I waited until he had finished chewing. "I've put this away for you," he said and retrieved a magazine from under the counter.

It was one of the popular teen magazines, and this issue had a small picture of him on the front cover; and underneath it said, 'full pictures inside'. Taking some money from my purse, I paid Paul for the magazine.

As I went to leave, I spotted a notice on the counter, 'part-time assistant wanted' it said. Paul saw me looking, "If you know of anyone," he said. Staring back at him with a stupid look on my face I said "Me," then went on to explain that I had been finished from my job, asking him if he would consider me for employment in his shop. He picked up the piece of paper, on which he had written the job advertisement and ripped it in half. "Does that answer your question?" he laughed, "Can you start tomorrow?"

Walking out of his shop, I felt a lot happier than I had been when I had walked in ten minutes earlier. Although I would be receiving anywhere near what I had earned in the mill, at least I would have some income rather than nothing at all.

Thankfully, the house was empty when I got in. Pulling out the magazine, I threw my bag onto the floor along with my coat, glancing at the small picture on the front, then turned to page four which showed the main pictures.

The headline stated that he had '*a new love in his life*'. There were four separate pictures of him with a girl who looked much older than him. Knowing not to make too much of any photographs I saw in magazines or newspapers, he had told me that if he had to attend any official event, he would need to be accompanied by a female.

Studying the pictures, although I hated seeing someone else by his side, I knew it was me that he loved, and that this was for publicity. On all four of the pictures, the girl was holding his arm, with her face close to his. Smiling, even though looking at him made me want him so much, I knew he was hating being in this position. It was there in his body language.

Kissing the page, making sure my lips were on his face; I whispered, "We love you, please come back to us, we miss you."

I had been working at the newsagents for two weeks. Paul was a great boss, and I was starting to enjoy my job. He would go out to wherever he had to go and leave me in the shop, making sure I had no heavy lifting or anything strenuous to do. Serving customers and keeping the shop tidy was well within my capabilities.

At least I didn't have to buy the magazines now; I could read as many as I liked, when the shop was quiet.

Chapter 56

It had been just over a week since the disastrous party at Simone's house. My brother had been to see how I was, but apart from that, I had kept a low profile; only going out if I had to go to the studio or anything else related to work.

He had looked puzzled when he walked into the house; and once we had settled down in the garden with a cup of coffee, he had said to me, "When you made your '*speech*' why did you say you were in love with a girl in the UK? Was it so that Simone would stop bothering you?"

Looking back at him I sighed. Not having told him about my girl in the UK as I didn't want him or anyone else telling me that I couldn't possibly be in love after one night and trying to talk me out of it; not that anyone could have done, I just didn't want the hassle. "No that wasn't the reason, I said that because there is a girl," I answered, "The most beautiful girl ever, we spent a night together, and I am totally in love with her, as is she with me."

I went on to explain what had happened in London and our plans for when I was back in the UK, asking him not to try and change my mind as it wouldn't have any effect. He smiled and squeezed my arm. "I'm not even going to try; he said, "I can see from your face how serious you are; I just hope she feels the same." I nodded, "She does. I'm one hundred per cent sure of that."

Two days later, I awoke to hear my brother's voice again. This time, however, it was seven in the morning, and he was banging on my door, shouting for me to wake up. Once I realised who it was, I legged it to the door; thinking it was a family emergency or something equally as urgent.

He was through the door almost before I had opened it. Walking into my kitchen, he threw a newspaper on to the table. "Read page six," he barked, "You're not going to like it." As I walked over to the table, dreading what I was going to see, I opened the paper at page six.

What I saw made me gasp; a photograph of myself and Simone underneath the headlines, *'MEGASTAR TO MARRY LOCAL SOCIALITE'.* My stomach flipped, and again I wanted to be sick. Reading a few lines, I sank to the floor; dropping my head in my hands. "Look," my brother said, "We can contact the paper and try to get them to print a statement deeming all this as untrue, it doesn't mean it's going to happen just because the papers have printed it to sell more copies."

By this time, he was on the kitchen floor beside me. I looked up at him, tears rolling down my face. Through my sobs, I somehow managed to speak. "I don't care what anyone here thinks of this, but if it gets to the UK papers, she'll see it, or she will get told about it." I wailed loudly, "She'll think my promise to her meant nothing. She won't come back, and I'll never see her again."

The thought of this was so utterly unbearable I wanted to curl up and die. Why was this nightmare happening to me? I had met someone, fallen in love, and made a promise which I knew I wanted to keep with all my heart.

It was still only 7.30 in the morning; however, ten minutes later, I was sat outside with my brother drinking a large brandy; the newspaper on my lap. I had made myself read the whole article. As devastating it was, I needed to know what lies that bitch Simone had concocted.

The whole article was a pack of lies, and although it didn't say it outright, it hinted that we would be getting married as soon as possible as Simone was pregnant.

I was physically shaking now as I thought of my girl reading the very same article in a UK newspaper. She was strong, but all the same, I knew what she would think. She would assume that I had come home, forgotten about her and slept with the first available girl. I had to think of something. Leaving it to chance wasn't an option. Although I knew she loved me, she was also proud, and I knew she wouldn't come to see me if she thought I was married.

My brother sat by my side, listening to me crying, trying to comfort me. I knew he felt guilty as he was the one who suggested I take Simone to the events. He said he didn't realise how cunning she was, or that she had wanted to meet me for quite some time. It seems she had designs on me before all this; so, I had played right into her hands.

He also went on to tell me she had paid the photographer who had taken the picture that accompanied the newspaper article. Remembering it now, he had insisted I put my arms around her and get closer, and although I hadn't wanted to, I had done as he asked to get it over with and get away.

Another thing my brother said, "The waiter following you round the games room trying to get you drunk was Simone's cousin. She arranged it so that you would be so drunk you would agree to the engagement announcement."

I was speechless, did she think I was so stupid that I would agree to marry her because I was drunk?

After my brother had left, I lay on my bed with my eyes closed. Feeling sick with worry, I also had a blinding headache from the crying and the brandy.

I wanted to get on a plane to the UK to find my girl, but I wouldn't have a clue where to start looking when I got there. How I wished I had listened to her when she had told me in which part of England she lived.

I needed to sleep, and when I woke, I would think of a way to get a message to her. More than anything, I had to let her know that there was no engagement, no wedding. Nothing but my love and my promise, that meant as much to me as it did the day we parted.

I eventually fell asleep, troubled and uncertain.

Chapter 57

A few weeks after I had been working for Paul, I arrived at the shop for my usual early shift. Paul had already sorted out the bundles of morning papers and sent the paper girls and boys on their way with their morning deliveries.

"You okay?" he said to me, "I need to go to the wholesalers and then I've got an appointment at the accountants." Putting my coat and bag in the back room, I answered him. "Yes, you get going; I'm fine."

For the next forty-five minutes, I was busy serving mothers and their children on their way to school; other mothers calling in the shop on the way back from dropping their children off.

At last, the customers had thinned out. After tidying the shop and making myself a cup of tea, I walked over to the magazine section, looking for one that I hadn't already read. The newspapers were in a row below the magazine racks, and as I scanned them, a newspaper caught my eye. In the top right-hand corner, I saw the words 'Celebrity Gossip' and a picture of him underneath.

Forgetting about the magazines I was looking through, I picked up a copy of the paper and took it behind the counter. Sitting on a stool, I turned to the page indicated on the front.

Assuming it must be news of forthcoming concerts, I was starting to get excited. What I saw when I opened the paper at the right page, was as far from what I had been expecting as was humanly possible. My body froze as I stared at the headline. 'TEEN HEARTTHROB TO MARRY'. Underneath was a picture of him alongside the same girl that he had been pictured with in the magazine.

Numb inside, I started to read the article below, hoping and praying that there was some mistake. Reading through it three times, knowing the more I learned that there was no mistake. He had gone home, forgot about me, got some girl pregnant and was now doing the honourable thing by marrying her.

Admiring him for facing up to his responsibilities; what he didn't know was that he had the same responsibility here in England.

And yes, she was only a girl, not much older as I had thought; she was two years older than I was although she looked much older. What hurt more than anything was the promise he had asked me to make which I had been only too happy to agree to; yet it had meant nothing to him. Within weeks of leaving me, he had been in bed with someone else; the words of love and promises had been forgotten.

Putting my hands across my growing bump, I sobbed. More than anything I wanted to hate him, but as I looked at his face smiling up at me from the newspaper, I knew I would love him forever, whatever he had done.

It was 12.30 when Paul walked back into the shop. I was in the backroom, washing my face, trying to get rid of my red eyes, not wanting him to think I had been crying while serving the customers. "It's only me," he shouted, so that I wouldn't rush through to the shop.

As I came out of the backroom, thinking I looked okay, he gasped "Oh my god," he said,"

What on earths wrong? You look awful. Thinking I was ill, he led me to the stool and made me sit down.

The newspaper was still on the countertop, open at the page of the article. As I looked down at it, his eyes followed mine. He was as shocked as I had been. "I saw the front page earlier when I was getting the paper sacks ready," he said quietly, "I thought it was about more concerts in the UK and knew how pleased you would be, that's why I didn't tell you. I thought it would be nice if you found it yourself while I was out. If I had known it was this, I would have told you before I went out."

He closed the paper and put it to one side. "No way would I have left you to see that while you were on your own."

By this time, I was crying again. "Go home," Paul said in a concerned voice. Your due to finish in forty-five minutes anyway. He went to get my bag and coat from the back and waited while I put my coat on. He had the newspaper in his hand. "Here," he said, "I know you don't want to read it again, but you need to explain to your sister and show it to her." Thanking him, I left for home.

The house was empty when I arrived home, which I was thankful for, needing time to think and come to terms with what I had found out, wanting to be alone with the devastation this had caused me.

I knew now; I wouldn't be going to watch his concert when he came back to the UK. I would have my baby and bring he or she up on my own. He would never know that he had a child in England, a child that was conceived during a fantastic weekend in London.

He would be a married man and have the child his fiancé was expecting. He had forgotten about me; all I had been was a day and night of fun and sex.

Yet, in my heart, I knew the love I had seen in his eyes was real and that he hadn't forgotten me. Okay he had broken his promise and slept with someone else, and now he was paying the price.

Opening the newspaper, I looked at his picture with tears in my eyes. "Oh, what have you done?" I said to the paper, "Love you forever, be happy my darling,"

Chapter 58

It was five days since the article had been in the paper. My brother had been an absolute star. He had gone to see Simone's parents on my behalf. Her mother had thought it was funny, assuming I would eventually come around and agree to the engagement, saying, 'Her daughter was a good catch, how could any man refuse'.

Her father, however, had been entirely different and was full of apologies for how his daughter had behaved, asking my brother to pass on his apologies to me. My brother had also told Simone's father that I didn't want anyone from the family contacting me whatsoever as if they did, I would be seeking legal advice.

After a few days, I was starting to think this was the last of the nightmare when I got a call from my brother. I knew as soon as I heard his voice that it wasn't good news. "Sorry," he said. "The story's been published in two British dailies', one last week and one yesterday."

The story appearing in the UK papers was the worst possible news he could have given me. I knew there had been pictures of Simone and myself in one of the UK teen magazines, but that had been okay; I had explained about having to take someone to various events.

If she had read the story and seen the picture, the one with my arm around Simone, she would believe that I was getting married, even that Simone was expecting my baby as the paper hinted.

But the most devastating thought of all was the promise we had made to each other. I knew in my heart that she would have kept it, I did not doubt that; only now she would think that it had meant nothing to me. She would think I had come home and jumped into bed with the first available girl.

Moping around for a few days, I thought of nothing apart from my girl reading the news that I was getting married. Wracking my brain for a way that I could let her know that it was all a lie; that I still loved only her and that I had kept my promise to her.

She would have seen the newspaper article; I knew that for sure. Or at the very least, she would have heard someone talking about it. I had many fans in the UK, the story that their 'idol' was marrying would be big news, talked about by many people.

Thinking of her reaction when she found out what was in the newspaper broke my heart. I knew what it would do to her and would have given anything to be able to hold her in my arms and tell her it wasn't true.

But there was nothing I could do. We were on opposite sides of the world.

After a while, an idea started to form in my mind, and although I didn't like it one bit, there didn't seem to be any other way of at least trying to sort this mess out.

As I drove through the gates of Simone's house, I wanted to throw up. Parking in front of the enormous front doors, I closed my eyes and pictured my girls beautiful face.

This idea had to work; it was my only chance.

Ringing the bell, I waited, my heart beating madly in my chest. As the door opened, I was faced by Grace, Simone's mother. Looking surprised, she opened the door wider and smiling she said, "Do come in, Simone is relaxing by the pool. Go through, and I'll send out some iced tea."

Staring at her, I wondered what went through the heads of people like these. I had stood on a chair in this house and said that 'I wouldn't marry Simone if she were the last woman on earth', and yet this woman was greeting me as though I was already married to her unbearable daughter.

Following her through the house, and out through the patio doors, I could see Simone lay on a sun lounger, beside the swimming pool. She was facing away from us and didn't turn round even when her mother spoke, saying, "Look who's come to see you, darling."

Simone didn't move at all, that was until I walked in front of her. As she realised who had 'come to see her' she jumped up, throwing her arms around my neck. "I knew you would come back," she squealed. "I knew the newspaper story would work." God, this girl is really stupid, I thought to myself.

Unwinding her arms and stepping back, I said quietly, "Sit down Simone; I need to talk to you."

Sitting back down, still with a big smile on her face and her hands clasped on her lap, I had a feeling she thought I was going to agree to marry her. My idea was going to be harder to put to Simone, than I had thought, wondering if I should forget the whole idea and go home.

But no, I was here now, and if this worked, it would be worth all the grovelling I was about to do.

Pulling a small stool across, I sat facing Simone and starting to speak; I asked her how she had got the newspaper article printed in the paper when it was a pack of lies.

Pouting, she answered me with, "You humiliated me in front of my friends and family, I wanted to get my own back," and then laughing she continued, saying, "I have connections who work on the newspaper. But it doesn't need to be lies. I still want to marry you."

Shaking my head at this spoilt, silly girl sitting looking at me with hope in her eyes, I knew I needed to be brutally honest with her, whether she liked it or not. "No, Simone," I said. "It's never going to happen. I don't love you, and when I said I had met someone in the UK, it was true. She's the one I love and the one I want to marry. The story that you have concocted has got to the UK papers, she will think I've forgotten her and that I'm marrying someone else."

I knew I had tears in my eyes. My tears, however, didn't seem to matter to Simone.

My thoughts drifting away to thoughts of my girl, I wasn't immediately aware that Simone had started speaking again, until I heard "...don't want to hear about your English bitch. If you don't want to marry me, just get out." "Please Simone," I pleaded. By now, I was crying, but still, she didn't seem to care. "Contact the paper and get them to do another article saying it was a mistake that there is no wedding. I need this so much; it's the only way I can get a message to her."

Looking at me, she started to laugh—a loud evil laugh. "You want me to sort out your love life, after you refused even to kiss me?" she sneered. "Not a chance."

At that moment, a woman who I presumed was the maid appeared with the jug of iced tea that Simone's mother had promised. As she placed it on the small table beside Simone's chair, she proceeded to pour it into two glasses.

As I waited for her to finish and go back into the house, I looked at the expression on Simone's face. From the look of anger on her face, before the maid had appeared, her face had now changed. It was now somewhere between a smile and a smirk.

Thinking this was because she had refused to help me, I took a long drink of my iced tea to calm myself down, and then said, "I'm going, thanks for your time Simone."

As I stood to leave, she grabbed my sleeve. "Sit!" she said. Shocked by her demand, I pulled my arm away, saying, "What? You've made it clear how you feel. I'm going."

As I started to walk away, she shouted after me. "Sit down; I'll help you," she retorted. I was immediately suspicious. After all, this was Simone. The girl who didn't do anything for anyone, unless there was something in it or her.

Sitting back down, I reached over to the table and picked up my drink, giving me a moment to think. Looking at her, I saw the sickly-sweet smile that she wore when she wanted her own way. "Okay Simone," I said, "out with it. There must be something in this for you if you're offering to help me."

Leaning over and touching my knee, making me shudder, she answered me. "Yes, there is. It's simple. I'll make sure another article is printed in the paper, stating that there is no wedding, on one condition."

Suddenly I went ice cold inside, knowing just what she was going to say next. Taking her hand from my knee, she stood up and bending down slightly; she whispered in my ear, "You sleep with me. Then I will contact the newspaper."

Laughing at my expression, she said in a nasty tone, "I'm going to the bathroom. You've got till I come back to give me your answer." And with that, she walked away towards the house, her laughter fading away as she disappeared through the patio doors.

Dropping my head into my hands, I couldn't believe I had put myself in this position. I would rather walk over red-hot coals or lie on a bed of nails than sleep with this horrendous, unbearable girl.

And no way did I want to break my promise to the girl who I loved with all my heart. But if I agreed to her ludicrous ultimatum, then I could get a message to her, letting her know that I wasn't getting married.

What did I do? Did I say no to Simone, hoping that my girl didn't see the newspaper article, in the UK papers? Or did I give in to her and get a message to my girl, making sure she knew that there was no wedding.

I knew one thing for sure, if I did give in, I would be honest about what I had done, and hope that my girl would forgive me. The last thing I wanted to do was to start our life together based on lies, having secrets from each other.

Sitting in the same position, still with my head in my hands, I hadn't realised that Simone had returned and was now back on her sun lounger.

Hearing her laugh, I jumped and looked up at her. "Why the gloomy face? Is it such a big decision? Your English bitch doesn't need to know, and you'll get the best screw of your life!"

Making myself speak, even though I didn't want to, I heard my voice say, "Okay Simone. I'll go along with your bribery. Not because I want to, because it's the only way I can let my girl know that I still love her and that there is no one else in my life."

As I finished speaking, she jumped up, threw her arms around me and before I realised what was happening, she had kissed me, long and hard on my lips.

Pulling away, I knew the look on my face was full of horror, but all Simone could do was laugh.

NO! What had I done?

Making the arrangements for our sex session was horrific. Simone wittered on about what a good time we would have and how I would see her differently afterwards.

Asking me when I wanted her to come round to my place, I went cold. No way was she coming to mine. I wanted my girl to share my place when I eventually brought her home with me and knew how bad I would feel if this insufferable girl sat opposite me had been in my bed.

Suggesting I book us a 'nice' hotel, she clapped her hands together and squealed "Oh how lovely; you're spoiling me already." What on earth was she talking about? I would book a hotel room, go there, have sex and then leave.

And...this would be back to how I had performed before I went to London. No making love, just sex!

Lying back on her sun lounger with a silly smile on her face, she gave a big sigh and then reached her hands behind her back;

unfastening her bikini top, she threw it to the ground.

Seeing the look on my face, she ran her hands over her bust. "Want a taste of what's to come," she said coyly.

I needed to get out of here now, and so I stood and said, "Got to go, Simone," and looking at my watch, "got to be at the studio in ten minutes."

Jumping up, she blocked my way. "Kiss me," she demanded. This idea was turning into my worst nightmare, but if I didn't, I was scared that she would back out. Closing my eyes, I leant forward and kissed her as she pushed her semi-naked body against me.

I had never vomited into someone's mouth. But there was always a first time.

Chapter 59

My life felt completely empty, and I spent the next two weeks in a trance. I went to work came home, made myself eat something, although I had no appetite. But knew I had to think of the baby and try to eat something, but the best I could manage was to would nibble at a sandwich or a piece of fruit. I thought of nothing else apart from the man I loved, and what had happened.

After how he had been in London, I had no understanding of the reason that he had immediately forgot me and slept with someone else. His love had seemed so real, and the promise was what he had wanted.

My sister had put it down to men being weak-willed. She had said that some men needed sex more than others, and this was probably the reason that he had given in so easily, sleeping with this girl. It made a lot of sense, as I knew he had a massive sexual appetite. It broke my heart to think that was what had happened as I knew if it was, it wasn't what he wanted, and maybe he did still love me.

It was now two weeks since I had discovered the article in the paper. Finishing my shift one Tuesday morning, I walked home deciding I would try to eat some lunch, then go into town to buy a few bits and pieces for the baby.

I already had most of the main items, a pram and a cot, but there were some other items I needed to buy. For the first time since the newspaper article, I felt a little hungry, cheered by the fact that I was going to buy the things I needed for my baby.

Up until I discovered he was marrying someone else; I had always thought about the baby I was carrying as 'our baby'. Now, however, I had started referring to him or her as 'my baby'. I wondered, if he knew I was carrying his child, if he would ditch his fiancé, marrying me instead. We were both in the same position, both pregnant with his baby. So surely, he could then choose which one of us he wanted.

Letting myself into the house, I went into to kitchen to prepare my lunch. Turning the radio on, I went about making my sandwich, singing along to the song the radio was playing.

I wasn't aware that the front door had opened until I heard a voice behind me. "So, he loves you, does he? It looks like it." My mother laughed, "you stupid bitch. He was stringing you along so that you would drop your knickers, otherwise why would he be marrying someone else." She had startled me, making me drop the plate I was holding.

All the time she was yelling at me, she was waving the newspaper in the air.

As I stared at the smashed plate at my feet, she carried on screeching at me, "Why on earth would he want a nobody like you, all he wanted was sex. He's getting married to one of his own kind, a rich girl. Why would he want a plain thing like you when he can have a beautiful wife like this?"

As she screamed this to me, she pushed the newspaper towards me and laughed.

Before she could continue, I snatched the newspaper from her hand and threw it across the kitchen, before screaming on the top note,

"Yes I know what's in that paper and it's got nothing to do with you so just fuck off and get out."

I didn't usually swear in front of either of my parents, but I just wanted her to go, not caring a hoot what I said.

As she started to speak again, I screamed, even louder, "GET OUT NOW." By this time, I was in tears and ready to push her through the door.

However, before either of us could speak again, a voice from behind her, said quietly, "I think you had better do as she says." Cath from next door had heard my screaming from the street outside.

My mother had been that excited to tell me what a silly bitch I had been, that she had left the front door wide open.

Looking at Cath with contempt on her face, my mother answered her with, "This is my daughter's house. I'll stay as long as I want." As Cath walked over to me and put her arms around me, she turned to my mother. I had never heard Cath raise her voice, but making me jump, she yelled, "Go, or I swear I won't be responsible for my actions. You're an evil woman. How can you be so cruel to your beautiful daughter?" My mother started to speak, and as she did, Cath moved towards her. With a scared look on her face, my mother turned and disappeared through the door.

Sitting on the sofa with Cath beside me; my sandwich forgotten, I brought her up to speed. She didn't know anything about the newspaper article as they didn't buy a morning paper. I told her he was marrying a girl he had gone home and met; she held me in her arms as I cried.

After talking for a while and making me a cup of tea, she cleared up the smashed plate in the kitchen and then left for her house next door; telling me to 'get some sleep'.

Lying there sobbing into the cushion, I finally fell asleep.

The sound of my sister coming through the front door woke me, the girls laughter jolting me awake. Rubbing my eyes as they came into the room, I was about to speak when my sister suddenly grabbed the girls and ushered them into the kitchen, telling them to go and get a packet of crisps each and some biscuits.

As she closed the kitchen door and turned to me, I asked her, "Why are you giving the girls snacks when it's nearly teatime?" As I tried to sit up, she pushed me back, telling me to keep still. "What?" I cried out, trying to get up again, until I followed her eyes, seeing where she was looking.

"Noooooooooooo," I screamed.

My work trousers which were a light grey, were stained with blood, between the top of my legs and halfway down my left leg. "Stay there," my sister said, "Please don't try to get up, I'm going next door to ring for an ambulance.

By this time, I was shaking and crying hysterically. Please, no, not this. I had lost him to someone else; I couldn't lose my baby; it was all I had left of him.

By the time my sister came back into the house, closely followed by Cath, I was sobbing and holding onto my stomach. My sister sank to the floor and cradled my head in her arms. "The ambulance will be here soon, lie still. I'm coming with you, Cath's going to make tea for the girls, so I will be with you for as long as you need me," and with that she hugged me tight.

I knew I could see tears in her eyes, however hard she tried to hide them.

The ambulance men arrived shortly after, asking me a few questions, one of them being how many weeks pregnant I was. When I said twenty weeks, I saw the look that passed between them. I knew what was happening to me, I wasn't stupid, but I didn't want to believe it. Wanting this baby so much; it was his, and at that moment, I knew how much he still meant to me.

I was then lifted on to a chair and wheeled out to the waiting ambulance. My sister climbed in behind me, sat by my side and held my hand. I looked up at her, "I know I've lost it," I sobbed, "It was all I had left of him, and now it's gone." She looked back at me; there were no words she could say to console me, the look on her face told me that she knew it too.

Arriving at the hospital, I was wheeled into a cubicle and examined by a doctor almost immediately, then I was informed that I was being taken straight to theatre. Knowing what this meant the sobbing returned and as a nurse prepared me, I lay with my eyes tightly shut, praying I would die while I was under the anaesthetic.

Seconds before everything went black; I heard myself say, 'love you forever.

Waking from the anaesthetic, I felt a hand in mine and looked up into my sister's face. Trying to smile at me but failing miserably, she squeezed my hand and said, "I'm so sorry." Looking back at her blankly, I replied with, "Why am I still alive; I don't want to live without him. However much I try to hate him, the love won't go away, and without my baby, I have no reason to live.

Burying my head in the pillow, I sobbed until I drifted back to sleep.

Waking later, I found my sister still at my bedside, sitting up, I hugged her as she stroked the back of my head. "Two things could have caused this," I said sadly. "Shhh," she tried to stop me. "No," I needed to say it out loud, "Drinking too much before I found out I was pregnant, far too much, or the stress of finding out he was getting married, knowing I will never see him again, could have caused it."

"And what about what happened earlier today," my sister said, "the stress 'she' caused you. I hadn't told her about mother coming to the house, but realised Cath must have told her when she went to phone for the ambulance. "Don't you think that could have caused you to miscarry.

Staring up at the ceiling, I thought to myself it didn't matter what had caused it, it had happened. Although I knew I would never see him again, while I was carrying his child, I had something left of our love. Now there was nothing. Nothing but sadness and a broken heart.

I had no idea how I was going to go on living a normal life after this. In the space of less than six months, I had fallen in love, fell pregnant, lost the man I loved and lost my baby.

Life didn't seem worth living anymore.

Chapter 60

It was three days since I had been to see Simone, agreeing to sleep with her. During this time, I had done nothing but cry and worry like hell, not eating and drinking far too much. No way did I want to do this. I didn't find Simone in the least bit attractive. She was stick thin, wore too much make-up, and her manner was loud and vulgar. These were the three things I hated most in a girl.

Thinking of my gently spoken girl with her sexy, curvy figure, I could feel tears forming at the back of my eyes, again. Telling myself, I was doing this for us didn't justify my actions or make it at all acceptable. I knew in my heart how wrong it was and if there were any other way, I would ring Simone without hesitation and call the whole thing off.

Getting up on the day of our 'arrangement', I showered and tried to make myself eat breakfast. I had most of the day to myself as I had arranged to pick Simone up at 5.30, the hotel was then a forty-five-minute drive. She had suggested that we go early in the day, as the hotel had a spa and pool. Saying, in what she must have thought was a sexy voice, "We can get to know each other before we start fucking." Did she really believe that this would turn me on? Not a chance! I had lied and said that I was busy with work until late afternoon and that 5.30 was the earliest time I would be able to collect her. I'm usually an honest sort of guy, and yet lying to Simone seemed to come naturally.

Constantly watching the clock, I was dreading the time approaching when I would have to leave. But with a heavy heart at fifteen minutes past five, I climbed into my car and set off for the ten-minute journey to Simone's house.

Driving through the gates and up the drive, my stomach was in knots. How on earth was I going to get through the next few hours?

As I pulled up, Simone ran down the steps with a suitcase in her hand. Suitcase! How long did she think she was going to be at this hotel that I had booked? The agreement was for me to sleep with her. Not take a vacation with her; I hadn't even brought spare pants. As far as I was concerned, we would go to the hotel, do what she had asked, I would then drop Simone off back here and go home.

Deep in thought, I didn't realise that she was standing behind the car waiting for me to open the trunk for her, until I heard her voice. "Get out and help me, will you, you're not much of a gentleman, are you?" she yelled at me. Now I knew why she didn't have a boyfriend or husband. She had no idea what manners were or how to speak civilly to people.

Opening the door and getting out, I walked to the rear of the car. "What on earth have you brought a suitcase for Simone," I queried.

Smiling her usual silly smile, she answered, "I need an outfit for dinner, clothes for bed and clothes for breakfast. I've packed six outfits for this evening, so that you can pick the one that I look sexiest in." Staring at her, I thought I was going to throw up – again. She was trying to turn this into a romantic night in a hotel; when all I wanted was to get there, get it over with as fast as possible and get out. Away from the hotel and away from the horrendous girl who was trying to manipulate me.

And dinner, breakfast, no!

Being close to telling her that I was calling the arrangement off, as I closed my eyes for a moment, a face appeared in my mind—a girl with long blonde hair, wearing a black vest top and jeans; my girl. Climbing back into the driver's seat, I started the car and drove out onto the road.

As we drove to the hotel, I wished I had booked somewhere closer as Simone talked incessantly for the whole journey. Although I wasn't listening, I did hear, "You won't be interested in your English bitch when you've had me, you will have forgotten her by tomorrow."

Swinging into a layby, I turned to Simone. "Call my girl that once more and I turn round and take you home. In fact, I don't even want you referring to her at all," I said, and then louder, "DO YOU UNDERSTAND." Pouting her lips, she turned her head away in a sulk. Pulling back onto the road, I smiled to myself. At least I could have some peace for the rest of the journey.

The hotel I had booked had not come cheap. Not that I wanted the luxury, but it was in a remote area, meaning it would be less likely that I would be recognised. The last thing I needed was even more pictures ending up in the daily rags. However, when I had rung Simone to tell her what time I would be collecting her, she had asked the name of the hotel. As I told her, she squealed with pleasure. "Oh, I knew you would book somewhere nice." Which was when she had suggested we go earlier in the day.

Now I wished I had booked a roadside Motel as I realised, I was giving her the wrong impression. She was now under the impression I wanted to lavish her with affection and spend time with her.

Arriving at the hotel, I parked up and before I could speak Simone had got out of the passenger door and was halfway to the hotel entrance. Shaking my head, I wished I dared to start the car, drive away and leave this rude, selfish girl, stranded here alone.

I needed to put a stop to how she was behaving, or the whole episode would be even worse than I had anticipated. So, catching her up as she was walking across the reception area, I pulled her into a corner. "This stops now, Simone," I said through my gritted teeth. "This is not a romantic liaison in a luxury hotel. You asked me to sleep with you, nothing else." Giving me the big sad eye look, she said, "You could at least buy me dinner and champagne. I'm marvellous when I've been drinking champagne."

NO! I really was ready to turn and run.

Having dinner in the hotel's restaurant wasn't a bad idea. By now, I was a complete bag of nerves and desperately needed a drink. A few large brandies and I might just be capable of actually doing what Simone wanted.

As I walked towards the reception desk, Simone following me, I turned and held out the car keys to her. "You need to get your suitcase out of the trunk," I spat at her, "I'm not your servant." Then turning away again, I smiled at the receptionist and proceeded to attend to my booking.

Standing next to the lift, I waited for Simone to return from the car. As she came through the hotel doors, I wanted to laugh. She was pulling her suitcase across the floor of the hotel's foyer, making out that she couldn't lift it—the same suitcase that she had been carrying as she ran down the steps of her house. Now, suddenly it seemed that it was too heavy to lift off the ground!

Not offering to carry her suitcase I called the lift and getting in, I pressed the button for the floor we had been allocated.

Unlocking the door to the room, I held it open as Simone dragged her suitcase in behind her. Walking over to the bed, she started to take her clothes off.

Shuddering inside, I wondered for the umpteenth time what I was doing here. I had created a situation for myself that was getting more out of hand by the minute. By now I wasn't just dreading what I had agreed to, I was scared. Okay, I hadn't been terrific in bed before I had met my girl, but I had at least fancied the girls I had slept with, if only for a short time. I didn't even like this girl, and I certainly didn't want to see her naked; clothed was bad enough.

I had to do something and quick.

Walking towards her, I spoke quietly, "What are you doing Simone?" Turning to me, now in her bra and pants, she answered, "Getting undressed, what does it look like. We can have a trial run before we have dinner, so that you will know exactly where I liked to be touched and what you need to do to turn me on."

Typical Simone, I thought. All about what she wanted; not giving a thought to what I might want. Throwing her arms around me, she pushed her body into mine and said, "Well, kiss me then, I liked to be kissed before you get me ready to be fucked."

Now I had gone beyond scared, I was terrified, and so unwinding her arms from around me, I tried to give what I thought sounded like a light-hearted laugh, "Let's have dinner first, I'm starving! Why don't you go into the bathroom and try your outfits on? Come out and show me them, one by one and I'll tell you which one looks the nicest," I said nervously.

No way could I say, 'Which one makes you look sexiest', which was what Simone had said earlier.

Asking her to do this seemed to cheer her up as she grabbed her suitcase and disappeared into the bathroom. Funny she appeared to have no problem picking it up!

Sighing with relief, once Simone had closed the bathroom door, I sank onto a chair, dropping my head into my hands. Why had I agreed to this? What was I doing in a hotel bedroom with a girl I couldn't stand, who was expecting me to sleep with her?

But I knew why? It was because I was in love with a girl who was on the other side of the world. A girl who wouldn't come back to me when I was next in the UK, because she would think I had broken our promise and that I was now going to be married to someone else.

Deep in thought, the bathroom door opened, and Simone appeared.

How I didn't laugh, I have no idea. She was wearing an outfit that would have looked cheap, even on a street hooker. Not knowing what to say, I nodded, telling her to change into outfit two. As her appearances progressed the outfits become more extreme, which at least cheered me up a little, wondering how bad the next one was going to be.

Now I knew why she had needed a suitcase. She had brought a separate pair of shoes and purse for each outfit.

After showing off all six of her outfits, I quickly plumped for a long silver dress with a split up the front. It was outrageous and much too old-fashioned for a girl of her age but was the only one anywhere near suitable to wear in the hotel's restaurant.

As she turned to take off her last outfit and change into the one that I had said she would wear, I stood and made my way to the door. "I'll make a reservation in the restaurant Simone; I said, "We can have a drink in the bar before dinner. I'll wait for you there."

And with that, I disappeared through the door.

After reserving a table in the restaurant, I made my way to the bar and ordered myself a large brandy. Sitting in a seat by the window, I took a mouthful of my drink as I thought about this horrific situation, I had put myself in, wondering how I could handle what was to come. Yes, I wanted to let my girl know that I still loved and wanted her, but this wasn't right. My hands were shaking, and all I wanted to do was to run out of this place as far away as possible from this mess I had created for myself.

Simone had eventually sashayed into the bar, trying to walk seductively towards where I was sitting.

Looking at her, I knew; I couldn't do this, however, much heartache I faced. I didn't find her at all attractive; in fact, she repulsed me. But more importantly, I couldn't break the promise I had made to the girl who meant the world to me.

Now all I had to do was tell Simone that I had changed my mind.

Sitting on the seat facing me, hitching her dress up so that I could almost see her crotch, she gave me a sickly smile. "Champagne!" she demanded. Frowning, I wondered; had she ever been taught that 'please and thank you' actually existed. Smiling back, I answered, "No, Simone, no champagne, you can have anything you want but no champagne."

Now that I had decided to back out of this ludicrous arrangement, I was actually feeling a whole lot better and much more confident.

Pouting again and turning her head away, I asked her if she wanted a drink, hoping she had got the message regarding the champagne.

It wasn't that I didn't want to pay for it, or that she had said she was 'marvellous' after she had drunk this. Champagne made my girl giggly and silly which I loved as she was 'giggly and silly' between the sheets, which turned me on, but the thought of Simone acting any more ridiculous than usual made me shudder.

Grabbing the drinks menu off the table, she quickly looked down the list of wines and threw the menu back on the table. "I'll just have a bottle of Chablis Premier Crus," she said in an uninterested voice. Standing and walking to the bar I smiled, she had picked the most expensive wine on the menu, purposely.

Taking the bottle, ice bucket and glass back to the table, along with another large brandy for myself, I poured some into the glass for Simone, placing the bottle into the ice bucket.

When I had ordered at the bar, the barman had offered to bring it over, but I had declined as I didn't want any interruptions. Now she had her drink; I intended to inform her that I would not be sleeping with her.

I had no idea what reaction I was going to get from Simone. But now that I had made my mind up, I was beginning to feel calmer, and once I had told her, I knew how relieved I would be.

Simone was gazing out of the window as I spoke, "Simone," I said in as confident a voice as I could manage, "I've changed my mind, I won't be joining you in bed tonight. I can't do that to the girl I love, I'm sorry."

Staring at me with a nasty look on her face, she answered me with, "Why? Do you think you will ever see her again, and don't even think I will help you now? And giving an eerie laugh, she said, "In fact, I might go back to my friend at the newspaper and make up some other lies. I could say that you had told me that you had just used her for a night of sex and that you never wanted to see her again."

Feeling my stomach churn and with tears in my eyes, I replied to this evil girl sitting opposite me. I knew she was trying to wear me down, but no! I needed to stand firm. "If you do that Simone, I will take legal action against you. I have the best lawyer money can buy, and I will not stop until I win.

You will not ruin my life in this way."

As a tear rolled down my cheek, she laughed again, but not the nasty laugh from a few moments earlier, but a softer, almost human laugh. "Okay," she sniggered, "If you agree to my next proposal, I will not make up any lies to the newspaper."

No, I couldn't deal with this. Why couldn't she just go upstairs, pack and I would drive her home. And even though I was serious about suing her if she had any more untruths put into print, if it were sold to the UK papers again, then the damage would already have been done.

Reading what Simone had said she would have printed would completely destroy my girl.

"Do you want to know, or not," Simone spat. Although I was dreading what her 'next proposal' was, all I could manage to do was nod my head. Listening to her as she wittered on, she was counting out on her fingers the details of what she wanted.

My body started to return to normal, and I found myself heaving a sigh of relief.

Her greedy nature had now turned to spending as much of my money as possible. What she didn't seem to realise was that spending money didn't bother me at all. I was rich, but yet I cared very little for material belongings. As she went through what I was to spend on her, I wanted to laugh. Yes! I had to stay here until tomorrow with a girl I couldn't stand, but that I could handle.

Then tomorrow I would think of another way to make sure my beautiful girl knew for certain that she was my only love.

Chapter 61

I had been kept in hospital for two nights due to my high blood pressure. However, on the third day when the doctor still didn't want to discharge me, I informed him that he let me go home, or I would walk out.

The hospital staff were concerned about me as I had been screaming in my sleep, calling out for him and waking up crying.

A psychiatrist visited me wanting to find out why I was doing this, but I had refused to answer any of his questions, so he had shrugged his shoulders and left.

Two nights was more than enough in there, and after my ultimatum, I was discharged, with anti-depressant tablets and sleeping pills.

I went back to live at my sister's. My parents knew nothing of my miscarriage, and I couldn't face the way they would have treated me, saying things like, *'it was for the best'* and *'now you can get on with your life'*.

My life felt worthless right now. Having lost the man that I loved and then his baby; how could it get any worse?

My days consisted of playing with and looking after my two nieces who I loved dearly; this helped a little, taking my mind off what I was going through.

After a week I went back to the shop, although when Paul had called in to see me at my sister's, he had told me to take as much time as I needed.

Sitting at home wasn't helping; I was spending too much time going over what had happened to me in the last few months, which had brought even more tears.

Although I loved working for Paul at the shop, I knew I needed to get a full-time job and make some new friends and so one morning when the shop was quiet, I sat Paul down and explained what I had in mind.

He was sad that I would be leaving but completely understood why I had made this decision.

I had to stop thinking of the man who had now forgotten me. The man who was marrying the girl he had gone home and slept with, after promising me the world—the man I would love forever.

I had to stop torturing myself.

Chapter 62

Simone had demanded dinner from the hotel restaurant's premier menu, with champagne, (which this time I had agreed to). The hotel's luxury breakfast and then a visit to the spa with three treatments, facials, manicures etc. As I had refused to visit the spa when she had suggested we go, she would need a bikini, pool shoes and a robe from the hotel's shop.

What Simone had demanded would cost a great deal, I knew. Yet, it made me feel a whole lot better as I did feel as though I had brought her here on false pretences; saying I would sleep with her and then changing my mind. Splashing out to stop her from doing anything stupid regarding the newspaper was an easy way out.

Taking our seats in the restaurant, I asked the waiter for the premier menu. At this, he informed us that we would be designated a waiter who would be available to serve our table only. At this Simone preened like a peacock. Choosing the most expensive items from the menu, Simone managed to eat five courses. Looking at her, I couldn't believe she could eat that amount of food and remain looking like a stick.

I had two courses which I thoroughly enjoyed as I hadn't eaten since early that morning. As Simone drank her champagne, our waiter appeared at the table to fill her glass before it became empty. Filling it so frequently caused her to drink faster, and halfway through the meal, she had drunk a full bottle. Watching her finish off her last glass, I thought of my girl. A bottle of champagne inside her and what she was like afterwards. No, I had to stop this! The memories of how she behaved in bed were turning me on, making me long for her more than ever.

Being deep in thought about my girl, I suddenly realised that the waiter had brought over another bottle of champagne. Well! What the hell. It was only money and if Simone thought I was going to object she was wrong. I was in a relaxed mood now, having stayed on brandy and as Simone talked nonestop, I had pretended to listen while dreaming of being with my girl, holding her in my arms, kissing her and making love to her.

By the end of the evening, Simone was completely plastered, and as she tried to stand, I grabbed her arm to stop her falling. Picking her up in my arms, I threw her over my shoulder as she giggled loudly. Somehow, I managed to negotiate the lift and the bedroom door without dropping her, hoping she wasn't about to vomit down my back.

Entering the room, I threw her on the bed and as much as I didn't want to, I removed her dress, not realising she hadn't been wearing a bra underneath it. Looking at her bony, thin figure, at her breasts which were almost non-existent, I would have given anything to be able to reach out and touch my girls voluptuous breast, to hear her sighing with desire.

Hoping Simone wasn't getting the wrong idea I was thankful when I heard a gentle snore coming from the bed. Picking up the room key and retrieving my car keys, I let myself out of the room, went downstairs and out to my car. I would sleep there until morning.

Reclining my seat, I lay back, closed my eyes and in no time, I was asleep, dreaming of my future with the only girl I would ever love.

Waking to glorious sunlight, I made my way up to the room, after what had been quite a decent sleep, considering I was in my car. Opening the door, I found Simone sitting up in bed tucking into a huge breakfast as though she had spent the previous evening drinking orange juice. She had downed two bottles of champagne, a bottle of wine and three very sickly-looking liqueurs. I had no idea if she knew I hadn't slept in the room with her. But as I had refused to sleep with her, I supposed she didn't care where I had slept.

Not wanting to stay in the room with her, I said I would go downstairs and book her spa visit and treatments. Once downstairs, I booked what she had requested, and after having a light breakfast and coffee in the restaurant, I waited for Simone to join me.

Visiting the hotel's shop, Simone began searching through the racks of bikinis, and not wanting to join her, I made my way to the other side of the shop, gazing at a display of jewellery; wondering what my girl would choose from the goods on offer here. I knew one thing for sure - she would be astounded at the price tags.

Still thinking of my girl with a massive smile on my face, Simone joined me clutching her bikini, shoes, robe and luxury towel. She hadn't included a towel in her demands and could have easily used one of the hotel's, but I wasn't going to make an issue of it; I was now in a good mood. This difficult time here was almost over and feeling generous I turned to Simone and said, "Choose something, Simone. And not for any other reason other than I'm feeling generous and I am sorry for misleading you."

Her eyes lit up, and as they roamed over the items of jewellery, I expected her to choose the most expensive piece on display. When she decided on a pair of diamond earrings which were nowhere near the most expensive item, I looked at her in amazement. "Are you sure?" I queried. Nodding, she astounded me when she answered, "Yes, I like these, and I've spent enough of your money already, thank-you." Walking to the desk, I couldn't believe what I had just heard. She had sounded almost human.

Simone's treatments and spa visit took just over four hours. Collecting a pad and pen from my car, I walked to the back of the hotel and sat on the grass by a lake, watching swans glide along the smooth water. Opening the pad, I started to write the beginnings of a song; basing the words on my feelings for the girl I loved. Writing always made the time pass quickly, and before I knew it, I was walking back to the hotel.

Once I had checked out and collected Simone, it would be time to leave.

Walking into reception, I found Simone sitting reading a magazine. As one of her treatments had been a facial, she was now without any make-up at all. Nearly laughing out loud, I realised why she wore so much of the stuff; she needed it.

Driving back to Simone's place, we managed to have what was nearly a normal conversation. Asking me about my girl, I was wary of answering her. But when I told her what she meant to me and that I would never love anyone else, she sighed and said quietly, "She's a very lucky girl, and I promise I won't have anything else printed, but I can't tell the paper that the other article was a lie."

By this time, we had pulled into the drive of Simone's house. Turning to me, she said, "I won't say I hope it works out for you, because I don't. Maybe if she doesn't come back, you might come back to me." She hadn't said this in a nasty tone, just in a sort of sad voice.

vGetting out of the car, I got out of my side and lifted her suitcase from the trunk. Leaning towards me, she kissed my cheek, saying in a whisper, "I will always want you." Then she turned and walked away.

Driving home, I thought about the last twenty-four hours. I was so thankful that I hadn't gone through with what Simone had wanted. I knew she had enjoyed being at the hotel with me, and I felt a little sorry for her. She wanted me badly, and although I wasn't attracted to her whatsoever, I knew she believed that if I wasn't in love with someone else that I would be with her.

Now all I had to do was think of another way, to make sure I was with the girl who I loved.

Chapter 63

Now that I had told Paul I would be leaving my job at the shop I would need to visit to the labour exchange in the town centre, to find out what jobs they had on offer. As Paul didn't have anywhere to go on Friday of that week, I asked him if I could finish an hour earlier. In addition to visiting the labour exchange, I wanted to have a walk around the town centre to see if there were any job advertisements in the windows of the big stores.

Getting home later after picking the girls up from school as I entered the house, I picked the post up from behind the door. Putting my sister's letters on the fireplace, I opened the one addressed to me.

It was from the hospital, giving me a date for my appointment to check that everything was in order after my miscarriage. Feeling sad thinking back to this time in my life, I sat on the edge of the chair and thought about the man I had lost, who I still loved with all my heart.

Snapping myself out of my melancholy mood, I went into the kitchen to prepare the girls tea.

My sister was out with her new boyfriend, and so I had told her not to hurry back; I would see to the girls, feed them and get them to bed.

After giving the girls their tea, we played their favourite board game and then it was time for bed. Before I had finished reading their bedtime story, they were both asleep.

It was around 10.30 pm when my sister returned with her boyfriend, Rob. Asking them if they had enjoyed their day, we chatted for about fifteen minutes before I decided to turn in for the night.

I could see that they wanted to be alone, and an early night would do me a world of good.

As I climbed into bed, I remembered that I hadn't told my sister it was the girls school photographs the following day and that I had ironed their prettiest dresses for the occasion.

I left for the shop before the girls and my sister got up and wanted to make sure she sent them to school looking their best for their photographs.

Plodding quietly down the stairs I was about to open the door to the lounge when I heard

Rob's voice, "I know she's had a rough time, and I do like her, but I want to live with you and the girls, not your sister," he said. Freezing where I was standing, I felt tears rolling down my cheeks and turning around I made my way back upstairs to bed.

I knew my sister wouldn't throw me out with nowhere to go, but how could I stay here knowing she wanted to start a new life with Rob. I would be in the way if I stayed and could well end up ruining their relationship.

Sobbing into my pillow so as not to wake the girls, I felt like I didn't belong anywhere. And as usual, I clung to my pendant, wishing with all my heart that I was still the girl he loved and wanted.

After a fitful and restless sleep, I awoke to my alarm clock ringing under my pillow. I kept it there so that it didn't wake the girls. Climbing out of bed I dressed, and after leaving my sister a note about the school photographs, I left the house; deciding to have a walk before going to the shop.

Within fifteen minutes, I was walking down to the canal footpath, trying to make sense of my life. I needed to move out of my sisters to give her the space she needed to build a life with her new man. No way was I going grovelling to my parents, having them speaking to me like I was a child and laying down their ridiculous rules. And, even if I did find a full-time job, I wouldn't earn enough to manage a place of my own.

So now I belonged nowhere. I had lost the man I loved, lost my baby and would soon have nowhere to live. Could my life get any worse!

Arriving at the shop, I was still troubled but smiled as I greeted Paul and the three paperboys who were waiting patiently for their bags to be filled, before setting off on their rounds. There were no customers in the shop, so I told Paul I would go and make us both a cup of tea, giving me a chance to pull myself together.

Talking to Paul once the morning rush was over, I asked if would be okay if I stayed working for him until I had been to my hospital appointment as I didn't want to be taking time off from a new job. Beaming, he said, "Of course, take as much time as you want."

And so, life went on as usual. I worked for Paul, helped with my nieces' and continued to live at my sisters. I had told her I had overheard what Rob had said, regarding moving in with her.

She had been upset but hugged me and said to me that I was welcome to stay until I had somewhere to live that was satisfactory and affordable.

Two weeks had passed, and I was now sitting in the waiting room at the hospital. Since I had overheard what Rob had said about me living at my sister's place, I had become more depressed and unhappy. I just couldn't see a way forward, and as much as I tried not to, my thoughts constantly went back to why he had gone home and forgotten me.

As my name was called, I stood and made my way into the consultant's office.

Greeted by a doctor who was probably in his forties, he smiled at me and asked me to sit down. A nurse hovered at the back of the room, busying herself looking in a filing cabinet.

Asking me some questions and going through the details of my miscarriage, asking me if I understood the procedure of my visit to the theatre, he then stopped, put down the files he was holding, and his face took on a stern expression. Then he started to speak, "I'm sorry, but due to the procedure we had to perform, it's highly unlikely that you will ever be able to carry another child, this was most probably the reason why you miscarried." He went on to explain more, but by this time, I had stopped listening. Not only had I lost the baby of the man I would love forever, I would never have another one. I didn't realise I was crying until the nurse sat in the chair next to me and took hold of my hand.

Now I knew why she had stayed in the room and trying to put a tissue into my hand. I jumped up from my chair and ran from the room.

Rushing past the people in the waiting room, I ran down the hospital corridor and out through the doors. Sitting on a wall, I buried my face in my hands, my body wracked with sobs.

I had lost the man I loved. I had lost my baby. I had nowhere to live. And now I had discovered I would never be a mother.

What did I have to live for?

Chapter 64

After the fiasco at the hotel with Simone, I had to come up with some other idea to get a message to my girl. If I didn't, I knew - I would never see her again. I needed help, and I had an idea who I could turn to for that help.

The following day I visited my agent who handled my publicity, magazine photoshoots and other events. Having always got on well with him; I thought that maybe he would listen to me and suggest a way I could get a message to her before I went back to the UK to do more concerts.

He did listen and was sympathetic, which was more than my manager did, who just referred to her as 'the slapper'.

As I explained to him, he was sympathetic; having seen the newspaper article himself. He thought that the best course of action was to contact TV channels in the UK and set up an appearance on a chat show, which would be shown on *'prime-time'* TV. That way, there was more chance of her seeing it. Also, I could get a message across verbally while looking directly at the camera. So that she would feel as though I was talking to her personally.

It wouldn't be next week or the week after, but if he could set something up, there was a chance that I could get a message to her, making sure she knew that I still loved her and that there was no one else.

Leaving his office, I felt a lot happier than when I had first gone in, knowing that as soon as my agent heard back from the UK, he would contact me immediately.

There is no reason for her to be faithful to me now, Simone has made sure of that. And even though the thought of this makes me feel physically sick, I just hope and pray that she hasn't fallen in love with someone else.

Once I made my TV appearance, I would make sure she knew how much I still loved her and that I hadn't broken my promise to her.

This appearance was more important than anything else in my life. It was my only way to let her know what she still meant to me and how much I needed her.

Chapter 64

Walking home after my hospital visit, even though it was miles, I tried to come to terms with what the doctor had told me. I would never be able to have children; my body wouldn't be able to carry another baby.

At this moment in time, I didn't want another man, not when I was still in love with the one who had forgotten me. But, in the future, I knew that I wanted a family; my own children to love like I loved my nieces. How could I possibly get involved with someone, only to see him walk away because I couldn't give him a child?

After a two-hour walk, I arrived home, to an empty house; for which I was thankful. Wondering where everyone was, I spotted the note on the coffee table, from my sister. She had taken the girls to the hairdressers and was then doing some shopping. Flopping down on the sofa, I felt numb inside and wondered how I was going to cope with what now seemed to be my disastrous life.

My days living here with my sister were limited. No way on earth was I returning to my parents, and I didn't earn enough to pay for my own place and still wouldn't be able to afford it even if I found another job.

Deep in thought, I heard my sister and the girls outside and the key in the lock. Putting on a brave face I got up, and after hugging the girls, I went into the kitchen, shouting over my shoulder, "Cup of tea?" Busying myself as I filled the kettle.

I didn't want to tell my sister what had said at the hospital, not wanting her to think I was looking for sympathy so that I could stay. So, as she followed me into the kitchen, and said, "Was everything okay at the hospital," I answered, not looking her way, and replied, "Yes fine."

At that moment, the sound of the girls squabbling in the lounge sent my sister running to find out what the problem was, stopping her from asking me any further questions.

Heaving a sigh of relief, I made the tea, trying not to burst into tears again. What a mess, my life was. If I hadn't gone to London, I would still be working at the cotton mill, enjoying my life, without a care in the world.

But I knew, I didn't regret any of what I had done. Meeting him and falling in love, promising to be faithful and being with him when he came back to the UK was the most wonderful feeling I had ever experienced. The happiest I had ever been was when I had discovered I was expecting his baby, dreaming of how it would be when we were back together', bringing up our child.

Coming back into the kitchen after settling the girl's squabbles, my sister asked if I could babysit that evening as Rob wanted to take her out. Even though I never went out in the evening, she always asked, never taking me for granted. So, of course, I had said yes.

Feigning a headache, I said I was going upstairs to have a lie down while the three of them had their evening meal, saying I would have something to eat later.

I wanted to be alone, going over what the doctor had said to me, where I was going to live and if I could find a new job. Everything in my life had happened so quickly, throwing it into complete turmoil, making me feel that I belonged nowhere, and that no one cared about me.

I lay there sobbing into the pillow.

And even though he was now with someone else, I wanted nothing more than to be in his arms, feeling his hair brushing against my face. Would these feelings ever go away? Would I want him for the rest of my life? I couldn't go on like this, facing the hurt buried deep inside me.

When my sister had left for her night out, I took the girls to bed and read them a bedtime story. After kissing and hugging them, I made my way downstairs and found the sleeping pills that the hospital had given me after my miscarriage.

The bottle was almost full, as I had only taken them for a few nights. Taking a can of cider from the fridge, I went into the lounge.

Sitting on the sofa, I tipped the bottle of pills into my mouth and then washed them down with a swig of cider. They were only tiny pills and went down quickly. After gulping down the rest of my can, I lay down and closed my eyes.

It was better this way. I was an inconvenience to everyone and out of the way they could all get on with their lives.

He would never know what I had done, which I was grateful for; I still loved him with all my heart and would hate him to blame himself.

My sister wouldn't be back for at least two hours by which time I would be dead. The girls were settled and never woke up once they were asleep.

As I lay there waiting for sleep to engulf me, I thought about our weekend in London, as tears rolled down my cheeks. Every few seconds, I could hear myself saying 'love you forever'. At last, the pain inside seemed to be subsiding, and I felt like I was floating - then there was nothing.

Waking to voices all around me, I groaned. I couldn't even kill myself successfully.

I didn't have to open my eyes; I knew where I was. I was in hospital.

Keeping my eyes closed so that whoever was there would think I was still unconscious, I tried to make sense of what I could hear.

Suddenly I heard Cath's voice asking someone what time it was. Shocked my eyes shot open, and as they did, I looked at Cath as she burst into tears. "Thank God!" she sobbed, "I thought you were a goner when I found you. What on earth's wrong love, why did you do it?"

I felt so guilty. Her eyes were red and bloodshot, and she looked so worried.

Wriggling so that I was facing her, I took hold of her hand. "I'm so sorry, Cath," I whispered, "why are you here?"

And so, she told me what had happened.

Not long after I had taken the pills and fallen asleep, she had come into the house to bring the evening paper as she regularly did, usually staying for a cup of tea and a chat. Seeing me on the sofa, she had placed the paper on the coffee table and turned to go.

As she closed the door and made her way back next door, she had said that she had felt uneasy. She had come into the house when I had been asleep on the sofa many times and knew the sound of the door opening had always woken me.

She had returned to my sister's house, opened the door and called my name. When she got no response from me, she had walked around the coffee table; it was then she saw the empty pill bottle on the floor.

She had then run to get Andy, who had tried to rouse me while she went to phone for an ambulance.

She had travelled with me in the ambulance, holding my hand and talking to me. Andy was next door looking after the girls.

Although I knew my sister and Rob had gone to a local pub to meet friends, Cath and Andy hadn't known how to contact her.

Stroking my hair, she asked me, "Why did you do it love; you have your whole life in front of you." As I cried I told her how low I felt after losing the man I loved and then my baby, then went on to tell her about Rob wanting to move in with my sister but that he didn't me living there. Finishing with telling her what the doctor had told me earlier that day.

"Oh, you silly girl," she said, hugging me. "We have a spare room; it's yours if you want it. I can't help with everything else that's happened to you, but if you're under my roof, I can be there for you when you need someone to talk to or a shoulder to cry on. And as far as not being able to have children. I know lots of girls who have been told that and have carried and given birth to healthy babies."

All I could do at this point was to cry like a baby. I had been so selfish in trying to take my life. People did care about me, and I had no right hurting them like I would have done. I had been wrapped up with my problems and hadn't given a thought to anyone else. Least of all my two beautiful nieces who would have been heartbroken.

Once Cath had kissed and hugged me, she left for home. Lying there, I thought about my life. I knew Cath and Andy would welcome into their home and love me being there. Cath had never been able to have children of her own, and as a couple, they had so much love to give.

I knew I would be okay with Cath and Andy.

When I was discharged from the hospital, I would find a full-time job and try to re-build my life. I would live with Cath and Andy, where I knew I would be happy and content.

My sister could start her new life with Rob and best of all, I would be next door to my nieces; still being able to be in their lives.

I would always love him, and I knew that even if I met someone else in the future, I could never love anyone in the same way.

What had happened to me in the last few months had changed my life forever.

Gerry IV

It was now just over three months since I had returned from London. My wife had been full of questions when I first got home, wanting to know about the 'pop star' tantrums. When I explained what a nice person he was and that he didn't have tantrums, but was a thoroughly decent lad, I went on to tell her the part I had played in him finding the girl of his dreams, and falling in love with her.

Being a hopeless romantic, she had dragged every last detail out of me. I was frank with her about where his girl had spent her last night in London. We trusted each other, and as I explained that the trains had stopped running on the Sunday evening, I told her that I had offered her the spare bed in my room. She had hugged me and said how proud of me she was; that I had looked after her as I had promised him.

One Monday morning, about three months later, I had gone to work for the weekly progress meeting, which the company held each week. As I took my place in the board room, the door opened, and Sandra from the admin department stuck her head around the door. "Phone call for you, Gerry," she chirped, "It's the wife."

Apologising to my colleagues, I went through to admin and lifted the telephone receiver, worried that it was a problem with my daughters. Saying hello, I heard my wife's voice, "There's a story in this morning's paper about the singer you looked after in London," she said quietly, "I think you should read it, it says he's getting married." Telling me what newspaper it was, I told her I would buy it on my way home and that we would read it together later.

Taking my place back at the table for the meeting, I heard nothing of what was being said, my mind going through what my wife had just told me. What had happened; how could he be marrying someone else.

After the meeting had ended, I completed some timesheets I needed to hand in and then after collecting my coat and bag; I headed to the newsagents on the corner.

Buying the relevant newspaper, I walked to my car, resisting the urge to read it. I wanted to know what had happened in his life to prompt a newspaper article stating that he was getting married.

But I had promised my wife that we would read it together.

Arriving home to a quiet house, my wife greeted me with a kiss; informing me that the girls were with their grandparents and wouldn't be back until later.

Making us both a coffee, we settled down at the kitchen table with the newspaper, turning to the relevant page. With my arm across my wife's shoulder, we both started to read what the paper had to say.

The heading was 'TEEN HEARTTHROB TO MARRY', a picture underneath of him with his arm around a female much older than himself.

As I started to read what was written underneath the picture, it said although they had not known each other long, they would be getting married within the next month; not wanting to wait any longer, as they were so much in love. There were hints in the story that this girl, (discovering that she was only a girl, although she looked much older) was pregnant; this being the reason that the wedding was to take place within the next few weeks.

Finishing reading the article, I dropped my head into my hands.

He wasn't in love with this girl; I knew that for sure. Looking at the smile on his face, I could see it was false; I knew him, and I had seen the way he had looked at the girl he had met in London. This smile staring out at me from the newspaper was nothing like it; it was a publicity picture, nothing else.

Although he had promised her that he would be faithful to her, it seemed that he had given in and slept with this girl he was about to marry, she had become pregnant, and he was doing the right thing by marrying her. I also knew that when the girl he had met in London read this, how heartbroken she would be.

She wouldn't go to his concert when he was next in the UK as she had promised him; not when she knew he was married with a child.

"Oh, what have you done?" I said out loud. "One moment of weakness and two lives have been ruined forever."

Chapter 65

I am still waiting to hear from my agent regarding my appearance on a UK chat show. It has now been two months since he said he would contact the TV companies—two months of worrying every minute of every day.

I am trying my best to carry on with my life. Recording, writing and generally being the person the public expect me to be. I smile for the camera, when inside my heart is breaking.

At night I go to bed and think about my girl. Did she read the newspaper article, or get told about it? Has she fallen in love with someone else? Has she forgotten me?

All these thoughts and many more go through my head every night; before I eventually fall asleep and then the same fears fill my dreams. Some days I feel as though I am going insane, and the tears I cry would fill an ocean. Oh, how I long to hold her in my arms, tell her how much I love her, that I have kept the promise I made to her in London; and that I want no one else.

I try to convince myself that she will watch my TV appearance and realise that the newspaper article was all lies and that nothing has changed. That I still need her to come back to me more than anything else.

I have to get her back in my life; this is all I'm living for.

Chapter 66

It is now almost six months since the day I set out for London.

I have an interview in a few days for a full-time job which will earn me a decent wage. Hopefully, I will make new friends and put the hurt of the last few months behind me; make something of my life.

I am now eighteen years old, meaning that I am now an adult and although I haven't seen either of my parents since the day my mother came to my sister's to wave the newspaper article in my face, my adult status meant that they can no longer dictate how I live my life.

I spent my eighteenth birthday with Andy and Cath, visiting a local Italian restaurant. They had given me a lovely silver cross and chain in a beautiful presentation box, which had brought a tear to my eye. I had received cards and gifts from my sister and the girls and even a big box of chocolates from Rob. My parents hadn't even sent me a birthday card.

What had happened in London and the following months were locked away in my heart. He would be married by now and looking forward to the birth of his child. I hoped with all my heart that he was happy and that he would enjoy being a father.

I still love him and have long since stopped trying to hate him; knowing that to try and deny my feelings for him are useless. He had been part of the most fantastic period of my life.

I knew, without a doubt, I would 'love him forever'.

If you have enjoyed reading 'Forever'. Find out what happens. Does he manage to let her know he still loves her during the TV interview. Does she watch it. Read on for a sneak preview of the sequel.

'Forever Lost'.

FOREVER LOST

Chapter 1

Two weeks later I was ready to start my new job in a mail order warehouse. I would be earning a good wage and mixing with people my own age. Leaving the shop only the day before, I had said a sad goodbye to Paul and promised to go in and see him often.

Trying to put the last few months behind me would be hard but I knew if I wanted to live any kind of a normal life I had to try.

On my first day however, I realised that it wouldn't be as easy as I thought. As I was shown round the building and walked into the locker room the first thing that I saw was a massive poster of him on the wall straight facing me. Stopping dead, I stared at it as my stomach turned somersaults. "You a fan then?" Michelle who was showing me round had notice me staring at the poster. I managed to mumble "Er, yes." "He's gorgeous aint he," she continued. "We have the radio on out there and if one of his songs come on, we turn it up full blast." She giggled, "What I wouldn't give to meet him," she gave a big dreamy sigh looked at the poster again, turned and walked out of the door.

That was when I realised, I had to get used to him still being in my life, if only through pictures and music on the radio.

Settling into my job quickly I made friends with several of the girls who I worked alongside. I had told no one about what had happened in London or of my miscarriage.

As Michelle had told me that first day, his songs were played on top note and he was the general topic of conversation at break and lunch times.

It was quite funny in a way as the only information they had was from magazines and newspapers, which didn't portray the real person I had got to know and love. They all thought they were in love with him, like I had thought before going to London, nothing like the real love I now felt for him.

All the teen magazines were bought every week as they avidly waited for pictures of his wedding, they couldn't wait; I was dreading it.

Friday and Saturday nights were spent going out and getting drunk.

Eagerly joining the throng of girls who met in town and went around the pubs, there was just one difference; while they chatted the lads up, I stood on my own. I knew it was stupid, but I didn't want anyone else. How could I fall in love with someone else while I still in love with the man who had now forgotten me? I joined in with the conversations and laughed along with everyone else, then went home alone.

How long was I going to feel like this? I didn't want to be on my own when all my friends had boyfriends, the problem was the man I loved didn't love me anymore and why that was still breaking my heart I had no room for anyone else in my life.

Although I still didn't feel ready to date anyone, I gave in somewhat. Brian, one of the lads who we met up with at weekends had shown an interest in me. He was good looking and quite a few of the girls were after him. Making sure he was in the same bars as me throughout the evening he would make a point of coming over to talk to me.

One Friday evening he had sat next to me and asked me out. My heart didn't want to say yes, but I was lonely on my own when all the other girls met up with their boyfriends at the end of the evening; and I had drunk more than usual that evening so I agreed to meet him the day after.

He looked really pleased and hugged me.

It wasn't what I wanted but I had to stop thinking about him, it was over, he had made his choice and I needed to get on with my life.

Chapter 2

It was two months before my agent had contacted me. He had been in talks with the company that produced one of the UK's current chat shows. They were more than happy for me to appear but had wanted to know when I would be back in the UK to perform in concert, wanting this to be the main topic of my appearance.

Armed with this question he had contacted my management company wanting to know when this would be.

Eventually my manager had rung me with the dates. It was to be a full European tour. As his voice droned on with dates for central Europe, I could feel myself becoming increasingly impatient and blurted out "England, just tell me the dates for England, you can tell me the others later." He laughed and said, "Still hoping the slapper will come and see you. I told you she'll have forgotten all about you by now." I was so angry with him, why did he have to keep putting her down like this?

I had no idea if she had seen the newspaper article and met someone else, but one thing for certain I knew deep down was that she would still love me. No way could feelings as strong as we had for each other just disappear overnight. Somehow, I had to get through to her when I appeared on this chat show, she had to watch it and believe what I was saying.

One thing in my favour was that it would be going out live so anything I said wouldn't be able to be edited out.

Sitting in the airport lounge waiting for my flight to the UK I rehearsed in my mind what I was going to say during the show, how to get my message to her. Knowing what I needed to get through to her, but just how it would pan out when I was in front of the camera could be a completely different matter.

One thing I knew was that I now felt like I was doing something to amend what had happened in the last few months.

By the time I got to my hotel in London I was whacked. How I wish she knew I was here, or that I knew where to find her. The chat show would air live tomorrow evening and then I would be flying back home, having studio recordings the day after the show.

Due to this I wouldn't be able to spend any longer here in the UK.

Trying to sleep but knowing I was in the city where we had fallen in love was whirling through my mind, making sleep impossible.

After an hour of tossing and turning I gave up, had a shower and got dressed. Still not being able go out in public without being recognised I pulled on a hooded rain jacket and decided to chance it.

Stepping out of the hotel foyer and pulling my hood up, I tied it as tight as possible around my face and put on a pair of sunglasses. Keeping my head down I started walking, while looking out for tourist signs. I wanted to see one part of London only. The Thames.

To re-live the moment, we had both said, '*I love you*'.

It took me a while to find, but somehow after crossing over Tower Bridge I managed to navigate myself to the exact spot where we had stood together.

As I stood against the railings, I knew I shouldn't have done this. Although it felt wonderful being here where we had shared so much it also hurt like hell not knowing what my future held.

Closing my eyes, I could almost feel her body up against mine. Sighing I turned to make my way back to the hotel, but not before whispering into the river, "Come back to me my love. I need you so much."

At last I was standing outside the studio where the show was being aired. I had decided to wear a black and gold shirt with black jeans. Black and gold were her football colours and I wanted her to realise I had done this for her.

Hearing my name announced, the guy at the side of me gave me a nod and I walked on set to screams and deafening applause.

Waving and smiling I sat down in the chair facing the host. My heart was hammering in my chest worrying me like hell at how I was going to get my message through.

After the preliminary introductions and small talk, the host turned the conversation around to my *'engagement announcement'*.

Host: It's now several months since the British public read about your engagement and imminent marriage, so I take it you're now a happily married man? Although we haven't seen any wedding pictures here in the UK.

Me: I took a deep breath, looked straight at the camera and spoke as calmly as I could. "No," I tried to smile but I couldn't manage it, "I am not married, happily or otherwise. The whole announcement was untrue, it was not my doing. I am still single and still in love with the same girl I was before the ridiculous engagement announcement.

Host: Okay, so there was no imminent wedding, but tell us….the papers hinted that there was a baby on the way. How true was that part of the story?

Me: I managed to answer with more conviction this time as this made me angry. "There isn't and never was any baby. I never slept with or even kissed the girl who was the subject of the 'so called' engagement. I then looked straight at the camera again and said as lovingly as I could possibly manage. "I'm still here waiting for you." I couldn't say anything more without starting to cry.

Host: "Wow, powerful words. Would you like to let us in on the secret and tell us who the lucky lady is? I'm sure your army of fans are as curious as I am about who has won your heart.

Me: "No, not at this moment. She knows who she is, and I hope she now knows how I feel." I looked at the camera for longer than was expected, willing her to understand. "When the time's right I will happily tell the world."

The show went on to talk about my forthcoming concerts in the UK and giving the dates for each one. I was pleased that this was one of the topics as she would now have the dates for all the UK concerts.

If she had watched this show, she would now know that the whole newspaper story was untrue and that I was waiting for her to come back to me.

The promise I had made to her was still in one piece; I could only hope and pray that she had kept the one she had made to me.

Printed in Great Britain
by Amazon